THE KEYS OF BABYLON

THE KEYS OF BABYLON

Robert Minhinnick

Seren is the book imprint of
Poetry Wales Press Ltd
57 Nolton Street, Bridgend,
Wales, CF31 3AE
www.serenbooks.com

ISBN 978-1-85411-550-8

A CIP record for this title is available from the British Library.

Inner design and typesetting by littlefishpress.com

Printed by Berforts.

The publisher works with the financial assistance of
the Welsh Books Council.

Robert Minhinnick is glad to acknowledge a Creative Wales award that has enabled him to undertake the writing of *The Keys of Babylon*.

Contents

At a dictator's grave

1

Mic remembered his father's hand tousling his hair, or pulling him across the road. A hard hand, cracks in the thumbs filled with dirt. He loved to examine his father's hands, to spread the fingers and trace all those roads worn in the skin, the whorls like the galaxies in the teacher's big book.

That atlas of stars was the only book in the classroom. There was no paper, no pencils. The windows held no glass, only sometimes the stars and maybe those galaxies like the calluses on his father's palms. On Friday afternoon, the teacher read from this single book. Mic could only remember that the sun was a yellow dwarf.

But his father was not a labourer. He worked in an office and his mother always said Dada had beautiful penmanship. His hands were hard because he had to break up the concrete gun emplacement behind their house, to grow vegetables on the land. The concrete was four feet thick, his mother said, and father a thin man, if wiry. Smashing the huge concrete mushroom was illegal, but there was no one left who cared.

They would walk to the cemetery. Two miles Dada always said, but it felt longer. His father didn't talk much, but once, Mic remembered, he told him the name of a flower. It was growing in the grass at the side of the road.

Chicory, his father said. Remember chicory. Some people make their coffee with chicory.

Why do they do that?

Because they're poor. Because it gives a taste.

Coffeeweed, his father then called it. That's its other name.

Mic thought he would hate chicory, and scowled at the flower.

Usually they'd catch the bus back. A man used to sit at the stop chanting a poem. He never caught the bus. It was a great poem, he always said. Even the Greeks had forgotten it, the poem was so old. Dada would scrabble a few qindarka out of his trouser pocket for the fare but often the driver merely waved them aboard. On that bus journey back to the city Mic always hoped to meet Pjeter. Usually the bus was full of headscarved women with bundles of sticks and trussed chickens, and soldiers in their green uniforms winking at the girls. Sometimes Mic and Pjeter could sit together, whilst his father stood.

Pjeter wanted to be a priest. Mic made little of this. Pjeter was pale with big eyes. He was skinny and could climb trees and hang by his long legs, making faces.

Do priests play football? Mic asked.

Pjeter shrugged. Dunno.

I want to play for Roma, Mic said. Pjeter sneered. How many Albanians play in Serie A? he asked.

I will be the first. Anyway, what do priests do?

Pjeter shrugged again. Eat three meals a day, he said. Touch up the girls.

Once his father took Mic up the hill to the warehouse. A lorry had arrived, full of aid. It was Catholic aid, but the Muslims were getting some too. It must be equal, the lorry drivers said. No favourites. Everyone laughed at that.

They stayed in the warehouse all day, fetching, carrying. Mic had never seen such bounty. So many things. There was a mirror. He loved it at once, that cracked oval mirror with a rainbow at its edge. He stared at his face in its glass, scowled, smiled. He wished Pjeter was there to blow out his cheeks and look like a monkey.

Who gets the mirror, Dada? Mic called.

Not you, said a woman, flour on her hands from a burst bag.

Mic's grandada was buried in the cemetery. That's why they visited. One day, his father took him to another part of the graveyard. The plots here were edged with marble and there were low marble headstones.

Look, his father said. On one of the stones were two words in capitals: ENVER HOXHA. On the grave bed were vases with brown bouquets, and a jam jar with dandelions in the green water.

But the boy wasn't interested. He was looking across the cemetery to where two young men were teasing one of the mad people. All the mad people had been chased out of the asylum and now everyone was scared of them. They wandered the streets begging for food. The mad people slept in doorways or down at the bus station. They were lost.

This mad boy was big as a bull. He was making strange bellowing sounds. The young men were pretending to beat him with bunches of dead flowers. Earlier his father had picked ox-eye daisies and placed them on Grandada's unnamed plot. Now he was muttering to himself. Mic looked back to the three figures on the other side of the graveyard. They were pulling the mad boy's trousers off.

His father had sat down by the grave and taken out his bottle. Now he would drink a little arak and continue talking to himself. Arak tasted of the worst things in the world. It smelt of rotten potatoes. Mic had seen his father spit a mouthful over Hoxha's name.

Once Mic and Pjeter and Flutura and some friends were playing round the mushrooms in the park. The mushrooms were the concrete gun emplacements, and they were spread all over the city and countryside, over the hills and in the gardens. They were grey and round and looked like they had sprung up overnight, even though they had always been there.

Some people kept goats in the mushrooms. Some people even grew mushrooms in the mushrooms. He remembered Pjeter was on top, larking about, sliding down with his lanky legs, wearing out the seat of his pants. There were no socks in his shoes. And then a woman came out of the entrance. Get off, she said. Go away.

She was one of the mad people, she must have been. Or that's what Mic thought. She was wearing a soldier's overcoat tied up with string. Her hair was yellow as bonfire smoke and she had yellow eyes, like a goat's in the dark.

Flutura screamed. They all scarpered because they thought she might have been a witch. A mad witch. You never knew what you'd find in the mushrooms. Dead bodies, guilty lovers. There were millions of mushrooms everywhere.

Another time, a man showed the gang his card. *BBC* it said. They took him round to see the tank traps, and he filmed them with his camera. He filmed the children too and wrote their names down. Once he told them to gather round, and opened a bag. It was full of chewies and sweets in their coloured cellophane. He gave everyone a handful, plus a dollar each. A dollar!

Mic ran home and showed his father, who came in with his sleeves rolled up and concrete dust on his shoes. But it was mother who took the dollar. She folded it up small as a postage stamp.

But where did you spend a dollar? Mother had only leks for the market. Sometimes she let Mic count the notes. Mic thought they must be rich, but the money was torn and dirty and smelled of dirty people like the witch with yellow eyes. Witches killed babies, Mic knew that. They could suck the breath out of children's bodies. Pjeter had made one of his rubber faces at the witch as they ran away.

2

Mic preferred the tongs to the grabber. After an hour's use, the grabber grew slack and was difficult to control. So it would be the tongs for Mic tonight.

The concert was supposed to end before midnight. That was the rule. But there was Paul McCartney running on to the stage, and there was Neil Young welcoming him, Neil Young with his ancient face, Neil Young, not a young man now but as ravaged as the alkies and the homeless Mic was supposed to roust from the park benches in the dark.

Not that Mic rousted anyone. Too dangerous. Because where would they go, those dangerous homeless men, the big Nigerians, the skinny Roma, the thin and whiskery Irish? They were sleeping in Hyde Park because they had no homes. Yes, that was the problem with the homeless. They never went home. And then on the big screen Paul McCartney was singing, singing his part of the song, his part of *Day in the Life*. And Neil Young, fearsome as some Hyde Park vagabond, rolling his eyes like a horse, spittle on his lips, was also singing *Day in the Life*. Neil Young's drummer, looking ill and decrepit, an older man the drummer, surely another homeless man there tonight in Hyde Park, a broken-down man, was drumming and drumming, and the song, that *Day in the Life*, coming to a crescendo, its last chord building and building and taking so long to die away, and the crowd standing and cheering, none of them sitting now, everyone whooping and waving, and Neil Young playing the xylophone, no it was the vibraphone the crowd said, a mysterious sound, silvery and slinky, and then he was gone, Neil Young gone, Paul McCartney gone, the drummer with his broken-down face gone, all gone from the screen, the screen in Hyde Park, and they would be starting their party now somewhere in a fabled West End hotel, and the crowd was making its way home, the thousands, the tens of thousands, and only Mic to stay, Mic and Stanis and the others to stay and clean up after the crowd, after the party and the concert in Hyde Park, the last chord of *Day in the Life* still echoing over the grass, still vivid in the crowd's shining eyes.

Already Greendown's electric trolleys and vans were travelling the park roads, and Mic was filling bags with polystyrene cartons and plastic glasses, cartons that had held Thai green curry and Thai red curry, glasses drained of Tiger and Kingfisher and Old Speckled Hen.

Mic wiped his brow under the floodlights. He stepped around figures in sleeping bags, figures in plastic bin liners, figures sprawled half-naked on the grass. People were not supposed to sleep in Hyde Park but he understood why they had to lie down. It had been so hot all day, hot throughout a day of uppers and downers until the downers won and the mind gave in.

Take your pick, Mic thought. And the sleepers had chosen, pot and coke and speed and kefatine and the blissful pethidine, the white tablets, the blue pills, the capsules full of rainbow granules, the Red Bull and the Jagermeister. Yes, they had chosen. Some of it, all of it, and these were the victims, the blithely dreamless sleepers under the Hyde Park trees.

Look, here was a couple asleep in one another's arms, a couple who had collapsed against the mottled trunk of a plane tree, a tree Mic decided he could not like, a leper's tree the plane tree, a couple asleep amongst the plane leaves fallen out of that parched midnight, a pale and sacrificial couple amidst the thousands and thousands of plastic water bottles that waited for his tongs.

So much food had not been touched. So much was abandoned half eaten. Mic and Stanis sat on the grass in the dark and shared a picnic. The red curry. The green curry. They drank from the plastic bottles and gathered the empties at their feet. Stanis had Yorkshire Spring, Tesco Fountainhead Spring, Surrey Down and Highland Spring. Mic found Hydr8 and Lomond Spring, Ty Nant and Ice Valley, Vivreau and Asda Farm Stores. Mic won because Stanis gave up and lay down under a hedge with his tongs and said he was too tired to work, too tired and his head was buzzing with the noise Neil Young and his evil drummer had been making. Yes, a wicked old man that drummer, someone he could imagine meeting in a forest, an old man who ate children, cooked them in a cauldron and ate them as the legends described.

Mic said don't be stupid. The Greendown superintendents were all over the park. They would drive up silently on their electric trolleys, and Stanis would lose his job. Then he'd have to go to the hostel, and he knew what that was like.

Mic thought Stanis had taken some chemical and he pulled

him up and put the tongs back in his hands and said at least pretend you're working. But Stanis only laughed and wandered off with a plastic bag over his head towards the screen being taken down from the stage.

As dawn broke, Mic surveyed the scene. They had worked so hard but it still resembled a war zone. Paper and bottles everywhere, sheets of plastic grey and blue, as if the sky had fallen, a tattered sky in ruins upon the grass.

He picked up the silver stomach from inside a wine box. Half full. He picked up a pair of jeans with a belt made of rope. Yes, he would take the jeans home. He picked up a tee shirt with a picture of Neil Young, whose face was huge and cruel. Yes, a cruel god, Neil Young, who had made such a terrible noise. What could have possessed him to make such a din? But Mic took the tee shirt too. It was useful.

Dawn's smoke rose in every direction. There were figures moving through the haze, Greendown's cleaners in their dayglo tabards, barefoot girls creeping over the grass dressed in gauze and mist and almost nothing at all, barechested boys who wandered about in thought, as if they had mislaid something marvellous that had been there a moment ago.

At 7 a.m. the sun was shining and the new shift was arriving, Obi Wan and Obi Two were there. The Ivorian was there, tall as a tree. Mic and Stanis stowed their tongs in a trolley and walked to the Marble Arch exit and into Orchard Street, then north and east towards Pentonville and eventually Hermes Street. It took them ninety minutes to get home.

They shared a room at number 37. Mic went to the shower cubicle down the landing, then back to the room to change. Stanis was already asleep on his couch, still wearing the yellow tabard.

Mic made himself a cup of coffee and put a slice of bread on the hot ring. It burned before it toasted, but he was used to that. By 9 a.m. he was changed into different jeans and a clean shirt, and at 9.30 he was entering the Champagne Bar at St Pancras Railway Station.

He could see himself in the mirrors. Hair combed, face clean shaven. Thin, a thin man, but worth a look. Yes, the girls might look. Or the women now, some of them at least. And a few might catch his eye then glance away from that slim figure, the dark man with grey speckling in his hair. Greek, they might think. Italian perhaps. A waiter on his day off. But as with all waiters it was hard to say how old he was.

Mic never played for Roma. But he had visited the Emirates Stadium and the Arsenal Museum, heard the crowds marching down the Holloway Road and stepped out of their way. A few times he sat in that pub near Varnisher's Yard and watched Sky Sports all morning, sometimes *Serie A*, sometimes the tall Totti leading the line, Francesco Totti who appeared in the mobile phone adverts.

Presto, Totti would say, Hey Presto, which made Mic laugh. Once Totti lay on the pitch after he scored a goal, the ball under his jersey in tribute to his pregnant wife.

How the crowd had roared, amazed. How Mic had cheered with the other Roma supporters in the bar, the rival Lazio fans shrugging it off, and everyone speaking their streetwise Romanesco in that London pub, and Mic happy for a moment. Because sometimes even an Albanian was allowed to cheer. Poor as an Albanian, that's what the Italians said. In Italy, Albanians were scum.

But this was not Italy. This was London and everything was different. Mic lived in the centre of the world. King's Cross was that centre, where the British queen was buried under platform nine of the railway station. The British queen who had fought the Romans, fought Totti's people with scythes on her chariot wheels. And platform nine was where Harry Potter caught his train. Sometimes Mic went to watch the Japanese tourists who thought Harry was a real boy. How he pitied them.

Then she was there. Only a little late. Thirty minutes late, her average. Suddenly, on the stool beside him, sat Li, Li in red, a tight red dress, Li boyslim, smiling, smiling despite her sadness, Li with her tiny handbag, narrow as a knife, her teeth shining, her eyes bright as a blackbird's even as she said hey, hey hello, hello to you, Mr Mic.

And Mic looked up and the barman came over once again and the bar hostess who has been watching him at last, looked away. How Mic wanted to order Dom Pérignon White Gold, 1995. Yes, a jeroboam. For £6500.00. That's what the menu said.

Instead, he asked for De Nauroy Brut NV. Two glasses, please. It came in at £7.50 a glass. Li always said Chinese people could not drink alcohol, but perhaps one glass would be allowed. And Mic knew that Li would take one taste and leave the glass untouched for the next hour, and then finish the champagne in one gulp when it was flat, oily and flat, then splutter and shriek and complain that she was drunk. Yet it seemed to Mic that Li could get drunk on nothing at all, so brightly did her eyes shine for that hour they shared.

But Mic understood that Li needed the drink. Her work started at 11 a.m. and anything that helped her deal with work was welcome. Li took other things to help her cope because so many men wanted to visit her. Mic understood that.

They had met three times this way. Champagne was Mic's

idea, although the cost was cruel. But here they were at the Eurostar departure floor, and who could say they were not on their way to Paris with champagne flutes waiting aboard the train? Certainly none of the others who sat along the bar that curved for one hundred metres like a gleaming rail. None of them cared. Yes, the hostess cared, who saw everything and acted as if she knew everything. But Mic's money was good.

Li went first. Always first.

Okay, she said. Okay. Once I remember we went all the way from Huangshan to the Yellow Mountains, up into the air on the cable car, higher than I ever thought I could go. How the cables groaned. The mountains had sharp points that came through the clouds. But the mountains were purple and green; I don't know why we called them the Yellow Mountains. And we had our picnic and then it was time to come down. But it was a public holiday, said Li, and Mic thought her eyes were black moons. So more and more people had come up in the afternoon. The paths were too crowded. We walked on the ledges and were pushed to the very edge. And more and more people were coming down through the trees to our trails, and more and more people coming up the tracks to where we stood.

Soon we were stuck. There on the mountainside. No one could move and it was already evening and I remember the evening star above Golden Turtle View of the ocean. It was winking at us like a warning. Children were crying and women fainting. Some westerner had a panic attack right next to me, a tourist, a fat white man, weeping. That made me feel better. Feel strong.

And then I heard a voice. It was a young woman in uniform, party uniform, telling us what to do. She was telling us to sing and what songs to sing, and soon after that the pressure began to ease.

I knew we'd be safe then. How beautiful she was, the party girl, how gallant. We all loved her, up there in the mountains in the mist, so close to the edge. Yes, we loved her and her strong voice, singing about our heroes. It was a miracle. I was ten years old and in love with the party girl. The boy next to me, with his flat Mongol face, flat as a plate it was, he loved her too.

The party, laughed Mic. My father was in the party. Not that he cared. In the end nobody cared because only the black market made sense. Once he showed me the dictator's grave and I saw him spit on it. At night in the capital we used to walk across Skanderbeg Square, my friends Pjeter and Flutura and me. Sometimes we saw Chinese people. They were the businessmen who were building our factories. My father said it couldn't be right; it was crazy to have Chinese factories. But Li, maybe I saw your people from Huangshan, wandering the square.

Li's eyes were heavy now. Something she had taken was wearing off. Or kicking in. But she roused herself.

Squares are dangerous places, whispered Li.

Under the few lights, Mic continued, the square looked like a frozen ocean. Pjetr said Tirana meant tyranny in English, and sometimes the army boys in their green uniforms would chase us away. It was something for them to do. It's boring being a soldier.

But that's what I always remember, looking out across the square and shivering. It was so empty, so huge. I felt crushed, but now I understand that's what they wanted me to feel. And the dogs were barking in the night, the dogs with rabies, the dogs with mad eyes out there in the dark, the darkness where the witches lived, where everything was broken and spoiled and all used up.

But we still took the BBC man we met to a bar where he could buy arak. He bought everyone in the room a drink. Even us kids. All he had was a card that said *BBC*, but to us he was like a god. I remember he took a quince from his coat pocket and gave it to Flutura. A golden quince. Like a magician he seemed to me then, that BBC man. And soon he was gone.

Mic looked around. The Champagne Bar was busy now, and the announcement for the Paris train was being made in French.

Li, he said. Li?

She was picking at a thread in her red dress. If Mic looked closely he knew he would see the dress was stained, that the crimson paint on her toenails was cracked, that there were scabs on the insides of her arms. Li's fingernails were bitten to the quick. As to Mic, his hands were now his father's hands. Mic had built the Tirana apartments, he had knocked them down. His shirt was from Age Concern, his jeans the blind shop. At least the hostess had moved away.

Li, he said. Li? Please marry me. Marry me, Li. You can escape and we'll go to another part of London. London's so huge no one will ever know where we are. We can go today, Li. Now. Go now.

He touched her arm.

Don't go back, Mic said. One day they're going to kill you. Li raised her glass and sipped, gargled the warm champagne like mouthwash, swallowed and made a face.

I'm drunk, she said, getting up unsteadily from the stool. Mr Mic, you got me drunk again, you fucker.

In those days there were lions in Iraq

Poole in Dorset, that's Dorset, UK, is not a strange place. But perhaps it's a peculiar setting for this story.

I'm Macsen, Max to you, and I've been part of what you call the environmental movement for thirty years. That's long before it became fashionable or cool. Or dreary.

Now, in those days, start of the 1980s, if you had told me that campaigning against new roads or pollution would become a career choice, offering a good pension, a car, ha ha, opportunity to travel and the rest of it, I'd have slapped your face.

Yet most of the people I've worked with over the last decade never did a day's volunteering in their lives. They certainly haven't waved a placard or organised a protest meeting. Or got down and dirty with a multinational trying to opencast a Scottish hillside.

Funny, isn't it. We won the battle. People like me. We bloody won. We raised the profile of all things environmental. Showed how everything was linked – clean air, good food, humane values. Raised the awareness level to such an extent that there's not a telly programme without some greenspeak in it. Chefs and weathergirls spouting off.

Well, great. Sort of. Sustainability rules. Now no one can claim ignorance of climate change or junk food. No councillor, no MP. Not anyone with power. We won.

And as proof of that, there are all those jobs in all those environmental organisations. Everybody saving the planet. But claiming time in lieu. Everybody with a computer and broadband someone else is paying for. With offices. With office cleaners for Christ's sake. With parking spaces. With the internet to do their thinking for them.

Yeah, but without the remotest clue about the people who created it for them. The pathfinders. The originators. That's right. People like me. And don't tell me I'm wrong because you can't. I was there. On the front line. And I don't remember seeing you.

These days, if I walked into that new Greenpeace office there's not a soul would know me. Friends of the Earth? They'd call security. Should have seen it coming, I suppose. But I was too busy saving your arse.

After a while I became more like your high-street green than a campaigning type. Fair trade, local and organic stuff. That was where the action was. I was part of a co-operative and we had this place in Cheam. Coffee bar, radical bookshop, performance space all in one. Ahead of its time? I'll say. That's been my curse.

Well, okay, after a couple of years, I left. Disagreement, you understand. Us greens are notorious for knifing one another in the back. And I was knifed. The Cheam place was awarded a Lottery grant and that really messed us up. There was money to pay a co-ordinator. Frankly, it should have been me. Unquestionably. What it created instead was internecine warfare. Divide and rule? Works every time.

Been around, haven't I? Communes, squats. That tipi village in west Wales? Couldn't stand another rainy summer there. Or the ayatollah who ran it. Tarifa? Extreme climate. It's where

Africa makes the jump into Europe. But try talking eco-politics with surfers and hang gliders.

Since then I've been writing, for *Resurgence, Grave New World*. Had some luck too, and that's what I want to do now. Writing's giving me the biggest kick I've had in a long time. It feels good.

And that's why I'm in Poole. Canford Cliffs to be precise, looking at how the new money is spent. Down there, in the harbour, are the bankers' yachts. Above me, the bankers' mansions and apartments, their second, third homes. Yes, Canford Cliffs is the place to be. An English Monaco. Paid for out of the credit crunch.

I've done a bit of filming too, with Earth First and others. There's some great indie operations out there. But there would be wouldn't there? Everything's digital. Just point and press. Not like when I started.

So filming is where the story begins. In a way it is the story. Of the film I made once. And the man who made it possible. Because this is his story. Mine will be told another time. You haven't got time for mine.

Ever hear of depleted uranium? DU? Back in 1996 I hadn't either. But out of the blue comes an invitation. A friend of a friend knows somebody. This rich Egyptian, she's a campaigner, a believer. She's trying to get a team together to film in Iraq. I'm like, known to be up for things. Will give anything a go. And I can write, can't I? I'm a journalist? Well, sort of. And I've all the green contacts haven't I? Yes, well... Jonathon Porritt owes me a fiver.

A week later there's blossom all over Queen's Gate. The colour of old bones. My mouth is at a silver intercom. Then I'm in a room lined with portraits of Saddam Hussein. He's saluting.

Hand in greeting, hand on heart. In a corner is a TV tuned to the news, but we ignore that because a clerk is matching photographs to papers and then something is being printed in purple ink. It permits me to spend ten days in Iraq.

Two weeks later I'm in a Baghdad hotel room reading a manual on how to work a Sony movie camera. I've got it on charge but the electricity is dodgy. From the balcony I can see the Tigris. The green tigress I call her. I have this feeling I'm already out of my depth. That I could drown in Baghdad.

Well, I say to myself. It's better than the tipi. Beats pissing out of a tree on Twyford Down. There's a knock on the door. It's Fatima, the Egyptian who's paying for everything. Who believes I'm a BBC hotshot.

Max, I'd like you to meet Mohammed, she says. He's our government guide.

Goon, I think. But next thing I remember I'm lying on a divan. I've just quit smoking this najila a yard long, hung with falcon feathers. Mohammed had chosen the pipe specially. You know, I thought I could take my draw. I stayed in Amsterdam's Bar 98 for a while and even the white widow didn't phase me as long as I kept off the wine. But that Baghdad hashish? I dreamed I was that falcon drifting over an ocean of dark stone. A black speck in the endless blue. Or maybe it was a 109 Tomahawk with a nosecone painted like a draughts board. Coming to a street near me, courtesy of McDonnell Douglas. And no, they don't make shortbread.

Then the next thing I recall is I've got the runs and we're filming an hour's interview at the Department of Transport. Still got the complete thing on tape. Mohammed's in the room. Mohammed has set it up. He's our ticket to ride, our official heavy with influence. And when he smokes he tells jokes about

Iran and the US. The stupid countries he calls them. Schools? hospitals? We film them. Crowd scenes? Safe on tape. Babylon? I've got Babylon coming out of my ears.

Had this Babylonian party once in a place in Cornwall. Films showing empty temples. Weird creatures on the walls. Euphrates kingfishers faster than Scuds. Look at this, I kept telling the guests. You won't see this again. What you think this is, the Discovery Channel? This is fucking real.

Well, we made our uranium film. Ten hours cut to twenty minutes. So sometimes I think about what we left out. There was this British soldier we interviewed in Birmingham. Depleted uranium victim. His friends said his nickname was Prettyboy. Well, I tell you, Prettyboy wasn't so pretty anymore. They'd given him thirty thousand pounds compo for everything that was wrong with him. Not that the words 'depleted uranium' were ever used.

Want to know what Prettyboy did with thirty thousand quid? He drank it. That could have been thirty thousand cans of Special Brew. Or ten thousand bottles of bad Rioja. Well, forget all that. Prettyboy cut to the chase. Necked five thousand litres of Krazy Kremlin. In three years. That's why he's not so pretty now. His mates told us they would take him to the Fox and Grapes in Digbeth and ask D U want another vodka? Good joke, eh?

With hindsight, he should have been in the film. With a lot of other material. Anyway, it was shown at CND meetings, a few arts centres. Didn't win an Oscar. But did it make a difference? Of course it did. And still does. If you don't believe that you might as well be a fossil. But as I keep saying, this is not my story. Or Prettyboy's. My story comes later.

So I'm in Poole for a few days, billeted with friends out of town. The Canford Cliffs area is exclusive and I've become used to seeing the same people. But there is one man I notice having coffee on the cliff, surveying the ocean, who is differently familiar. One morning I decide to act. I take my cup to the next table on the patio and look out.

Hello, I say. A decent morning.

The man turns to me. He's puzzled.

How are you these days? I ask.

He looks closely at me then.

Oh, he says finally. Takes him a while, like. I expect him to be embarrassed but he's not.

The last time we saw each other, he says carefully, I believe I was crying. You might think that a difficult thing to admit. But it no longer matters.

We're alive, Mohammed.

He lifts his cup in a brief toast.

Remember that hotel room in the madman's capital, I ask. (I know that's an odd thing to say but in Baghdad everyone told me never use the boss' name. And don't even think of pointing that camera at one of his statues.)

Yes, Mohammed replies. You and your companion laid out the money on the bed. Black dinars I wouldn't wipe myself with. Royal Jordanian pounds that were more like it. But no dollars, my friend. Not a George Washington to be seen. And I needed dollars. All that work I had done. All the special services.

But the government paid you, I say.

Pistachio shells. But to repeat, it doesn't matter now.

How did you get away?

From the insanity? Surprisingly easily.

We order more coffee.

Do you know, says Mohammed. I was in a restaurant in

Amman when that fool, the Information Minister, came on television and said there were no Americans. And no American tanks.

What's that then? the journalists asked. There was a Challenger coming down El Rashid Street behind this oaf. A Challenger tank with a barrel long as a palm tree.

Oh, pardon me, gentlemen, says the minister, I have an urgent appointment. And he disappears.

How we all laughed in that café. Or maybe I was still crying, but the coffee was very strong. Yes, that café was an excellent place. There were CIA there, braying and bragging, but I wasn't afraid. Small fry, you see, I was never more than that. My picture wasn't on their screens. Not one of the playing cards, not even close. A different game entirely.

How did you get here? I laugh. Poole!

Mohammed smiles again and looks into the harbour.

I live here, he says.

Now that just blew me away.

And I live well. You must come up to the apartment.

He looks at me tolerantly.

You will remember the museum? I had it opened especially for you and your friend.

It was unbelievable, I say.

Yes, a marvellous place. But walking with you there, something occurred to me. So before I left I paid the museum a visit. And then another visit. By the end I knew every corridor. The storerooms too, the crypts, and what they held.

It was a privilege, I say.

Now Mohammed produces his wallet and from it a plastic wrapper three inches square. Out of this he takes a piece of bubblewrap. Within it might be a dark coin.

It's a stamp, he says. Or a seal. A stamp, a seal.

I look at the broken disc. He doesn't let me touch it. There are designs of antelopes upon it and men who might be hunters.

Pretty isn't it, he smiles. And, guess what?

What?

It is six thousand years old.

He sits back, the bubblewrap on the table between us, the disc catching the sun. It waits like a tip for the waiter.

Such a charming thing. And there is so much more, so much you wouldn't believe. You see, we Mesopotamians are a civilised people. Six thousand years ago there were kings who craved such fine art. When your people were rubbing sticks together, our artists and craftsmen were learning their trade.

You looted the museum?

Loot? Of course not. I went with a friend who knows Nineveh, who understands how Babylon and Ur were built. Who knew what wouldn't be missed and what the country could afford to lose. Oh, we were careful in that. We were scrupulous.

We both look down at the harbour.

You see, says Mohammed, we walked along the aisles of the museum and were the only people there. Just like when you paid your visit. No wardens. No professors muttering or students sketching. And no glass on the floor as there soon would be. We came to a hall. In a cabinet was a copper mask, a king's head. The king's beard was cut in curls and ringlets. There was a copper crown upon his head. But his lips were a woman's lips, red and royal and alive. I looked at that king in the twilight and thought, yes, I could love that man. For that man is an imperial leader, maybe a cruel man, perhaps a murderer of his people, a sacrificer of children, a lunatic, a psychopath. But here he is; here is the king. After five thousand years, here is the king.

And my hands were on that cabinet and I said we must take this, we must. And you know what my friend did? He touched me on the shoulder. Such a beautiful touch. It explained everything. And the passion passed. And we walked on through the museum and we left Nebuchadnezzar's dragons and the Assyrian magicians with their square whiskers and we took what would not be missed.

Tiny gods. It was only the tiny gods we took. The smallest gods who never really mattered. Do small gods matter? To small people perhaps. We took not the gold gods but the alabaster gods. As tiny as chessmen, those gods. My gods now. And seals like this. Some tiles from Babylon. A sphinx from the back of a cupboard. And a red cheetah that fits my hand.

Because I am silent, Mohammed thinks I am critical.

I saved them, he says. I saved them for the world. Where is the great king now? Where are the lions of Uruk or the golden bulls? Where are the chariots? Where are the tablets with the world's first writing? Gone my friend, gone with the smugglers who lacked my sensibility. Gone with the idiots who exchanged eternity for cigarettes. I sell what I took to dealers who make ten times the money I could ever do. But my tiny gods will be safe in Tokyo or Los Angeles when the rest of it is dust in the street.

Yes, I say. I agree with you. And I wish I had done the same.

And I smile because I remember now a statue of a woman. I had stood before it and seen my mother's face, my mother's 1950s' hairdo frozen in Parthian limestone, the statue's drapes my mother's dressing gown, its inlaid eyes the eyes that would never grow old.

Another time, he says.

You mean for coffee?

No, says Mohammed. It was all another time.

He looks at me then.

Now, he says, you must come up. I want to show you my home.

We walk past a pub called The Nightjar which is opening its doors. I haven't heard a nightjar in thirty years. I was on a dark road once, listening for footsteps behind me. Crossing a moor. I heard it then, the nightjar. An old, old song. A lonely song.

My grandfather used to say nightjars sounded like knives held to a grindstone. In Cheam there was this travelling tool sharpener who used to pop in for coffee. Don't worry, all those trades are coming back. They have to.

Mohammed takes me into the foyer of an apartment block. The deskman calls him Mr Haifa. The lift feels as if it's made of glass, but it's burnished steel. I can see my own reflection, Mohammed's cotton jacket, thin and a pale mauve. Jaeger, I'd say. He was pudgy over there and has put on more weight.

I remember our last meal, eggs and figs in the hotel. Tea in a glass. We were all agitated, Fatima and I scared we'd miss the Jordan bus. She'd spent all her money by then. Turns out she had medical training and the hotel staff used to consult her in her room. She gave them money. We'd brought in boxes of medicines because we knew there was nothing in the hospitals. That was breaking the UN embargo, by the way. So I'm a smuggler too. A badge of honour.

But that last day we were stony broke. Think of it, broke in Baghdad. Mohammed didn't believe our backsheesh was enough and was sulking. I liked him better when there was coffee or hash inside him, and he told us stories. Mohammed was a survivor. Which means he must have been complicit in the murders, the disappearances. I had time to think about that on the way back through the desert. And, you know, I couldn't bring myself to condemn him. A plump man in a sweat-stained white shirt. Little moustache. Say he was fifty. The skids already under him.

The corridor was silent. Like walking on a lawn. And his apartment? The same thick felt in emerald green. I saw armchairs, a divan. That first room had a view over the harbour and cliffs. We stood on the balcony.

Yes, he said. I love to sit here in the dark and watch the lights, listen to the boats' rigging, the ships' bells. Mournful music to some, but remember, the sea is a wonder to me. For a man such as I, the ocean is a dream.

Are you homesick? I ask.

Of course. Always. Such is life. You know, when I was a boy I'd sleep in summer on the roof of our house. Every night I'd look at the stars. In Iraq, each star has a story but I'd make up my own. Even in the heat I would shiver. But with excitement. It's that excitement we feel homesick for. But I know I'll never find it again.

The bathroom is decorated in gold and onyx. But everything's black. There's a black whirlpool air spa bath. The toilet I piss into is black. It makes me think of an eisteddfod chair. Mohammed's bathrobe is black embroidered silk. When I come out I join him on the balcony.

What happened to the lion we saw? I ask. The great carved lion gnawing a slave?

No one knows, he says. But there are still people alive who remember lions in Iraq. So many of our artists have honoured lions. The sculptors of Babylon were hired out all over the world to make stone lions. Or lions of alabaster. Even gold lions. Dragons and lions guarded Babylon. But they couldn't stop the tanks.

He pauses and smiles. Listen, you are the reason I am here. You and your companion.

We only wanted to film the museum, I say. But we cut it out of the film.

Yes, but history roared in my head, answers Mohammed. I was in the museum crypt. The lights were dim. There was silence. It was a holiday and even the scholars were absent. Dust floated in the air and lay underfoot. Only Haji Abid was there. He had worked in the museum for fifty years but if he understood what was going on, he didn't say. Then there it was. A red lion on a desk. Its mouth open, its mane like armour. It sat like a cat watching me. A terracotta cat on a newspaper. I would have sworn it was alive. The museum cat, licking its chops. Mohammed sips his tea.

I stroked that lion's cold fur, he says. I'm told the statue was smashed in the looting. Knocked to the ground and trodden to pieces. All those idiots looking for riches. They didn't have a clue what they'd done. Some used hammers and saws to break up statues too big to move.

But there were others, hired by high-ups in the party. They came with shopping lists and explosives to open vault doors, emptying whole cabinets into ministry cars. What could old Haji do, holding his broom? I found him once hiding in a pot discovered in the temple of the sun god at Hatra. Old Haji, like someone from the *Arabian Nights*.

Mohammed and I come inside. On glass shelves are women, voluptuous in pale alabaster, men of clay like red chess pieces. A copy of *FI Magazine* lies opened on a cream leather armchair at a picture of the new Ferrari.

How did you escape? I ask.

Mohammed inflates his cheeks. By then, he says, we were a

nation of smugglers. I hired two men who owned a transit van. Cash, I said. One quarter now, three on delivery. It was a risk because I was using my savings. I told them we were going to Amman, so they had to have their papers. It was up to them if they came back. Neither turned a hair.

We actually used the museum's own crates. The hired men didn't understand what I was doing. Boxes of stone? The head of a boy with no eyes? At first I had the idea that we should hide it all. I was going to buy a load of watermelons and pretend we were farmers. Then I decided there was no need. Because I knew what would happen at the border.

Delay, I said. Two check points.

Yes, said Mohammed. I recall you were detained there. But on our side they didn't care any more. Maybe they had never cared. All those grandmothers sitting in the dirt, looking through their bundles for a scarf to shield their eyes. And the children crying because of the wind, the men standing together, smoking, the buses unloading, reloading, the empty petrol tankers parked up.

Then no-man's land, I said.

Indeed. That stinking part of the desert between two nations. As if both refused it. Razor wire, a burned-out car. Then more old people opening their cases. Doing it all again. Half the time the officials didn't bother to look. They were dead with boredom, sick of that screaming wind full of grit. It sounded like metal tearing. What a place. The road was scattered with shredded tyres, there were glaciers of black sand behind black rocks. They knew what was going on and that there was no way of stopping it. Some people slaughter a sheep and look at its liver. No need there. We all understood what was coming.

The Jordanian troops were smarter than ours. Not hard. Our men were the scum of the army, illiterates off the streets. They lifted the sheets and opened one crate. Builders' rubble? they asked.

To decorate a villa in Amman, I said.

They shrugged and waved us through. Jordan did the same. We were part of the convoy. The troops even made jokes with my companions.

After that we only stopped to take a leak. Why else would we? That's a wasteland where nobody lives. Not a tree, not a house. I remember we passed a Bedouin shepherd. There must have been a wadi somewhere about, but God, that land looked as if it had never known rain. Everything the colour of ash. Pebbles like peachstones burned black.

The shepherd stared down at us from a rise, and I could feel it didn't matter to him where the border was drawn. Because he was the desert king and his fathers had always been rulers there. They lived in some scrape of the ground. At night they were cold because there was no wood to burn. So they slept in goat skins. Maybe a lammergeyer would take a kid. But what did it matter if it was camels or tankers on the road? Bedouins don't need roads.

As far as I was concerned he was welcome to his wilderness. Badiet esh Sham? It means the desert of the left hand. No Babylon there. No astronomy either, though the stars sparked like coals when a pipe is lit. Where would that shepherd find a wife and not a goat? I like houses and automobiles. A city glow spreading out before me, headlights heading home.

There was petrol where the road forks to Damascus and we reached Amman not long after dawn. It was like a dream, and everything since has been a dream. Amman, the white city out of the black land. Amman on its hills, as I think Athens must be. A big Marlboro sign. People at the roadside offering tea and coffee. We stopped on the outskirts and bought bread from some Palestinians. They had baked thyme into the crust and it tasted good. The first taste of civilisation.

Looking back, it was so easy. But everything was easy. I was a man of some importance. Sometimes I forget that. We drove to my cousin's home who lived near the bus station in Abdali. I remember the van drawing up outside his apartment. The streets were busy, people were going to work. It could have been Athens. Or New York, maybe. Buy this chewing gum, a boy was shouting. Buy this chewing gum, he called at us, as if it was the most important thing in the world.

We took fifteen crates of Mesopotamian history up in the lift to the apartment. Nothing really heavy. My cousin's wife had a feather duster, trying to brush away the dirt of the left-handed desert. Hey, what's in the boxes, Mohammed? she asked. I need a food mixer.

I was exhausted and thought the drivers would want to rest. But no. We gave each a can of Sprite and I paid them in the lobby. Then they went back to the transit and drove off. Just like that. Good business men. They took a risk and were rewarded. I paid them well.

The leather of my chair is cold. It feels like no one has sat in it before.

So you live here alone? I ask.

My wife and I were apart, says Mohammed. It was my son I cared about. But my son was a soldier. He had been admitted to the Imperial Guard. A great honour, some would claim. Others might call it a curse.

One of his first duties was to patrol the British Embassy. Oh yes, the irony is not lost on me. Exquisite is it not? The unit sergeant at the gate would let me through because of who I am.

Or was. But a small consideration smoothed the way, destined for the captain, whose office lay in the embassy itself. After all, gentlemen understand one another. The protocols must be observed.

I remember those walks up the embassy drive. There were unusual palm trees in the gardens, loaded with dates. The soldiers harvested them and had a good business going. Sometimes they played football on the lawn. Yes, the World Cup had been held in France, and bloody Saudi was part of it. Iran too, for God's sake. So it was Iraq against the Rest of the World. All the boys wanted to be Ronaldo or David Beckham. Michael Owen scoring that goal. His greatest goal, they tell me. They couldn't remember our own golden generation. And what a pitch. The croquet hoops were still in place. But that's where the captain organised his own World Cup. On the croquet lawn. Sometimes he'd referee. Said it let off steam.

I remember once I brought him a tin of Russian Caravan tea. It had come from Fortnum and Mason in London. The captain called me into his room and we shared a pot. He looked at me, then at the tin and read aloud: 'Its light, almost nutty flavour and distinct character evoke the unique position of Imperial Russia on the world's crossroads, and its rulers' domestic passion for really superior tea.' Hmm, he smiled. Rather like imperial Iraq. World's crossroads and all that.

He offered it the English way, but the milk was sour because the electricity was off. Tea with milk remains a curiosity. By the way, that's the tea we're drinking now. But what an office the captain had. Wood panelling and a glass-topped desk with a reading light under a silver scroll. A picture of the queen on the wall, a picture of Margaret Thatcher. Fine women. They were much admired in Baghdad.

He was an immaculate man, the captain, his uniform spotless, his holster gleaming like oxblood. We shared Turkish cigarettes and once a pipe. But when the time came, he disappeared with the rest. Hid the imperial uniform, walked away a civilian. He already knew that at the crucial moment, it was not the black Mercedes or the deposit box in Geneva that would save him. Wily Bedouin blood still counted in the capital.

Your son does well, he would exclaim. He scored against Brazil.

How we laughed.

He will make a soldier yet, he added.

We both knew this was nonsense. But the game had to be followed. The real game. The end game.

You play chess? Mohammed asks me. Well, the end game had not yet commenced. But we guessed it was very close. All of us would have to escape, each after his own fashion. A little like death, I suppose. But it was understood without speaking. Saddam's picture also hung on the wall. In this incarnation he was a civilian in a double-breasted suit that might have come from Savile Row. But Baghdad used to have the world's best tailors. A handsome man, Saddam, I always thought. You could see why the women loved him.

Now please, the captain would say. Your son is waiting. And I would meet Tariq in the banqueting room, the table still polished every week, the lords, the ladies with their hunting dogs looking down at us from the walls.

You see, unlike the British, we remember our history. And we do it honour. In Baghdad there is the British cemetery, from the 1920s. All those young men were killed by cholera and sunstroke. And yes, some by bullets. But we have tended it ever since, cutting the grass, revering the dead. Again, unlike you, we remember the dead. Our tribes study their genealogies like you do your scratch cards.

We sat together at that banqueting table, Tariq and I, exchanging pleasantries. It is hard for fathers to talk to sons. I gave him chocolate and money. But he had changed. No, not because of the army. He had met a girl. Just at the wrong time, he had met a girl.

They used to see each other when he was off duty. I explained as carefully as I could that it was wrong to tie himself down. The day was coming when he too would need to get out.

But Tariq laughed and spat date stones into an ashtray. The woman had turned his head, as women will.

And yes, I confess, I followed him once. It seems she worked in an office. I watched them go into a tea house near the old baths. No hijab, nothing. And I approved of that. Oh, but she was a gorgeous creature, black eyes with long lashes. To me her high cheekbones meant an Iranian family. Yes, she had the blood of Shiraz within her. Irresistible. I understood exactly his excitement. God help me, I still picture the gold thread she had woven into her hair.

When Tariq gave her the chocolate her eyes grew even wider. Like a schoolgirl's. The sanctions meant the people were starving. There were beggars on the street and malnutrition in Baghdad. One of the world's great cities. It was unheard of.

Tariq, I thought. She will pull you back. She will hang chains on your soul when you need to be free. Those eyes will work a spell.

What happened to Tariq? I ask.

Oh, another irony, says Mohammed. Irony followed him until the end. He became a tank commander, in charge of a T-72, the

Arad Babil. You know what that is in English? The Lion of Babylon.

I gaze at the gods on the glass shelves. I'm still unsure how Mohammed reached the UK, but he senses the unspoken question.

Yes, this is home now, he says. Maybe Amman was a little fraught. Eventually I hired other drivers and took my belongings to Beirut where I have a friend. Then, when the money started to come in, I decided to travel. See the world. This is a pleasant apartment, no?

Canford Cliffs means money's no problem today, I say. But it was in Baghdad.

Mohammed looks hard at me. He is a man of sixty now, his moustache grey.

I apologise, he says. For crying that is. How crass it must have seemed.

Those were strange times.

No, my friend. Those were good times. Well, better times, despite the embargo. These are the strange times. The dangerous times. He whose name we could never speak, he whose photograph was in every room, he was maybe not so mad after all.

You miss those times?

The certainties? Yes. Being able to sit in a restaurant or walk down the street without some imbecile blowing his useless carcass up beside you? Yes I miss those times.

There are no terrorists in Poole, I laugh.

Not on the London Underground either, he says.

We're silent for a while. Mohammed has served almond biscuits. They're too hard for my teeth.

You know, he laughs, they bombed our national archive. Most

of the old documents went up in flames. What was left was put into freezers but the electricity was always off. On, off. Then, a little later, the Americans arrived in Babylon. They built a helipad there. Bulldozers flattened a site in the immemorial earth. America, the stupid country, the new Mongols, brought history to an end.

We're quiet again and I'm still looking around. The leather, the tiny gods. On the plasma widescreen a dancer in a yellow bodystocking is silently circling on a black stage. She looks like an ash key falling to earth. Round and round in the darkness she goes.

Mohammed has made the best of things, I think, glancing up. He understood what was valuable. The time to stay, the time to leave. But when have I ever done that? That Lottery job would have sorted me out. Given me a chance to show my strengths. And the bloody film. All those hours we recorded were reduced to a fragment. At night in Baghdad I would lie awake and look at the green light on the battery charger. If it winked I would panic. But the film we cut doesn't tell the story. How could it? Ten hours of tape wait unseen in an attic and nobody gives a damn. It might have been a masterpiece. Maybe it still could.

There was a doctor I filmed. He took us to view the terrible twins. These had just been born and lay together in an incubator. Something was wrong with them and they weren't going to live. They looked like two halves of a walnut.

In my experience, the doctor said, they are unique.

I remember their wizened faces. Ugly as cicadas. Whatever their illnesses, we thought uranium was responsible. When we arrived home we offered the footage to all the news channels but nobody wanted to know. The parents lived north of Basra.

That was where Prettyboy and his mates had been chucking DU around.

There is an intercom buzz. Mohammed's lunch is arriving. Steak and salad from a local restaurant. A quiver of frites.

I hold out my hand.

Extraordinary to meet you again, I say, but his attention is on the food. The silent screen shows cricket now. Sachin Tendulkar in blue and orange is batting for the Mumbai Indians.

Yes, goodbye, says Mohammed.

In the lift I look at myself. I've forgotten to shave again. I decide to have a drink. Yes, I'll go to The Nightjar. I need to think about things. And there's an article I have to write.

In Goliath's country

Her Honda makes the turning and she drops down slowly into Black Canyon City. But what she remembers today, for no reason she can understand, is something that happened further up the highway.

Somebody had told her there was work in Flagstaff. Boomtown. So what was there to lose? She shared a room with a deaf woman. There was no air con. The office where she cleaned held a thousand desks and every time she clocked on she wondered what the desk people did all day in their miles of metal and glass. Crunch paper? Spill coffee? There were famished flies in the double glazing.

Years of night shifts had brought her down. Daylight sleep meant lethargy. And the TV was on all the time. *Bonanza* in the mornings, *I Love Lucy* any time. You'll wonder where the yellow went when you brush your teeth with Pepsodent. Maybe that was why people went to work, fleeing to their desk islands and the Aqua Chill cooler. The deaf girl would sit and goggle, eating peanuts and drinking milk, a yellow mash in her mouth. With the money she'd saved, Maria decided to try north of Phoenix.

The bus had dropped her at the railway station. She had stood outside and waited for the line to clear, for that Santa Fe with its mile of iron carriages to go wherever it was going. She had looked at each freight car as it passed. Each a casket. A coffin. Sealed tight as an airplane hold. No riding that. No way.

There was a man looking at her from the platform. Blue and white bandanna, dark glasses. She could see his body through the singlet. He was old but he was fit. Or so he might think.

The next day she was sweeping thc pine needles off his floor while he made the Impala roar through a cloud of sawdust. They had slept on a mattress in the back and in the morning he had cooked onions and eggs together in a skillet. She used Pillsbury sweet bread to soak up the grease.

Be back round five, he had said. Adios.

And she had kept sweeping because there was nothing else she knew how to do in that place. When he came home she was still there. Her choice.

The house was a shack above a new lot being cut into the trees. Juniper, pinot pines. Early on, when he wasn't there, she would walk out as far as she dared, climbing a hill in the forest where there were slabs of moss-covered rock with seams of crystal in it. She watched the lizards there, walked higher and stared out at the tops of the hills. All green. All smoking. Each hill with its rocks, its lizards.

Don't get lost, he had told her once. There's fifty miles of it outside. Lion territory.

From the rock she watched the jays, blue and black. Their voices reminded her of the travellers who had raised their puppet theatre one weekend in her home village. Mad voices. Whiny, stupid voices. She and Juan and the other children pointed at the shapes of the ventriloquists through the curtain. But how people had laughed at the puppets' cruelties.

She had thought the jays couldn't see her but maybe they could. How dazzling they seemed. Jays in their jewels. Such crowns they wore. But they were thieves, weren't they, the jays? The greatest of thieves. And out there in the forest were fifty miles of thieves and robbers. Of silent lions. On her fingers the pine needles had smelled of orange peel.

Thirty years ago? Close enough. Thirty years ago, she'd been standing on the station. A man regarding her. She had felt his eyes. Yes, thirty years of feeling eyes upon her. Thirty years waiting for the knock. The man was still staring. What did the bandanna mean? The leather vest? The Santa Fe passed and there were the empty rails.

He was dark as adobe, this staring man. But still an American. And she had sighed. Flagstaff was higher than six thousand feet, the signs said. It would be cold. There would be snow. Deep snow covering the red pine dust. Star-shaped lion footprints coming out of the rocks. Over the crossing she could see a sign for the Lumberjack Café.

Looks like you could do with a drink, the man had said. Poco aqua?

Yes, she had replied. I'm thirsty. Because by then if she knew anything at all she knew there was no turning back. And beyond Flagstaff there was nowhere. Or nowhere big enough to get lost and still survive.

What she's driving is a powder-blue Civic with red primer patches. Up in Flagstaff it would have rusted through by now, but, as she always said, Phoenix was bone dry. Not as dry as where she came from, but getting there.

A woman she knows in the nursing home had told her she should fly. 'Not to go nowhere. Just to see the swimming pools.' Apparently landing and taking off in Phoenix was some experience. A thousand, ten thousand swimming pools were strung out like Zuni turquoise. Like jays' feathers in the dust.

She'd never asked Frank what he was doing at the rail station. Old man had he been? Sort of. If the Luckies hadn't killed him, he'd be seventy now. Lean and red with a little pot belly.

And now it was her turn to be fifty. Only a little younger than the man who had picked her up on the platform. She could remember him pouring iced water in the Lumberjack and buying hotcakes, the syrup in a little jug. That night he left a spot of bloody drool on their shared pillow, his rifle standing in the corner.

Of course, she hadn't loved him. But there were times when she thought she might. Down in Cottonwood once they had danced to a bar band and some boy at the counter made a remark. Wetback, was it? She knew the word but had never heard it said. Not like that. And never about her. Maybe it was went back? Yes, that was it.

With dignity, Frank had told her they were leaving. Going home to the house in the trees. That there was no point. Let this one go, he said. They had other troubles to meet.

Yes, she had loved him then. His silver hair and a different bandanna. Kate, the bar owner, stayed silent and watched them go. The familiar betrayal. Yet what was Frank but a man looking around that bar and noticing, maybe for the first time, how the world had changed. And making the best of it. Facing it with the courage he could muster. Because when a man's time has gone that's all a man can do.

The young drinker had smiled at the room with both elbows on the bar. The stance that meant he owned it now. Owned the time. And Frank, humiliated in his heart but not in hers, coughed as they drove north. How their shadows had swung when at last the oil lantern was lit, the darknesses full of coyotes yapping and some kids driving pickups down the loggers' road.

She had all those years in that cabin and each day the black and white TV flickered in the kitchen. The Osmonds. Richard Nixon. And the Cardinals, the Cardinals who played all the time, and one day were miraculously red.

Hey Maria?

Hey, she said.

Buenos dias.

Hey, she said again.

No rest for the wicked.

I'm not that wicked.

You on afternoons all week?

Yes.

It's not so bad.

No.

They say it'll hit 100 today.

Oh boy.

See you inside.

Okay.

The Sunset was one of the smaller nursing homes in that part of the state. It had been bulldozed out of the hillside south of Black Canyon City, and yes, the evenings could be spectacular, black shapes of the saguaros against the orange sky, and then the town lights pricking the rapid nightfall.

Maria had worked there ten years, starting one year after the Sunset opened. Long enough for the home to get comfortable with itself, the rules to relax.

Finding the job had been easy. She was on time for the interview and said yes to every question. Welcome to the Sunset, the man had said. We'd like you to start soon. And remember. No chilli in the chilli con carne. Our clients don't go for the spicy. So the Sunset doesn't do the spicy. Set menu always.

And he'd laughed. Then she laughed too.

For the first six months she worked in the kitchen and learned to do everything. How to keep the mashed potatoes and meatloaf warm. How to ensure the rice pudding wasn't wasted. Yoghurts were the problem. The staff waited till the tops started to bulge. Then waited one more day. Then disposed. It was her job to see all the wasted food ended up in the aluminium wheelie that was collected every other day.

But it wasn't her job, she considered, to stop staff pilfering. So she always turned a blind eye. To fit in, she took a little herself. But only apple sauce. Only salad leaves. Maybe some of those *tomatillos* that no one ate. Little green strangers.

Yeah, no chilli, the head chef had said when she started. No cinnamon. No nutmeg. And he'd smiled a bitter little smile. No cilantro. No garlic.

That first day he had told her to stand on a chair. Then he ran his hands up her skirt. Up and down the cool insides of her thighs. While he did this she regarded the bald patch on his head. The greasy comb-over.

Thanks, he had said, eventually.

You're welcome, she said.

He never touched her again.

Then there was another interview. This took place in a corridor, everybody standing up. Again she said yes, yes, except to the query about using the defibrillator. Don't worry about that, the man had said. Nothing to it.

Now she taps in the entrance code and uses the antiseptic rub by the door. Really she knows she's not supposed to wear her uniform outside, but all the staff ignore that, and she starts clearing away the lunches.

Afternoons are pretty good. There are already some visitors in and the edge has been taken off the day. Off the residents too. There is a sprinkling in the television lounge, but most are already in their rooms. Doing what they do. Which is mostly sleeping. Or crying. Yes a lot of them cry. But then, she would too, wouldn't she? Wouldn't anybody cry who wound up in the Sunset, watching that big fiery sky? Ending up. Ending up in BCC. Which was nowhere, everybody knew that. A scattered town on the way from somewhere to somewhere else. Ribs and a Corona in the Badass BBQ? French toast at the Amish Kitchen? Then what? You'd move on. Past the saguaros. Move away.

No, of course she wouldn't cry. Ending up at the Sunset was a Hollywood dream. The Sunset was one thousand dollars a week. She couldn't have afforded one hundred. Fifty. Ending up was something she never thought about, like winning the lottery or UFOs in the desert. Ending up was nothing to do with her.

On her way back from the dining room she notes the bell in 42 has been ringing for some time.

Everything all right? she asks, entering.

He'd like to urinate, says a tall, bald man, gesturing at another man in a wheelchair. We've been ringing for ten minutes.

Of course, she says.

While she pulls the old man's tracksuit bottoms down and puts the plastic bottle in position, the bald man goes into the corridor.

Never seen his father piss, she thinks. Never seen his father's sweet little, dead little cock. Kind of mauve colour. Like a jalepeno.

The spurt is rank and dark and there's not much of it.

Hey Larry, she says. I keep telling you to drink water. And you keep not drinking water.

She pulls his pants up. Drinking's good. Water's good for the kidneys. Flush all those nasty poisons away.

On the television screen is a freeze-framed DVD image. She has to look at it. For some reason it jumps into life. There's a soundtrack too, a tune she likes, 'The Breeze and I' played on a Wurlitzer organ.

Her mother had sung it to the family, using the Spanish words. All about far-away Spain. About Andalucia, mythical kingdom.

Maria had once sung it for Frank who had smiled and danced her round the room. Before even Frank's era of course. He told her he remembered Caterina Valente and the new English lyrics on every radio station in the country. But Frank was no dreamer. He played driving music. Little Feat and the Allman Brothers were his choice, the house in the trees awash with that tuneless guitar squall. Frank catalogued the songs on the tape cards, his writing too big for the spaces. Strange that. She'd never thought him a man who made lists. But it passed the time, she assumed. She recalled the old Impala pulling up in the slush, 'Dixie Chicken' playing until the engine died. Frank always liked the rock stars who died young. That Lowell George. Poor Greg Allman, coming off his motorcycle. He spoke about them as if they were role models, though he was an older man, a grey-haired caretaker dressed like an outlaw. Tongue between his teeth, making his lists.

He doesn't urinate enough, does he? said the bald man.

Urinate, she thought. Why not say *micturate*? Why not pull your own father's jogging bottoms up just one time. And weep for his yellow loins.

Larry was eighty-five. He complained about his pants. About them rucking and twisting. Or coming down. About something he called *sting ring*. About not being able to take a crap. Yes, pissing and shitting. That's what it came to in the end. In the ending-up type of end. The real end. Which was no type of end she could imagine for herself. Because ending up cost money.

Maria smiles. Mr Chernowski, your father has good bladder and bowel control. But he doesn't drink because he feels the bottle is an indignity. He tries to avoid it. But a bottle's better than a catheter.

She turns to the television.

Where's that? she asks.

Oh, little treat for Dad, says the son. Our premiere. Folks in the office clubbed up for my retirement present. Bought Mrs Chernowski and me a weekend in Rocky Point. We took some film so dad could see where we were.

Rocky Point?

In Mex. Sorry, Mexico way. About an eight-hour drive from here. We stopped in Gila Bend for lunch and were there by early evening. Went through a place called *Why*. Stopped the car and took pictures by the sign. Why not? ha ha. But there was nothing there. Then we crossed at Sonoita. Bad roads at the other end. Dogs with no hair. But what can you expect.

Maria watches the film. Mr and Mrs Chernowski are on a promenade. The Sea of Cortez is violet behind them. There are palm trees, pelicans perched on bushels of kelp, an old man with a machete cutting mangoes into flower shapes. Mrs Chernowski is holding her mango flower to her face, and now Mr Chernowski is choosing an oystershell at a fish stall and the stall holder smiling and opening the shell with a stiletto and squirting sauce over the oyster and Mr Chernowski saying no, no, don't make it hot, I get heartburn. Phew, I can't eat that.

There are fishing boats in a harbour. A low stone posada with the couple outside, a panorama of the town from some high place.

We put the organ music on because it's my father's favourite, explains Chernowski. Polka too, he likes a good polka. Hey, look, this is the next morning.

The Chernowskis are at breakfast in a bar called Mickey's. A beaming man has brought plates of eggs and bacon and glasses of orange juice, plus two small bottles, to the table. The camera homes in on these. They say 'Mickey's Tequila'.

Yes, that's Mickey, says Chernowski. He served us himself. Speciality of the house, Mickey said. Free tequila with your breakfast. Mrs Chernowski looked at me, she said Jacob, you even sniff that stuff you'll be inebriated. And I bet she would have been right. Oh yes. The people on the next table asked if we were going to drink it. No way, we said. So we passed it over. Phew, it just vanished. And at that time in the morning. Takes all sorts but you need to keep your wits about you down there. Yip, there's Mickey. What a ham. You just wouldn't believe how cheap it was. Look at those sunny sides now.

You're retiring? she asks.

Well, that's the idea. I'll be a retiree. Funny word. Moving up to Anthem, out of the city. I could keep going of course. In accounts, experience pays. Everybody tells me that. But they're always changing the software. Like, why? And Mrs Chernowski says she wants me home. Says it's a long day on her own, though she has her magazines.

Anthem's nice they say.

Well, yes. The great outdoors. And the golf's going to be good I suppose. I've actually played the Ironwood. Well, first nine. Six.

Company's paying the membership for three years, which is a fantastic deal. But you know sometimes I just stroll around and can't believe it's so green. Everywhere else burned off, but the course like the Garden of Eden. And those red birds flying about.

Would you take Larry, I mean your father there? He might enjoy an outing.

Chernowski smiles. In theory, fine. I'd love to. But even in his new wheelchair, even with those straps, he slips down, and with my hernia, you know, it's hard to make him comfortable. I get this shooting pain. And there's the bottle business. What if he needs to go?

The son looks old. His glasses are pebble-lensed. Maria thinks he's Jewish, but maybe he's too tall. Are there tall Jews? Even here in the room, the room smelling of his father's piss and pine-scented disinfectant, he's stooping. She notices the waste bin is overflowing with tissues, and opens the second window.

Okay, says Chernowski. And sits down. I'll come clean. Truth is, golf's not really my bag, as they used to say. It's tougher than it looks. And it takes so long, phew, out in that sun. Then there's a drink at the clubhouse. Those nibbles they lay on, they're to die for. But then I'd never want lunch, would I? And all the time there's Mrs Chernowski fretting at home, thinking I'm in an accident. I got blindsided once on Buckeye and she's never forgotten it.

He crosses his long legs.

Tell the truth, she didn't really like Rocky Point. You know, there were beggars there. Grown men and women, out and out begging. We both wore money belts and stayed on the main drag. Hotel had a safe, no messing. But you even wonder about that these days.

You didn't enjoy Mexico?

Well I did, says Chernowski. I certainly did. We saw a good show there, the Saturday night. You know, those mariachi guys, in those suits they wear, all gold embroidery. Big sombreros too. Called themselves Los Burros. And a girl, just a kid really, dancing on a table, lifting her skirt right up over her head.

Sounds great.

Oh yeah. We bought their CD. Brought it in for Dad to hear. But, you know, what was disappointing was this woman we met. Outside the hotel. She was selling rugs, these Mexican rugs, traditional design and all that. And you know what she said?

Yes, I do, smiled Maria.

You know? How can you know? What did she say?

Maria steadied herself. She was being forward. This was unlike how she behaved. In a way she had transgressed. All those years ago she had vowed to agree with everything she heard. Never to stand out. That was the rule. Wasn't that how she had survived?

She says that the rugs aren't made by Mexicans. That they come from China. And that the Chinese make them cheaper than the local women.

Wow, breathes Chernowski. Hole in one. And the thing was, they looked… authentic, those rugs. Like they were just off some country loom. You know, like tortillas in the ash. Like home weaving. All that Mexican schtick.

The next day at 4 p.m. Maria walks into room 42. Larry is sitting in his armchair, head down. Someone has put the Rocky Point DVD on for him, but there's no one else there. 'The Breeze and I' is playing, his waste bin overflowing again.

Hey Larry, she says. You didn't eat lunch.

He looks up and scowls. Then he smiles.

That crap? It's invalid food. What about a steak one time?

Well Larry, you know we don't run to steaks. You're trying to bankrupt the organisation. And have you really got the teeth for it?

That's my problem, not yours. Just a steak one time. Porterhouse, like we used to eat. Hanging both sides off the plate.

And gravy?

Sure gravy. Why not gravy? With red wine in it and a glass of red wine. French wine. Fancy. And Bohemian crystal. On a white tablecloth. Yeah, that's Bo-hem-ian.

How Larry loves that word in his mouth. Its smooth jewel. He licks his chops.

Maria sits down. You know I used to work in the kitchen and I can't remember us ever serving steak.

Larry's son is on the TV screen holding Mickey's tequila. He's giving the bottles to the people on the next table. A barechested young man with military tattoos, a girl in a bikini top, her hair wet and pulled back.

Now those two look like they're enjoying themselves, says Maria.

Sheesh, sneers Larry. Get a load of the jugs on that.

Hey mister, she laughs. You're the lively one today. I think we might take a walk.

A colleague helps her hoist the old man into his wheelchair and they go down the cool corridor. Larry has his ballcap and dark glasses, but when Maria taps in the code and the door opens, he recoils. The air is a hotplate.

A concrete path with passing bays has been built around the Sunset. There's no meat on the old man, but it's an effort to push him up the incline towards a cottonwood and a bench of recycled plastic. On the bench is a plaque that says 'to Ben & Martha, who loved this place'. She parks Larry and sits down.

So, Maria says. Rocky Point.

Larry shrugs. Surprised they went, he says. That's some drive you know. Through the National Monument.

Oh I know, she says. It's a long way to Puerto Penasco. Or Rocky Point as you call it.

I was down there one time, says Larry, looking up at last.

Around them the low hills are studded with iron-pointed cholla. There's a Chevron gas station sign next to the road.

We stayed in this hotel. They claim it was where Al Capone used to hang out, trying to smuggle booze and guns north. Alphonse Capone. Died of the clap.

With Maria's help the old man sits back and lets the sun do its job. Soon it will be too fierce but now it is balm and benediction. She looks at him. Old tortoise in fashionable Ray-Bans, his red Cardinals cap too big.

Hey, he says. What's that smell?

Maria looks around. It's fresh air, she laughs. Good Arizona air. You're just not used to it.

Larry's paralysed down one side. He used to give the staff hell but soon realised where the power lay. She's had to promise Chernowski that the night nurses take his father's mobile away. Before that he would ring at all hours, describing his nightmares. Recently they've started giving him an 8 p.m. Temazapan that sends him off till morning.

Now, Larry, says Maria at last. I'm going to break my pledge. My pledge with myself. I'm going to tell you my story.

Behind his shades she cannot tell if the old man is listening. Sometimes he's spot on, talking about Obama or the gangs in Phoenix. Sometimes he's drifted right away.

We came north, she says. Out of the desert. We stood on a hill and could see Rocky Point. See Puerto Penasco glittering in the distance. Right then, on that rise, we thought it was the Promised Land.

We had been walking for five days. The three of us. Juan, me, Juanita. Coming from somewhere you've never heard of. The sand was like flour, but there were tracks to follow. Keep north, everybody told us. Keep the idea of the ocean, the ocean air on your left.

So far, so good, we thought. We hadn't even used much water. So we spent one more night in the rocks and got a lift on a farm truck the next morning, hauling watermelon. We were dropped at the seafront, as the fish stalls were opening. Juan bought fruit and bread and we ate it with the pelicans, the fishing boats all coming back with the night catch. Hey, you listening Larry? You listening?

But it's impossible to tell if Larry's listening. Maria decides he is.

There was a man we were supposed to meet. He was called Vincente and he was right on time. He bought us coffee. But we were all surprised by Penasco. There were Americans in the street and tall cranes across Cholla Point. They were building apartments all over the peninsulas.

Why not stay here? I asked. There's work. But Juan was for pushing on, as we'd organised with Vincente. Juanita said we could even catch the bus to Sonoita, and cross there, but that's the free trade area and it's full of army and police. So we had to do what Vincente said. It was like a pledge. As if we'd signed a paper. Oh we were good Mexicans. Good Mexicans always do what they're told. We had to go across El Gran Desierto del Altar.

Below them the Goliath laundry truck is delivering. Bags of dirty linen are stacked at the sides, waiting to be hefted on. All those pissy sheets, she thinks. Those bloody, shitty sheets.

She shuts her eyes and lets the sun press her down. Her mother used to scatter camomile flowers in their washing at home. As a girl she had pressed her clean underwear to her face and discovered a garden. Here, the cottonwood bark is rough and grey, its dead leaves at their feet. She sits with a dying man, telling her story. Telling her story in the country of Goliath.

Vincente drove us north-west. Into the Pinacate and the volcanoes. There were eight of us now, but we stayed together. Our little group. I was with Juan. Juanita was coming too. Vincente looked at us as if he had something important to say. Then he turned away. We never saw him again.

They had told us to walk at night but that was crazy. Yes, any fool can read the stars but no one can walk that country in darkness. There's lava sharp as glass. There are craters that cut your shoes and are hard to climb down, climb up. And that darkness is total darkness. Juanita was terrified. *Los Indios*, she kept saying. She thought we'd meet indians who would scalp us. Now that scared the others. Only Juan laughed and put his arm around her. Chucked her chin. There's nobody out there in the Altar, he laughed. Only the ghosts. But that scared everyone too. Country people believe in ghosts.

But we also knew the stories. About the people who died trying to cross the border. About the fools who were looking for gold. Everybody talked about that big nugget someone had found. The biggest nugget ever. So there was gold in the desert. There were old mines we could explore. One man with us had even brought a shovel. He didn't carry it long.

Yet Juan was determined to go and where Juan went, I did.

We were together. At night we'd lie rolled up in the same blanket. One dawn I remember, I woke and Juan wasn't there. He was standing on the crest of the dune, looking west. The sand was smoking around him. He called us to come and see the Pacific Ocean. We all stood there and gazed out. From that dune, pink in the first light. Pink sand all around. Shadows behind the rocks like pools of ink.

Juan said not even Cortez had seen such a sight. Not even Cortez and his horses and his iron army had glimpsed what we did then. Juan was our hero now. Juan was our conquistador with cracked lips on a sand dune red as fire. Juan pointed with the ocotillo stave he'd fashioned with his machete. And we all looked where that stick pointed. Where Juan told us to look. We did what our leader commanded. And that leader was Juan who the Indians or the ghosts or the *jaguares* would never catch.

We had this silly dream, the two of us. We would live in LA and take the train to Union Station every day. I'd become a teacher and Juan an engineer. And one day, coming home together, talking so much, we get on the wrong train. And we end up in Hollywood, and as we're walking across Sunset to Vine, we see Raquel Welch and Martin Sheen just ahead. And Raquel drops this envelope she's carrying – the script for *Bandolero*! Or something like that. And Juan picks it up, and yes, we've saved the day. So they take us for cocktails to the Brown Derby. And they think we're so cool that they want to stay in touch.

It was Juan drove us on. He had maps. He seemed to know the way. But how could that be? We came from the same little town, far away. We studied English together. There were eight of us. Then there were seven. One of the other men just disappeared. I didn't even know his name. Then there were six.

You know, there are legends about the heat. It's hot now, here at the Sunset. But nothing like the Altar. They said this boy, from Guadalajara, got lost in the *gran desierto* once. He was trying to make the crossing. He said there was no space for him in his city. Even in his own home, no space. So many children. He was desperate. They said that to keep cool he pushed his head into the sand. That his brains boiled.

I've heard people laugh at that story. But those people have never been in the Altar. Maybe our companions who vanished turned back. They were good people, honest people. They believed in God. We used to hear them praying in the darkness. They shared their water with us. One of them carried the water in a calfskin on his shoulder. Walking behind him I used to watch that water on his back, as if there was an animal writhing there. How soon it became just an empty sack.

Maria touches Larry's brow.

Time to go in, senor. They're making supper. No garlic. No chilli. And no steaks for you. Sorry. But yeah, Larry, we could have died. Nearly did too. My tongue was fat in my cheek. It felt like a stone. Juan used to cut cactus open and we'd hold our mouths against the wet insides. Suck the shreds.

Then it all gets misty. Like it used to up in Flagstaff in the rains. The mists right down over the trees. But misty in my mind, Larry. We were in the organ pipes, you know, real cactus country. Trees of knives we used to call them. They were razor sharp. Twice as high as Juan. Maybe we strayed into the Barry Goldwater Airforce Base. We could see the military in the distance. And at night we heard their dogs. Juan had the maps and by then it was just the three of us again. Juanita in the blanket, too. Me in the middle of course. Juanita was crying and Juan tried to comfort her. He gave her extra water, his water, while I kept a little black stone in my mouth. Sucking on a piece of volcano. A little hummingbird is what he called Juanita. That's when I knew.

At the end, Larry, they were chasing us. Getting close. We crossed a highway in the evening and there was a white pickup, bouncing over the rocks. First up a dirt road. Then where there was no road. It had a floodlight mounted on the top and I watched that light swing everywhere. A lighthouse in the desert.

And I thought, why are they trying so hard to stop us? Like we are really bad people. But we're not bad people. We'll work. We'll go to Yuma and spray pesticides in the polytunnels so people can have lettuce. Those crazy Americans who want lettuce in the desert? We'll do that for them. We'll scrub their filthy toilets in the Tucson Arena. We'll bring the trays of nachos and Monterey Jack to their seats. Just so Americans don't have to do it. But please tell me why are they trying so hard to stop us?

I looked at that beam sweeping the rocks. I could smell the mesquite around me, we'd been chewing it. And every inch of me ached and ached. I had cholla scratches all over. Every patch of my skin. There was a prickly-pear needle in my wrist. Look, there's the scar. Those thorns were like fish hooks, Larry. I know how a fish feels. I see the girls now who pierce themselves with studs and rings and I can't believe it. I have to turn away. If you've been in the cholla, you don't do that.

Our clothes were rags. We'd all run in different directions. What we had agreed, if we split up, was to wait till morning, then look around. So that's what I did. I could see a water tower in the distance, hear traffic on the blacktop. I searched everywhere. Then waited, looking out. But the others didn't come. Juan and Juanita, they must have been together. If they weren't, one or the other would have showed up.

That was it. I'd made the crossing. But I was on my own. On my own in a foreign country, Larry. Somehow we'd crossed the border but there was no sign on the ground to tell us that. The heat was the same. The thorns were as sharp. I watched an eagle overhead. It must have crossed that border twenty times a day. And you know, right then, I didn't care if they caught me and sent me back. What could they do? Take me to Sonoita and put me over the white line?

Yes, I could speak some English. Yes, I had a little money left. Hadn't lost my hat either. But I knew Juan was with Juanita. She was pretty. Like a cactus flower. Not like me with my big feet, my desert boots. Juan was with Juanita and my mouth was full of ashes. Maria touches Larry's brow again.

Okay, let's go in. That's my personal DVD for you. Enough for now, I think.

The next afternoon Larry is not so well. He sits in his armchair with head down. A mummy in a tartan blanket. The Rocky Point film is playing again, 'The Breeze and I' filling the room. Such longing in that music, she thinks. But a yearning for what? How the chords cascade. For two minutes she allows the old-fashioned organ sound to swell the hollow of the heart.

On the bed is a scattering of CDs, a talking book of *The Grapes of Wrath*. But there are no real books or magazines in the room. Since his second stroke Larry has difficulty co-ordinating his eyesight. He can see well enough but cannot follow print.

Maria turns the volume down, glances at Mrs Chernowski outside Sonia's restaurant in Gila Bend. That day Mrs Chernowski did not touch the complimentary salsa but chose instead two little white hens' eggs that came from the battery farm. With toast. With coffee which proved too strong. A flan, no, a *crème caramel*, that she enjoyed.

Wasn't it today the Chernowskis moved into their new home in Anthem? Frank had told her about Anthem years earlier. 'A new community for vibrant seniors.' I'll stay in the trees, he said.

The city replanted the barrel cactus and saguaros around Anthem. But not the rotten ones, the dead ones, the colour of old men. Those were dangerous cactus that could topple and kill. She's seen a man once drive a Grand Am straight into a dead saguaro. It exploded into splinters. The whole tree, pale and bone hard, came up by the roots.

Maria can visualise the house in Anthem now. It's too big. There's too much space between all those houses. Outside is an empty street that will stay empty all day, and in the kitchen a refrigerator full of food the Chernowskis will throw out. All that lettuce in its polythene. Even though the blinds are pulled down, the chrome on the four toilet seats gleams in the desert light. Outside in the mailbox are national magazines that will never leave their envelopes, on the kitchen pinboard the couple's medicine regime in a laser-printed grid.

Hey Larry, Maria says. Look at this. She takes a towel off a casserole dish.

Yo. A present. For you. It's steak. But not like you mean. You know you can't chew steak. And I can't afford fillet. But you can eat this. Try a mouthful.

She tucks a napkin under his chin and offers the spoon. The old man stares. Then he takes the food and chews. Soon he looks ready for another taste.

You see. It's good. We know it as *nopalitos*. Little bits of meat. And onion. And *tomatillos*. And *jalapenos*. And *cilantro*, Larry. Fresh cilantro. I've heard it called Mexican parsley round here.

And garlic. And, guess what, Larry. Cactus. That's right. Pieces of prickly pear. Ever eaten prickly pear before? That's why they call this *nopalitos*. All this food grows wild here, all over the Sunset lot. Over every hillside. Be a shame if we couldn't do anything with it.

Now that's right, she encourages. Take another mouthful. And another. You see, it's not too hot. It just tastes. It has a taste, Larry. That's why God gives us taste buds. Such a clever God. But don't tell the others about this. They'll all be wanting some. Hey. You're eating cactus, Larry. Oh boy, you're eating cactus.

If Larry can eat, she reckons, he can listen. He's not been shaved and already shows a silver stubble. There's cactus juice on his chin.

Yes, Maria thinks. He looks better like this. He seems a real man today. Is a real man. The whiskers have sexed him up a little. Larry's not the neutered cat any more. Not the coiffeured corpse. Yet he hasn't spoken.

Try the pepper now, smiles Maria. I grew it in my window box. Don't worry, I scraped all the seeds out. And saved them.

A trucker took me to the Paradise Valley, she says. He was hauling lavatory pans, I remember that. I sat up front and he gave me a Hershey bar. Welcome to the US of A. Then another ride got me to Phoenix. Big, bad Phoenix. Belly of the beast. With all those swimming pools. You ever have a swimming pool, Larry? Hey, three cheers for swimming pools. All those cleaning jobs they create.

The lavatory guy dropped me near the Greyhound station and, you bet, there were others like me there too. Oh yes. I washed in the Greyhound toilets and talked to the cleaners. Everyone spoke Mexican. But there were Indians too. And these people who'd come all the way up from Chiapas. And some from Guatemala, riding on top of freight trains. Little brown people. Like dolls. Hair cut straight across their foreheads, wearing serapes as if they were back in their villages. Their language was strange. Couldn't read or write they said. But they could work. So where was the work? Let us at it was their attitude.

And at once I started to feel better. Because all these other people had done what we'd done. Me, Juan, Juanita. I had kept thinking we were unique. But others had come further. Puerto Penasco? they laughed. That's just down the road.

But what surprised me was that Americans were so good. People are good, Larry. Or they want to be. The truck driver who took me to the station even had a sticker in his cab that read 'The US is full up'. But he said I looked like I could use a ride. He knew, Larry. He knew.

And that was years ago and it's still not full. When I tried my luck in Flagstaff I lived in the forest. There's nobody there. When you've been in the Altar you might be scared of the forest. It's a different kind of loneliness. A different silence.

Maria pours him a glass of water.

In the desert we thought we'd never see people again. We slept one night at an abandoned mine. It was still the eight of us then. Juanita was afraid to sleep in the mine entrance; she said there might be dead people. I went in and found part of an old book. It was *Robinson Crusoe*. We'd never read it but we knew what it was about. Juan said there was a movie, *Robinson Crusoe on Mars*, that was filmed in the desert. Just over the border, he said, in California. We'd go to see it in Hollywood, Juan promised me. Or watch it in our own apartment when we owned a videotape machine. With popcorn and sundaes. Juan liked ice cream.

I worked everywhere. Cleaned up in Wendy's. It had just opened. Ever had one of Wendy's old-fashioned hamburgers? I might have flipped it for you. At Pizza Hut I crushed all the cardboard to be collected. Heated the plates. But I took the pizza crusts back to the room I was renting.

Larry looks up. His chin is shining. But after the third mouthful he hasn't touched his food.

You married? he asks.

No sir. No sir I'm not.

You should be married.

Why?

He studies her now. In her blue uniform with the Sunset crest. In her sandals that he hears slap down the corridor when she leaves his room. Bigfoot. He used to hear her on the night shift. Slap, slap. Before the new medication. Before they took away his phone.

Because.

Because what?

Just because.

I wanted children, says Maria. If I'd stayed home I would have had children.

How old are you? he asks.

Coming up to forty. Or is it fifty? Ha ha.

Larry sucks in his cheeks. I used to take my son to Wendy's, he says. Maybe not Wendy's but some diner in Phoenix. My son, Jacob. It was a treat. He liked root beer too. He always wore these big thick glasses. Made him look like a bug.

They're moving to Anthem this week, she says quietly. Exciting for them.

He prods the food. All my father brought to this country, mutters Larry, is a violin. A poxy violin. He played it on the ship coming over. He played it walking down the gangway, his ass hanging out of his pants. Then he never played it again.

He must have been proud of you.

The old man is scowling.

I bought a violin for Jacob. He never touched it. Always had his head in these encyclopaedias we had. He could reel off every president's name and dates. The capital of every state. Augusta, Maine. *Sheesh.* My wife bought them from a door-to-door salesman. Took up a whole shelf. You got kids?

No. I told you.

Why?

Because.

Because what?

Just because.

Maria looks out of the window. The Goliath truck is there again. The heaps of white sacks. From her pocket she takes the stone she had thought to show Larry. The black stone she had sucked in the desert. One round stone.

Hey, the sky's really red, she says. If you feel like it I'll take you out tomorrow. To our tree. Or you can watch the Cardinals game. Could be close, I hear. Now eat your *nopalitos*, Larry. They're going cold.

A welcome for the river god

It was on the blackboard. So, I thought, it must be true. On a little blackboard at the back entrance, facing the car park. I was coming out of the Spar and the Polski Sklep and I had my provisions already, if you know what I mean. I was stocked up, and feeling good about things.

Because the town wasn't bad, and the weather had been dry all month. But better than anything was the sea. I could hear it as I looked at the blackboard. A sucking, a sighing. Big swell, they had said, for the next few days. I could imagine the spray with the sun in it. The ocean showing its muscles. And the smell of it. That was the difference. The shock. Even after a month, I wasn't used to that smell. Salt and catpiss and redcurrant leaves. Or boiling tar. Tar popping in its barrel.

Dangerous, really, the sea. That's what I think when I walk the promenade. All these pensioners and school children come to gaze at it. But the sea is threatening. Imprisoned for a thousand years, but capable still of killing its jailer. Yes that's the sea. Whispering in its own language. Waiting for something to happen as it loiters under the green railings. That's what the sea does. It waits. The sea has patience and will never run out of time. But I can feel the minutes pass. The days. Gone like bubbles of black tar. Gone like pounds and pennies.

The day I first went in I'd been nervous. You never know what idiots you're going to meet in places like that. Or, rather, you do. The failed and the flakey. The ugly and the deformed. The men whose first instinct, even at that time in the morning, is violence.

Most especially the women. The women will be few but they will be noticed first.These are women who by their very presence are exposed immediately as beyond salvation. Because walking into a place like that is an admission of guilt. Or desperation. Being seen there incites a verdict. For a woman, the walk up that pathway, out of the car park and past the dented keg, over the fag ash thick as cinders, is a long road.

Eight a.m. the blackboard said. It was 8.05 when I first stepped in. Yet the place was full. I'd say it was seething. But not like a workmen's café at that time, when there's a frenzy to life. Where you see men in plaid shirts starting enormous breakfasts. Swigging tea out of white enamel. All the coming, the going, the familiarities. In a café, there's an expectation for the day. Unimaginable things are going to happen. Fateful things.

But at the Seagull Room it's a different busyness. The act of entering says this is the day's highlight. Reached already. That this will be for you, the one who dares enter, the best part of that day. Before even the school buses have appeared. The locks drawn in the banks.

When I went in I was carrying two plastic bags, my coat over my shoulder because it was already warm, and I had a three-inch bolster in a side pocket of my jeans. Heavy, blue steel. Edge of brickdust on it. Scabs of concrete. But I'd recently had it under the grinding wheel and there was no burring on the blade. It's not something you'd want waved in your face. Which, I'm afraid, I had to do last week. To some waster. Some wanker.

I was on the hill going down towards the fairground. They call that stretch the Ghetto. It was about eleven, throwing-out time, and I was just wandering off to watch the waves. What's wrong with that? Maybe buy chips. Then out of this alley come three of them. Two kids and their dad. It was obviously their dad. Stubbies of Stella in their hands, so not hard up. Money to piss away.

One of the kids shoulder-barged me off the pavement. For no reason. Believe me, I was sober and I was orderly. He was only a kid, but it hurt and I stumbled. The three of them laughed, but I had the bolster out in a second and under the father's chin. Blue steel, like I said. Heavy in the hand. Serious heft.

Okay, that was a stupid thing to do. But you can't let yourself become a target. I learned that a long time ago. He was fat, clean shaven, the father. Nice white shirt, properly ironed. And he smelled of cologne. As sweet as a lemon. As it was dark he couldn't have known what I was holding. Only that there was a cold blade against his Adam's apple. A very big blade. Something immediately dangerous.

I looked into his face and ignored the boys. Boys? Eighteen, twenty. Big, drunk, unutterably ignorant. They could have floored me then and there. Imprinted their trainers on my face. But they froze. Surprised by the unexpected. By my reaction. And dulled by the booze.

Hey, all right, he laughed. The fat man laughed but I could hear the shock in his voice. The fear. Sorry, butt, he said. Only messing like. It's all right.

And they walked off. Slowly, but they left. Swearing, red-faced, bollocky men. Dad bandy-legged as a pitbull in his powder-blue, low-crotched Levi's, his riveted belt, the Samoan tattoos on his arms. Yes, some role model. Dad dragging his sons away. I expected them to throw the bottles but it didn't happen. What they aimed at me were the usual words. And unlike glass they were impossible to avoid.

Ten minutes later I was down on the esplanade. The sea was under the railings. And I was shaking. I was nearly crying too, then laughing, then everything together. And there was the bolster in my pocket. A dead weight. A deadly weapon. A comforter. Get caught by a bolster's edge and it will excavate your face. Its blade will depress and fracture your skull. Yes, I was laughing because I had won, but I was crying because I might have killed that man. And I was shaking because he could have killed me.

But now I think they were just playing rough. Rugby men, used to the scrum, bulked up by the weights machines. The boys swearing vengeance, one of them foaming, the father thinking it all over and, if he's sensible, shrugging it off. Oh yeah. If he's sensible. With his cologne on my skin.

When I enter, no one speaks but the room acknowledges me. Already I am a familiar and already I have my place, my back to the wall, my eye on the door. The barman puts a pint on the counter. I feel the cold beads of its industrial dew. The barman is another shaven man. Bulging, implacable. He smells of smoke, this man, and a few of the customers have cigarettes. It's illegal of course, but so is the violence of their streets, the pills and wraps they deal here, up this track behind the car park, the render coming off the brick, the pipework oxidised in the salt air. The Seagull Room they call it, though there is no such name front or back. Yet its protocols are stern.

Now seagulls I understand. They crowd the landfill. They harry one another for foodscraps. Even when a gull has swallowed a morsel its companions continue pursuit. They swoop on its vomit. They cry like the insane in the hospital in Naujoji Vilnia. But even seagulls, they say, are rarer now. Endangered species.

What I pay for the one drink could buy me four in the Spar, the Sklep. But I like it here. Money is a problem but it's not the only problem. And slowly, the routine begins, the regulars' routine.

Pancho's in with his guitar. It's good busking weather and has been all month. So Pancho's flush. In more ways than one. Sometimes he even sings in here and is tolerated, a sixty-year old with a duct-taped guitar, the hair on him long and thin, a man in jeans and a denim shirt, a necklace, a bracelet, what few teeth he's got left tobacco-stained.

Pancho washed up here years ago and liked it enough to stop moving. I see him on the street and laugh and put some pennies in the open guitar case, a case with stickers of towns where he's worked the streets. Torquay, Torbay, Saundersfoot they say. And all that's left of that case's turquoise silk is a rag around the rim.

And Pancho will laugh too and go on with 'Visions of Johanna'. Every verse of that song. His great song he calls it. His prodigious feat of memory. Or I'll hear him tuning up on the gum-blistered pavement when I come out of the Sklep and then that line, the best line, the only line I listen to. *How does it feel?* Pancho who maybe once had a voice, still believing in that line. Still asking the question and knowing its answer. That's Pancho, who'll tell me this morning what it's like to be a rolling stone. And when he's finished he might add his own story of what it is to sit on the dock with the night fishermen, to lie under the esp and breathe good Moroccan draw into the lungs. Right down until it's too hot to hold. As if his body was full of sparks.

Pancho who's still asking how it feels. Cracking that word into four shiny pieces. *Fee. Ee. Ee. Eel.* Who should wash his hair. Maybe his shirt. Pancho with his caved-in chest. The only troubadour of this town.

Roly's in too. Strangely, I met him first on the street. I was doing what I do, I was watching the sea. Then this sports car hammers past, brakes, turns round. When it reached me it slowed and the boy in the front passenger seat shouted.

You fucking shit, he shouted. You ignorant shit.

Then the car speeded off again, did a handbrake turn and came back. A black Mazda. This time it was the driver who yelled.

You shit. You bastard shit.

I stared him in the eye. Seventeen maximum. Dark hair with blond streaks. Good-looking kid with Ray-Bans and a big gold necklace. In a wax-polished car. A car like a scarab. There's money here, you see. Villas with high hedges. Personalised number plates. Oh yes. I noted the number.

So I shrugged as if to say, you got the wrong person. But he shouted again, then gunned the Mazda down the straight road towards the beaches.

That's when Roly rolls up.

Take no notice, he said. I know his parents. I'll intercede.

I liked that word. That *intercede.*

No problem, I said.

No, he said. It's unacceptable behaviour. High spirits because their exams have just finished. They're under pressure at this time of year. But a poor reflection. I hope they haven't been drinking.

And here's Roly now. Who is certainly drinking. Roly holding court in the Seagull Room. The barman has taken the Dewar's off its bracket on the wall and it waits at Roly's elbow. His blazered elbow. Roly wears a striped cricket blazer and a red bow tie. Roly is a fat man and his white flannels are stained yellow. And yes, Roly is giving the room his rape stories. Roly knows a good deal about rape. He was once a lawyer and is now a bar-room barrister. His jury grins, winces. Or maybe Roly is an opera star and this his proscenium.

The detail Roly provides is unsparing. The ambushes, the underwear. Every loving spoonful the perpetrators can squeeze out of themselves. Girls used like tissue paper. The eighty year olds accosted with broom handles.

Madge sucks on her Rizla.

Get off, she says. He's making it up.

If Madge was a candleflame you would expect her to go out. She is a happy-go-lucky anorexic, red haired, arms like fire tongs. She sits on a barstool and I can see the cracks in her heels and the dirt in those cracks, the dirt that I know will be there for the rest of her life.

He's making it up, she cackles. He's never seen a minge since his poor old mother got rid. He hasn't a clue. Have you Rolyo? Not a fucking clue.

But as Roly subsides, no one else feels like talking. To me, they're a predictable bunch. A postman with his loaded pouch, bundled letters tied with elastic bands, orders a second pint. A supermarket shelfstacker is sipping the own-brand vodka he brings in himself. Dullards, for the most part. Stammerers and twitchers. Porn-addled doleys. A roomful of ghosts on this July morning with the sun already hot on the tarmac and the light unbearable on the sea. And yet, for an hour, comrades of a sort. They will nod, each to each, on the street. They might even go to the same funerals.

*

At two minutes to nine I walk out to the car park and at nine Justin arrives with the van. The doors are open and Justin slows down but he doesn't stop. I get in head first through the back.

Now perhaps this is the best time to tell you about a mistake I've made. A mistake about my name. My first name is Nerys. When I arrived I didn't know Nerys was a girl's name in this part of the world. My mother called me Nerys after the river that flows through Vilnius. I hated it. My father hated it. But my mother insisted on Nerys as she insisted on few things in her life. I was her river god. I was the water spirit. That's what she told me.

Even back home it was difficult. My name felt wearisome. Sometimes it plagued me. If it had been up to my father, I would have been *Andrius*. A good masculine name. A warrior's name. But my father was rarely at home. He worked in an office for the Communist Party and after work he sat in bars, smoking, drinking Bajoru. That's all I know. I suppose he commanded a desk and moved papers about. That he spoke into a big black telephone. But if being called Nerys was a problem, having a father in the party in Vilnius was worse. When he died, I tried to atone. For being the son of a collaborator. Who ate sausage when the others ate bread. Who wore good shoes.

That was a difficult time. The Berlin Wall came down, but in Lithuania we'd been ahead of the game. Everyone was restless. There were men coming into Vilnius who had hidden in the forests for forty years. There were writers speaking on the radio when they were supposed to be banned. Or dead. Everything was changing, and fast.

By then, my father had given up. It wasn't long until the cigarettes killed him anyway. My mother had already been put away, locked up in that gloomy castle on Parko, hidden in the pines. So I was the only one left, the river god looking at the green Nerys with its devious current as I look at the tides in this town, spray black against the sun.

I was already staying in Uzupis. That used to be the gypsy district. It was where the ruffians lived. The anarchists. I had a room in a house that was falling down. Outside, there were posts propping up the walls. Dishwater ran along the cobbled street and black flags hung on the lamp posts.

Yes, I can remember. Back in 1991, Gorbachev came to see us. There were crowds and chanting and the certainty, not the hope, the certainty, that things would have to change. That night a friend took me to the Writers' Bar. It was downstairs in the main square. You couldn't move, it was thirty minutes to get served. Some great poet had arrived. He'd come out of hiding upcountry. His children were there too, and everyone was dancing and singing, politicians, Russian-speaking prostitutes, students like me, and the poet sitting on a ledge, high off the ground, reading his poems in this crazy dialect that was ours. Ours.

Me and my friend had one beer each. But we were already drunk. Drunk on adrenaline. We just stood in the crush, laughing at the photographs on the wall.

Because our writers looked like rock stars. Like the Beatles had once, with beards, or the Band, wild as mountainmen, backwoods philosophers with axes and manifestos in their hands. At home we always played the Beatles. *Happiness is a Warm Gun*. Or *As my Guitar Gently Weeps. Okay*, old stuff, but better than techno. Better than poor Pancho's Dylan. More life to it. Oh yeah, the White Album had been Lithuanian nerve gas in the Kremlin. We knew it was changing. Even with the Red Army tanks in the streets, we understood it had to change. Yet it took so long.

What a night that was. I came out two hours after dawn, up

that steep flight of steps from the Writers Bar. And there was a girl with me. She came along and we'd never spoken. Just danced. I thought she was a prostitute, but she was a schoolteacher. She came with *me*. We took our shoes off and walked in the flooded gutters down to the Katedros Square. The square was a lake. And we danced in the lake, holding our shoes, the cathedral bells ringing seven or eight, and a woman on a bicycle going past, waving a flag.

Some time afterwards, when the dust had cleared, I was down in Drusk, near the Belarus border, working in an open-air museum. We were all determined to show the world what we'd endured. We wanted to publish our history. I was only a labourer but I did my bit, sleeping in a tent in the forest, or in the wooden huts that held exhibits. So the statues of Joe Stalin and Lenin and the rest of the crew were taken down and brought there. From all over the country. Some of them were already crumbling, the ferro-concrete breaking up, steel reinforcements rusting away.

And I was part of it. Building the huts, laying the paths, cutting grass. At night we'd go drinking under the birch trees. Build a fire and pass round the vodka and the magic mushrooms. There was a man there used to collect mushrooms in his shirt. Brought in these red ones once, with white growths on them. They were death caps, somebody said. Death caps in the death camps. How we laughed.

Because that's what we were doing. We were recreating a concentration camp. To show the world what had happened in our country. Hidden away in the miles of spruce, of birch. What Hitler did. Then what Stalin did. What Snieckus did to his own people.

By then I'd stopped thinking about my father. All the yellow files in his cupboards. The staples going rusty and the cigarette ash in the turn-ups of his trousers. Anyway, this man showed us how to eat them, the red mushrooms. They weren't death caps. They were another amanita. But everybody knew it was risky. And how far away was Chernobyl anyway? We'd often meet old women in the forest, picking berries and fungi to sell at the roadside. It was their only income. Everybody knew it was dangerous. That all the mushrooms were radioactive. But we ate them anyway, as we ate the red amanita.

Oh boy, I felt strange. Maybe it was wonderful but the strange is all I remember. I was inside out. I was a statue of Joseph Stalin with a spider web over my face. I was this old mushroom woman who had survived Hitler and survived Stalin and survived my father. She lived in a hut and grew Michaelmas daisies. And the colour of those flowers was the colour of my dream. Purple haze. *Mauve*. I've hated mauve ever since. I could murder mauve. She told us we should sleep with the red mushroom under our pillows. Then we could dream, she said. If you want to dream, she said, then sleep with the mushrooms. She didn't know we'd been eating them.

But that was the best time. We were a real team who lived there, the girls with money spiders in their hair, the men roasting potatoes in the fire. That's where Andrius really died. Killed by the red mushrooms. But I was never Andrius.

Instead I was the labourer who looked like Richard Manuel from The Band. That's what the others said. Wild and creative. Who took cocaine.Who played the drums and sang. Played the marimba too, the sound of a ghost. Hung himself three months before Chernobyl went up. But every day I went to work in a concentration camp. And every night I drank vodka in the forest. The amanitas put my inside on my outside. They shone the mauve into my mind. Yes, the strange is all I remember. Those mushrooms shook me up. Yes, I had black hair and a beard but I couldn't play one lousy chord on the guitar we passed around.

Sometimes I swept up the gravel at the camp entrance. Not that many visitors came. You see, it's not the kind of history people are proud of. If you are a certain age, from a certain place, it's better not to be asked questions. Because, look, not everyone can be a hero. Not everyone is a poet standing on a plinth telling the world how brave they've been. Holding out against the bad guys.

So, it's wiser not to ask. Over here, in this country, no one's a part of history. History is something you learn in schools and forget. But at home, you're involved. You're part of it, whether you want to be or not. Every thing you ever did there is a historical act. One day you sneak on your friend. The next day you save his life.

I would be at the camp entrance in the morning, and boy, one day, I hear a rumbling. This lorry is coming down the road through the trees. This low loader driven by a man in a tartan shirt. Just a little the worse for wear. He had a gang with him who jumped off and said, give us a hand here. We need a hand. It took us two days. Two days to put together this statue they'd taken from a square in Kaunas, I suppose, because it never came from Vilnius. Well I never saw it there. Must have been about thirty of us, mainly soldiers, with ropes and pulleys, digging foundations, unpacking the parts. With a professor from the national museum telling us what to do.

And it's there to this day. Near that entrance to the camp. It's called the Spirit of Spring, or the Goddess, though the Soviets weren't hot on goddesses, I know. And yes, I loved that statue, that Russian statue. It was graceful. I'd go so far as to say it was beautiful, though we're supposed to laugh at all those things now. Clumsy, dutiful, uninspired. That's what we're told by the critics to think. But there she was, a concrete dryad, pale as one of that old woman's mushrooms.

I never bothered to ask who was the sculptor. I just loved the sculpture. At dawn, I'd stand in the dew. The mist would be rising and I'd stroke her rough skin. She was chalky, that goddess, and she spread herself like a gymnast. Or I'd look at her from the trees, as the river vapours lifted. It was as if she made herself out of the sky. One week she hadn't been there. The next, there she was as if it had always been so. A miracle, sort of. Because maybe this was the real Nerys. Maybe this was how a river god might look. Not crowned with weeds. Not fanged like a pike. But a gymnast. With the chalk on her hands.

That was the time I'd eaten the amanita, and I was quiet. The strangeness had become a silence. So I'd stroke the goddess' white thigh and think about nothing and not even brush the pine needles off my arse before I clocked on.

As I'm clocking on now. I like Justin and I think he likes me. Not that I care. But you can always tell when a man likes you. Or when he doesn't. There's a humour, an almost undetectable regard. Tolerance, I suppose, and an interest. That's it. Yes, when one man likes another man he finds the time to be interested in him. A little curious. He's one degree warmer.

Back of the van is okay to sit in because I cleaned it last night. Swept out the cement dust and the Supercrete, the wet building sand and the sharp sand, the brick dust and the chippings, the broken plastic guttering, the empty tins and the tin lids. Collected the screws and the rawlplugs and saved them in a pocket of my jeans, saved any nail bigger than one inch, any bracket or hasp, any quillet because they're hard to get. Anything useful. Tub of seal and bond with a scrape left. A stainless-steel hammer fixer. That might come in. One day. There was also a new blade slipped from its dimpled Stanley haft. It went in my other pocket.

That's why I like Justin. He's small time but he's meticulous. He takes care of his van, or, rather, I've been doing it of late, checking the oil and water, adding a drop of brake fluid because he likes it just past the line. Safe side. Sometimes his kids travel in the van. Sometimes his wife.

First thing I did when I arrived here was ask Justin for work. He was parked outside the Spar, smoking, window down in the heat. Watching the girls go past in their little dresses, showing their tattoos.

Hey boss, I said, putting my pack down. Any work, boss?

Now *boss* is an interesting word. I found that out a long time ago. A local word but used everywhere. Kind of national patois. Multifarious meanings to you, to me. A word to be careful of, boss.

Justin's a thin man. Wiry as a weasel. He blew out Benson smoke and looked at me.

What can you do?

Point me at it, I said. And I'll show you.

That was a month ago. Money was never even discussed. Cash only of course. Divvied up on a Friday evening. But I show willing. And I don't complain. That's why Justin likes me.

See you at nine tomorrow in the car park behind here, he had said. Then a girl walked past with a butterfly on her shoulder and whispered something and Justin laughed and that was it. Settled.

Now Justin's driving. Furiously, like he smokes. Doesn't drink but the Bensons make up for it. Cled, the plasterer is in the front seat. Don't know why he's come because it's just hard labour today. And Si's in the back with me. Filthy Si, in broken Army and Navy steelies, their webbing ripped out, his jeans caked white with cement dust, his tee shirt paint-stained. He'll peel it off soon enough to show his scrawny back with its American bald eagle tattoo. Si's plugged into his iPod and Si doesn't speak. Si doesn't even look at me. So I look at him. His scalp is shaved up to the top of his skull. All that's left of his hair is a circle, gelled and dyed blue. He looks like a thistle.

How's the family, Nerry? shouts Justin, changing up.

That's a joke. Not malicious.

You might be seeing them soon, he laughs. The paper says you're all going back since the pound's dodgy. Going back home with your ill-gotten gains.

Yesterday I took four rolled-up copies of *The Sun* from the front windscreen, five silver-grey Benson empties and more crisp packets and Twix wrappers than I could count. An empty two litre plastic flagon of Tesco cola was wedged under Cled's seat, and five tropical-flavour Sprite cans rolling about. With one Lipton ice tea. God knows who was drinking that. Not Si.

Since last week Si and I have a bit of a problem. It won't be resolved. We were in Wickes, the builders' merchants, with a list of supplies we had to pick up. Si had the paper because he didn't believe I could read Justin's scrawled English. So he was leading, I was pulling the trolley, long and awkward to manoeuvre. That's the word I used that got Si going. *Manoeuvre.*

Si didn't like that word. Either I pushed the trolley or I pulled the trolley. What I didn't do, what I couldn't do, was manoeuvre the trolley. Because manoeuvre was a bad word. It offended protocol, and like I've said, I pay attention to life's protocols. When you're an illegal, protocols are life and death. My father was a man of protocols. Okay, I'm not illegal now. But I'm an immigrant. And even if I go home tomorrow, I'll be an immigrant there.

When I stood in front of Justin that first morning, I put my pack on the pavement. There was a dictionary in that pack, a dog-eared Concise OED. I love that book. In a Camden squat, a fire-ruined, three-storey Victorian townhouse in Cardiff, under the bridge in Bridgend, I've sat and read that book. Yes I love that book. I've seen *manoeuvre* in it and I've even heard people say it. I knew that word in college. But I made a mistake in Wickes. I should have pulled the bastard thing. Pushed the bastard thing.

It was a scorching day, lunchtime.There was a petrol haze across the roundabout to the McDonald's drive-thru. We went down the aisles picking up some Marble Tex. Some Powerkote. Then we were down where the timber was, that new wood still smelling sweet despite the plastic wrapping on everything. We wanted some tongue and groove.

What's wrong with shiplap, I said, thinking of the job.

Si looked at me then. The last time he's ever going to look at me.

Justin wants tongue, he hissed. It's on the fucking list. He's written it here.

Okay, I said.

Si kept looking. What's that rattling all the time? he asked.

Rattling?

Fucking rattling. In your pocket.

He was still looking at me. I was looking at the timber. Clean,

Swedish. Impossible to think it had been a tree. I thought of the birches around Drusk, of Drusk and the camp lost in the birches, the fungus on the birchtrees like rain-swollen bibles, the birchsap wine one of the gang passed round. Cloudy as piss. I thought of the goddess, clumsy, ecstatic. Then I pulled the shells out of my pocket.

What the fuck are those? asked Si.

Mussel shells, I said.

Shells?

Off the beach, I said. I picked them up the other day. I used to collect freshwater mussels when I was a kid. Looking for pearls.

Si was still sizing me up. He had his shirt off, and every step through the depot I'd been staring at the eagle on his back, the bald eagle in front of the stars and stripes. A tattoo that must have taken weeks.

Jesus, said Si. Your name is Nerys and you pick up shells. Jesus Christ.

That's when I turned to him. I saw the scorn in his eye. He was a skinny kid, twenty say. There was nobody around. We had walked all the way down that aisle on our own. I put my left hand in his crotch and lifted. The tuft on his belly was against my wrist. I had the newly-ground bolster in my right hand and I put it under his chin.

Listen, I said. I'm more than twice your age. But I was in the army, son. I was in the Russian Army. They sent me to Chechnya. Ever heard of that place? You know what happened there? Is still happening?

Si was white. Stiff as a lath.

If it's on the list we'll buy the tongue, I said. We'll get it all. Boss.

Then I stroked the hairs on his belly. Like I'd stroke a dog. Then I kissed him. Once on the cheek. Then I let him go.

That's when Si stepped away. When he looked away. And he's never looked at me since. We picked up the tongue and groove. Then ten bags of builders' sand. A chuck for the Black and Decker. Some sandpaper for chamfering. There was still no one around.

I pulled the trolley behind me and we went out wobbling through the yellow automatic doors to the van. Justin was smoking and reading the paper.

Okay? he asked, not looking up.

Si gave him the change. But he didn't speak.

Okay, I said. And got in the back.

Now we drive three hundred yards and pile out. All day I sand a floor in a house on the seafront. Its name is 'Hafan' and it used to be an old people's home. Soon it will be apartments. Justin's been sub-contracted to do a few things. So today I wear a mask and push an industrial sander over varnish that's thicker than treacle. Every ten minutes I stop and go to the window and take off the mask and suck the air. The sky's so blue it hurts to look at it. Below are the young mothers with their buggies, men in panamas and white flat caps, kids in long shorts.

The sander is worse than the Wickes trolley. I remember I drove an armoured car once. We went across a field of lupins. It was like a blue mist. A farmer shouted after us. There was a fox we scared out of a ditch. Our sergeant said it was a wolf but I knew all the wolves were dead. We were just driving around like teenagers with their dad's car. Nothing much to do.

This sander must be clumsier than a tank but by 6 p.m. I've finished a big room, apart from under the walls and around the washbasin. I'll have to do that tomorrow. The floor is pale and stained, a bit cut up, I'd have to say. But no one could have done this better.

There's a mirror in the corridor. That word 'Hafan' is carved into the frame. I've seen it in every room. When I look at myself, even I'm surprised. I'm black as a coalminer from some shithole in Donetz. In the corner are nineteen sacks of varnish dust and all the floorboard shavings the machine's rubbed up. All the filth of one hundred years. Paint and varnish and old people's piss. Si's doing the wallpaper in another room. I saw him at break, down on the esp with his iPod in. Cled's mooching about, and hours ago Justin was eating an ice cream, talking to the girls. Haven't seen him since. People say it's been nearly one hundred today, which might be a record. For here.

I wash the thick off in the sink then undress and beat my jeans, my pants, my shirt against a wall. I take off my shoes and empty the dust and I comb my hair until the needles are clogged with the crap and I wash the comb and repeat.

Up the street near the charity shops is a men's toilet. This old bloke's in charge and it's won prizes for cleanliness. They're on stickers on the door. *Loo of the Year*. Every year bar one for the last ten years. What happened that year? I wonder. All the fixtures are brass, the enamel a rosy white.

I speak to the attendant, who's usually looking for a compliment, and I have a shower. First freezing cold. Then as hot as I can stand. Then I get it just right and the water runs over me and I'm in my element. A kid, seventeen, jumping off the bridge at Uzupis, aiming for the only pool that's deep enough. A boy in his knickers, clutching his knees, smashing into a roof of green glass.

In Uzupis, there was always someone's washing in the trees

or on the bridge, a girl packing up her honey stall. That was Uzupis before it changed. That's where I learned what I know about building. How to keep a wall from falling. How to point.

You should see it now. I can imagine what it's like. Because the Russians have come back, the Germans have come back. They bought it up and cleaned it up and tidied it up. Now only rich people live there. Second homes. The gypsies have gone, the black and red puppets they used to hang in the street have gone. Or, maybe someone's selling them to tourists now. Maybe there are guided walks to show you where the anarchists lived.

I'm staying at a rooming house in Lifeboat Street. It's an attic, stifling this month, even with the Velux window open. And it's been open all month. I lie on the bed naked and look at the sky. There are swifts up there, one, two, twenty swifts. All of them screaming. I get up and peer out. The swifts live in the eaves down this street. There are nests under the slates and at night I hear the young scratching. Or maybe it's mice. People say the adult swifts never sleep but I don't believe it. How can that be? Now there they are. One almost seems in reach. Black stars like the stars on a thrush's blue egg. I found a thrush's nest in Drusk once and looked at the clutch. When I touched them the eggs were cold. There was dew on the shells.

I put the same jeans on but another tee shirt I bought at the car boot sale. Twenty pence it cost me. A Polish guy runs the stall, there are lots of Poles up there, on the old airfield. He was friendly. I looked at his tattoos. Some kind of Nazi insignia.

Oh yeah, I thought, as I gave him the coin. Everyone's coming in. Big orange cotton tee, with the words *Una Cerveza Por Favor Senor*, on the front. It's wrinkled at the neck but the best I've got.

Now, food. Sometimes I save up hunger. Save it till I can

hardly stand. Tonight, I'm ravenous. I buy double chips and one of those oggy pasties and mushy peas in a tub. Lots of ketchup. Two tubes of mayonnaise.

Hey, this is the life. I sit on the sea wall and as I'm eating I look out and there's nothing there, not a ship, not a wind surfer. Only the flat blue it's been all month. But the sky is whiter now. Like a hotplate, and the far coast a line in the heat haze.

When I was in the army, hunger was permanent. Like the sergeant it was always hanging around. Powdered egg and powdered potatoes. Black half moons of rye bread with no gravy to soak them in. Maybe the oil from a sardine tin. Sometimes we'd fry mushrooms in lard and wipe the skillet clean. Round and round with the black bread. So I became used to hunger.

Yes, that was the longest year of my life. Christ, we were a shower. No bootlaces. Wooden bayonets. We'd barter bullets for cigarettes. There was a boy in our unit who could make rotgut vodka from potato peelings. We swapped this plastic drum of the stuff for a big piece of belly pork. The fat on that pork was the best food I had ever tasted. We put it on a spit made out of an axle and cut open an oil can and watched that golden juice dribble out of the meat. I can hear the hissing now. That crackling was better a million times than this oggy here.

And that's all it was. Hunger. Hunger and boredom. Except when we were afraid. So afraid we would piss ourselves. Hunger, boredom and fear. It wasn't my war but it was my turn. I could have avoided it, could have run off like lots of the others. But that was my quiet time. I was having problems making decisions and so someone made a decision for me.

But I never fired a shot. The only Chechens I saw gave us gifts. We were passing a cottage and an old man comes out and pours us glasses of this homemade beer. There was a sunflower he'd grown as tall as his roof. One of the boys was going to cut it down but we stopped him. See, we weren't so bad. And that's no lie. But try telling that to the black widows.

College hadn't worked out, and I'd wandered away from Drusk. We'd done it all there, we'd rebuilt the camp and the gang had split up. Funny how your time comes and then passes. Richard Manuel was dead before I heard a note he played. It was a kind of in-between period. The end of days. But the days wouldn't end. The empire was taking time to lie down and die.

I roll up the chip papers, stuff them in a bin and walk into the fairground. Little Rhian's on at one of the shies and she tells me I look thirsty and gives me a can of Tango, one of the prizes. Rhian's all right but when you get close you see she's not so young. Like me. She has this feeling of loneliness about her. This aura. I know she thinks I have it too. So I wink at her and give her back the empty and she puts her hands on her hips and laughs and then our meeting is over.

Most people, you see, know me by now. I work on the Blitz, weekend evenings, the busy period. Justin arranged that too. He said there were Poles in charge of the rides now, but really they're Lithuanian. Justin can't tell us apart. Tonight it's Petr and Virgilijs and they greet me gravely. Yes, I could be their father. So we talk and they explain how badly they are treated but how much money they're earning, and then I buy an ice cream half price and lick it carefully down to the cornet and then I strap myself into one of the carriages and we're away. Very slowly at first. Only inching forward.

It's not the falling I seek. The descents make me sick. It's the climb I love, my carriage climbing to the top of the frame, high above the town. And then that moment at the summit, when the car is perched there trembling. When I know I cannot climb higher and everything is laid out as it should be. When the world is in its place and everywhere there is order. When the rider understands that the car ahead is already hurtling back towards earth and the car behind is still crawling to the apex. That this is the moment before the drop. The moment of stillness. The quiet moment, even though the girls are screaming and Virgilijs has More, More, More by Andrea True Connection louder than the rules say. Then I shut my eyes. Then the blackness roars. At the bottom I'm still holding the cornet and the ice cream has melted into the little crunchy squares of the rim.

By half nine it's getting dark. I walk down to the Point. A few cars are parked and I can see two people far out on the rocks. There's a long sunset tonight, the sky fiery even into the north, wrapping itself around the town.

Passing one of the cars I have to stop. It's a Mazda RX-8 and the registration is GAZ 101.

That boy, I think. The boy with blond streaks in his hair. On the dashboard is a pink scrunchy. It will be that boy over on the rocks, I decide. The boy and his girl friend. Her hair loose.

You bastard shit, he had called out at the world. Just a kid, as Roly said. Showing off. In the red light the car is shining. What polish it has. What expensive wax. But the boy doesn't polish it. His father does. I'd wager a week with Justin on that.

I would say they are a hundred yards away. Holding hands as the sea breaks at their feet. Or maybe his hand in her hair. And even as I look the sunset is fading, the sea turning violet, black.

Out of my jeans pocket I take an antique brass-headed mirror screw I picked up in the oldies' home today. You know, cleaning up. Because I'm always cleaning. Getting it right for Justin.

It needs a little force with my left hand to dig the screw in through the shell of wax and the coats of paint and the coats of primer on the Mazda. But in twenty seconds I have walked around the car and I finish my circuit at the bonnet insignia. Which is a tulip. Shaped like an M. My scratch runs all the way round. No, my *gouge*. Down to the metal. The bare steel.

When I reach the tulip the car alarm comes on. The indicators start flashing and there's a siren noise like the ghost train makes and the couple out on the rocks glance up. In the twilight they start to run this way. But I'm looking at the waves. It's funny really, this town. All the time I've spent here watching the tide. Because I still can't tell when the tide is going out. Or when it's coming in.

A bed on the prairie

He was a big man now. Too big. But still a little man. His thighs chafed, his belly bulged. Once a week he'd ride the number three bus up 8 Street and was conscious he took up more than half a double seat. More than two thirds.

Never mind. What could he do? Anyway, most journeys the bus was empty. People were going the other way. Sometimes he'd see the driver looking at him in the mirror and he'd put the brown paper bag below seat level. In the bag was a hip flask and in the flask a pint of Bushmills. Eye-watering, throat-sandpapering Irish. At 27 Street the bus would start to turn west and he'd pull the bell chord and get off and walk up the road. The driver still looking.

It was an effort. His back hurt. The road led nowhere. It ended in a mound of bulldozed turf and rubble. There were sheets of plastic, Caterpillar tracks in the earth.

It wasn't the prairie. The prairie was somewhere else. But tonight it was the best the Big Little Man could do. He stepped over the flattened wire and sat on the seat. Then took the whiskey out again.

There was a plaque on the seat. It read *In Memory of Walter and Ingrid McGovern*, who Loved this Place.

Strange people, he said to himself. For putting a seat here. A seat made from black recycled plastic. But if the developers didn't move it, the seat would survive until the next ice age. He thought about ice and he thought about the north, the north where the ice age still persisted. The ice age that would never end. The McGoverns had lived in Highland Place, off 8 Street. They would park their Fleetwood back on the road and totter out on to the prairie. Because this had been the real prairie then. Virgin land, never touched by plough or genetically modified canola. And the McGoverns would look up at the stars or at the northern lights, holding on to one other, the fat woman, the sticklike man in his ballcap and Levi's. They wouldn't speak. Just gaze out at the new world. The promised land where they had arrived and were about to die.

Eventually it was claimed, 27 Street would lead to the next mall the city was going to build. Another Safeway's. Another Sears. But everything was on hold. A bank in Toronto had gone bust. Tits up, people around here said. In Toronto, investors had queued along Yonge Street in the snow. Here they had lined up on 4 Street for news. The news was bad. So what? said the voice of exhaustion in the Big Little Man's heart.

The Big Little Man sat and held the whiskey under his nose. The day was ending. Another day ending. He looked north into nothing. Then his eyes grew accustomed to the light. The prairie now was pale with sage, the silver sage that seemed to reflect the starlight. Maybe there were coyotes out there, though he'd never heard one. Maybe the last of the wolverines. He'd read about those. The fiercest of creatures, not welcome now in the world of wire. Maybe a single wolverine still lingered in the grass.

Then he raised his sights. The stars burned so thickly they hurt his eyes. There was Mars, the Bushmills-yellow phantom that roamed the sky. There was Arcturus, a bonfire that never burned out. He knew if he looked long enough he'd see satellites passing in the dark, the red winglights of aeroplanes coming south from the pole. And maybe he'd see a craft. A saucer. An unidentified flying circus. Ha, ha, he thought. I've made a joke. It was cold now. He couldn't stay long. But he kept looking skywards. Take me, the Big Little Man would whisper. He wanted to wave the flask but even in the darkness he was careful. Behaviour was everything. But again he whispered. Take me. Here I am. I'm waiting for you.

Then he smiled again to himself. Tonight the Big Little Man was not convinced by his own desperation. Making a joke in a foreign language is difficult. But he was good at it now. He had had a lot of practice.

When the Big Little Man first arrived in the city he was still a little man. There were hoardings everywhere. There were signs. We're building a mountain together, the signs said. That was a good omen. The Winter Olympics were coming to the province. But there were no slopes for the skiers. So the city was building its own mountain out of rubbish. All the city's rubbish for three years was to be piled on the prairie, then earth poured over it and grass seed sown. When the grass grew, the city would be ready. All it had to do was wait for winter and the snow.

In this city the snow always fell on the last day of October. The Big Little Man didn't understand that, but it was always predicted and it always occurred. By now, he was used to it. As on the evening of that day, he was accustomed to children knocking at his door. Children dressed as ghouls and ghosts, with black lipstick or ice hockey masks like Michael Myers. There were whole shops now in the city devoted to fancy dress.

For the first few years he had bought candies for these Halloween children. Recently he had stopped. The children had started to frighten him, the children in the corridors outside, whispering at the apartment doors. Meanwhile, the children's parents would huddle on the sidewalk, eating Halloween food. The parents came in case the children were invited inside. In case they disappeared.

Strange, he thought, in his dark room, listening to the children scratching like mice. Why are they so afraid? Afraid of disappearing? There was a story that had been in the news. A teenage girl had vanished. Maybe she was abducted. Witnesses swore they saw a light on the prairie, a beam like a ladder reaching to the ground. Perhaps the girl had climbed the ladder into the indigo sky.

Lucky girl, he thought, his back to the door where the children were whispering. If they stopped and listened instead they might have heard him breathing. He could picture them in their hoods. In their cloaks. On the other side of that door stood a four-foot Grim Reaper and a Star Wars trooper. In the street their moms were eating taffi. He hated taffi. It glued his teeth together. The first snow was falling and it shone in the women's hair under the streetlight, the women in their scarves and ski pants, their furry boots.

After a while the whispering would stop. But he would not switch on the lamp. Soon there would be another knock, another scratching. Freddy Krueger with a green face would be asking for a treat, and Freddy's mom would be standing in the snow in her black lycra. In her zips and buckles.

He pictured the mother's smile. Her teeth would be Arm & Hammer white, her belly, if he might miraculously glimpse her belly, would still be tanned, the colour of prairie earth. And flat as a dinnerplate. How he longed to rest his face there. His lips upon the knife slit of her navel. Someone had told him you might hear the heart through the belly. The belly beating with blood. Yes, such were the mothers now. *Toned* was the word. A word he had never used.

The Big Little Man wondered where the fathers were. In their offices, he imagined. Doing the things office people do. Talking on telephones, scrolling down, always scrolling down, towards the next financial cataclysm.

These mothers and fathers were tough people. They lived in a city without bends in the road. A city without curves. Which meant there was no mystery in this city. That made it a hard place to live. The mall too lacked mystery. It was a small mall and not many people visited. They wandered the forecourt looking bewildered, as if they had misplaced something. Some of them stood in front of the sports shop and studied the numbers on the hockey shirts. What would it be like to wear a number?

The Big Little Man worked at a noodle bar in the mall. He had been there fifteen years. Sometimes he had to cook, but generally he waited on tables in the concourse. There were twenty tables, four chairs immovable around each table. Two banqueting tables had six chairs.

The noodle bar was called the Prairie Wok and it offered Chinese, Thai and Vietnamese food. But all the food was made together in the tiny kitchen. The Big Little Man had no idea what people ate in Thailand and Vietnam. In China, in Ann Hui province, in the city of Huangshan, in his street which was the street of clapping doves, if they could afford it, they had eaten pigs. All of the pig, the trotters, the brains, the long pale bellies with the hairy teats. Yes, all of it. The valves, the vulva, the hooves, the heart, the veins, the bristles, the brisket, the fiery arsehole and all the glooms of the gut. But usually, they didn't. Eat pigs that is. Pigs were precious.

He remembered scraping rice out for the pigs they kept in a sty behind their house. The house was one room up and one room down. The front door was made of planks and outside the door was a mud street where other pigs ran, and children ran after pigs, or played or peed. In their garden, no bigger than a table at the Prairie Wok, there was a melon vine and a persimmon tree.

This mall disappointed people but the Little Man liked it. He had his regular customers with their usual orders. Many of them ate singly. How lonely they looked at the tables, with their plastic forks and plastic chopsticks, dabbing their mouths and looking at their watches as if they had somewhere else to go.

Coffee? he would ask, passing to wipe the next table. Soda? And sometimes they did and sometimes they didn't. Outside, there would be spaces in the parkade, and the big neon sign for Red Lobster would block the sky. The snow was swept into khaki heaps like tiny ski slopes.

Most of the customers drenched their food in soy sauce. Standing behind the counter or pushing the broom, he'd smile as he watched them shake the Blue Dragon bottles over their crispy noodles. The Big Little Man hated noodles. He hated rice too. No, he ate pizzas and subs now. He took gyros home, and doughnuts with chocolate and hundreds-and-thousands on one side. That's why he was fat. It was no mystery to him. He would look at the bundles of pak choi in the kitchen and smile, in his quiet way. Those pigs, years ago, would have eaten the pak choi, those pink and chocolate-coloured pigs behind the house. But this was the great country of meat. Burgers wrapped in bacon. Chicken wrapped in bacon. Wings and ribs. Pak choi was peasant food, but meat three times a day was the emperor's carnivorous dream.

There was a woman who came regularly to the Prairie Wok. For his own amusement, in his own way of making sense, he called her Starwoman. She would sit alone, dabbing her mouth and looking at her watch as if she had somewhere else to go. The young women who sometimes came were different. They always talked on their cell phones. If four girls sat together, there would be four cell phones on the table. Often a phone would ring and they would all look at the screen, laughing.

Don't answer him, they would shriek. Be mysterious.

But nobody telephoned Starwoman. She would sit with her tofu and pak choi, which was 48 on the menu, and her own plastic chopsticks that she always reused. The Big Little Man liked that. In Huangshan, his family had eaten with their fingers. The riceballs were like moons. His little sister held up a moon and he had put out his hand and snatched it. He didn't think about it. It just happened. The rice moon filled his mouth. How his sister had cried until his father had smacked his cheek and grandmother hissed like a goose at him. Grandfather wanted a pig brought into the house. Mother sat with her face in her hands.

Sometimes, the Big Little Man asked customers, the older men, the women in pairs, about the terrible north. The far north where the prairie became lakes and trees, where granite seas rose and fell into the darkness and wolves howled in the tamarack. And sometimes the lonely men would tell him lonely stories, and he would pause with his mop and J cloth and nod his head and see the empty roads and the ice burned dark as marrowbone.

One day he picked up courage and asked Starwoman if she had ever been into the north. She raised her eyes, mauve as the prairie crocus. How she whinnied then, like a horse for its mealbag.

Why would I go there? she laughed. She laughed and laughed showing her square mare's teeth. Then she got up and never came back.

But the Big Little Man himself was already a traveller. He had made a great expedition and landed at the port on the west coast. In the day he mopped floors and cooked noodles and in the night he pored over his Jack London books. After a year, someone said there was work to the east. So he had taken the Grey Goose and arrived when the mountain was being built.

Sometimes he travelled further. He owned an old green Plymouth now, a barge of an automobile. The prairie galleon, people called it. One year, for his holiday, he drove to Moose Jaw. Another year to Medicine Hat. Then one year, he decided, he must keep going. Just continue cruising those straight highways. So he did. After a while he came to a place called Wild Horse. It was cold. He could cross the border here but there was nothing down the road that he could see. Nothing but the grey snow, the pelt of that desert, and a sky that would soon become a winking lid of water like the bottom of a well.

The Big Little Man got out of the car. Yes, he could see for miles in every direction. But so what? asked a voice of exhaustion in his heart. A cloud of dust lay ahead, as if a herd of bison had passed. Maybe there were coyotes on the prairie, maybe the last of the wolverines was looking at him from the prairie sage, a forty-pound, black and dirty white wolverine. But no, he thought. The wolverine would be asleep now, dreamless in its den of old bones.

The Big Little Man looked up. If there was any place in the world they would come for him, it would be here. On the road to Wild Horse, a road sharp with gravel and porcupine spines long as knitting needles, the road that crossed the border from nowhere into nowhere. Yes, If they were ever going to take him, it would be now. And he was ready. As ready as White Fang, as ready as Jack London himself, stamping outside his smoky bivouac. The Big Little Man got out of the car. He stood in the emptiness in his camouflage clothes, grey and brown, like the snow, like the wolverine's fur. Looking around, he thought the sky would surely fall.

The next day at the Prairie Wok, he was squashing boxes of stale prawn crackers into a rubbish bin made from black recycled plastic. A man came up to him and said he was sorry but the restaurant would be closing for a week. When it opened again they would be selling English food. English breakfasts and English teas. English Sunday dinners of roast beef and Yorkshire puddings. The fish and the chips. But we think you're a good worker, the man said. We want you to stay. The staff training is next Thursday. The new restaurant will be called *Rule Britannia*. Okay?

Okay, said the Big Little Man.

On the McGoverns' seat he wedged the flask of Bushmills between his knees. The sun was sinking and the sundogs flaring. He looked north. That was the sundog trail, that was where the sky would tremble and glow. The Big Little Man remembered running out of his house in the street of clapping doves and running and running down into the town. He could see the mist clearing from Nine Dragons Peak. He ran past an open room. In this room was an iron wok burned black upon an open fire. A few chairs stood around for the customers who always came. One strawhatted man was eating rice with yellow peas.

He ran past a redsmith who stood in the steam of a slack tub. He ran down hill and passed the chestnut peelers and a woman who always laid out sunflower seeds on a straw mat. No one looked up. He was running away from home and his mother's tears and away from the pigs who wore rings like half moons in their snouts. He ran with a stitch in his side, a thorn in his foot and the shape of his father's hand on his cheek. But after a while he ran only for the joy of running.

The Big Little Man ran past the men playing mah jong and the men playing checkers and he ran all the way into the square of Huangshan. He only stopped at the wall around the pool, the fire still in his side, in his mind's eye his grandmother's pigtail dragging in the soup as she leaned across the table. Ha ha, he laughed. Ha ha.

In the pool the carp spoke to him as they usually did, rising from the weeds in their peeling gold to bring him the news, the news of empires that had been, that were to come.

Ha, ha, he laughed again, as the fish blew him kisses, and spoke to him of poets and astronauts. He peered into the pool. The other children said it was miles deep and that a little girl had fallen into it and never been found.

The next day, or maybe it was the next month, the Big Little Man found himself standing under the television that hung from a wall bracket at Rule Britannia. There was a Union Jack behind the counter and a picture of the Queen. But the chairs were still bolted to the tables.

He felt sad. If Starwoman ever came again she would not be able to use her plastic chopsticks. Does it matter if she returns? asked the voice of exhaustion in his heart. But one of the lonely men was there, putting soy sauce on his chips. How he shook and shook the Blue Dragon over his plate. The four girls with the four cell phones had also arrived. They all wore half price Husky shirts from the sports shop that was closing: 26. 38. 76. 98. A phone rang and the girls pounced to see who was calling.

Don't answer him, they squealed. You're not ready to leave.

On the television an English king sat up in bed. Such a bed. The Big Little Man thought about his couch at home. How hard it was. In the street of clapping doves he and his sister had slept on a wooden shelf that was taken down in the day. But it was better than sleeping with grandfather in the pigs' sty.

The Big Little Man's back hurt. So did his legs. But he was planning his next holiday. He thought about Wild Horse. It had snowed there, a dry snow like polystyrene pellets, and the wind had blown. So why had he worn those camouflage clothes? No one could have seen him. In the next place he would not be hidden. He would drive his green car over the prairie, the only colour visible from above. And his clothes would be brighter than the dragonflies that hovered over the bottomless pool in Huangshan.

Yes, he would go north to where the great rivers met. How their ice would groan and grind, the grey floe meeting the brown floe, the grass snapping under his feet, his breath a beard of fish scales.

Ha ha, he laughed. With such whiskers he would look like his grandfather pulling the pigs by their nose-rings into the house. In the north the Big Little Man would find a seat like the McGoverns' bench and he would sit under the sky of inexhaustible stars. Or better still, he could build a bed. A huge bed like the English king's. He could lie amongst its furs and cushions and gaze up at the pandemonium of lights. Then he would whisper, as he always did.

Here I am, he would whisper. Please take me. I'm ready now.

The tunnel

The banknote lay at his feet. The man had paid for drinks and dropped a two-dollar bill. Nobody had noticed yet. But they soon would.

Juan drew a little closer, looking the other way. Then he glanced again. No, it was a twenty. When had he ever seen a two dollar in this country? It was a twenty, there on the floor. The man was talking to the woman, their barstools pulled together. Looked like tourists, tall and blonde. Swedes, he thought. Maybe Dutchies. Their clothes were good and they were showing off their English. But they wouldn't stay. One beer each and they'd head over to Time Square, stand in the neon noon, photograph themselves and send their Samsung smiles to friends at home.

Yes, it was now or never. As he passed, he bent over and palmed the bill. And kept going, heading for the restrooms.

No word of protest. No call. Of course not. Dave's Tavern was so dark sometimes you couldn't see five feet away. In the shadows, the perpetual twilight, nobody had noticed. This morning, Peevo had already arrived but he was standing out on the sidewalk, staring at something. At nothing. The open door was a dazzling slash, the only evidence it was, at the latest, 11 a.m. Yes, must be about that. The weekday ritual was starting.

Mary Mack slid the DVD into the machine. And there they were, straight into the movie. According to Mary the best movie ever made. Or fillum, as she called it. The greatest *fillum* of all time.

Mary Mack ran Dave's Tavern. Mary Mack had run Dave's for forty years and boy, she had run it down. Well, that's what Juan thought. Did he care? You bet. It was a job, right next door to his other job in the Port Authority. Handy. He walked from one darkness into another. Also, if Dave's closed, he would lose his lodging. Juan rented a room upstairs, a midtown room, smack in the centre of the centre. Mary told him he was a lucky little sod. Told him over and over that the bohos and the computer nerds and the artists would kill for such a room. Such an address. Manic midtown, throbbing with the heartbeat of America. All those Hell's Kitchen heroes wanting his ten by twelve, his mattress, the immovable mahogany wardrobe where his life was hung.

Yes, Mary, Juan would say. You been good. You been so good.

Old soak, he thought. But she was right. He had arrived two years previously. Arrived through the tunnel. The first thing Mary had made him do was clean the windows. Soon he would have to clean them again. He had borrowed a ladder from the Port Authority, taken the bucket from behind the bar, and climbed as high as he dared. The glass had been black. The grime was a centimetre thick.

American dirt, he thought, as he saw the water in the pail darken. You could grow money in it. All that traffic smoke coming out of the tunnel. All those buses lining up, their exhausts thick as drainpipes. That's where the dirt came from. And those windows not washed in years. In his own room he'd sometimes sit at the glass and stare outside. It always seemed foggy and sometimes there was a real mist off the Hudson, Greyhound headlights big and ghostly in the gloom, the cockpits of the coaches maybe blue lit from the on-board TV.

And if he couldn't see at least he could hear, hear voices below raised in terror or supplication, or the growl of buses he knew were coming in, the Montreal, the Chicago, delivering their riders into the darkness.

But mostly it was the crust on the windows that made things grey. The *crud*. How he laughed at that word. Maybe crud was his favourite English word. Mary relished telling him to clean the crud off the lavatory pan rims, the crud in the sink which was a mixture of ketchup and carbolic and that sweatsweet Gallo from the winebox. The inescapable crud that everybody left behind wherever they went. Evidence of their passing. Proof of terrestrial life. Blast it, Mary would say, waving her brown coffee cup with the Bailey's in it. Blast the fooken crud. And she'd cackle and go back to her fillum.

So Juan had wiped the windows and the glassy shamrock bolted to the wall that Mary claimed was a genuine antique, and then the letters above the door. *Dave's Tavern*, now white on green again. With a gleaming apostrophe. Just like a teardrop, Juan had thought. A tear for Dave.

Juan should have been cleaning the restrooms. He flicked the lights and waited for the roaches to hide, the waterbugs that seemed to be made of metal. They ticked like something electrical. But the rooms didn't look too bad. He put the twenty in his pocket and pushed a mop over the floor in the Men's. The Women's could wait. Or maybe he'd polish the mirror there. He breathed on it and swept the glass with his sleeve. If the Women's was used, the mirror had to be clean. In one of the cubicles the lock was missing and the hole in the door filled with tissue. The mirror was even more important than that. Someone had scrawled *Hilary for President* on the wall. Someone had written S*he is, stupid* beneath it.

Juan worked five straight nights in the bus bays under the Port Authority. Where it was always dark. That week all the underground staff were talking about what had happened on a bus in Manitoba. A madman had decapitated the passenger in the seat in front. Juan had shrugged. It was a crazy time.

Those nights in that nether world he scraped oil from the concrete, cleaned mud from wheel arches and polished windshields, removing the excess before the buses went through the mechanical wash. Sometimes a driver told him there was skunk meat on the muffler and it was stinking the bus out. Get it off.

Yeah, Juan thought. Roadkill. Singed deer hide. Racoon guts. On another shift he had been assigned the grille of the Trailways down from Binghamton. It was caked with black snow and rocksalt. When he looked closer there was a bird impaled in the frets. Some kind of hawk. He thought it was dead but saw its eye follow his hand. An eye like a papaya seed. Hey, he said. Where you get on?

One night he'd been told to roust out a woman sleeping in Bay 26. She was rolled in a blanket on a strip of C Town cardboard. Around her were remains of a meal: a Ray's pizza crust, a Snapple bottle.

Hey, he said. Hey.

She rolled over and looked at him.

Hey, she said. And smiled.

This morning he was tired. Even with two jobs he had no money. When Juan came out of the Women's, Peevo was back with his beer and installed in his corner. That corner, between counter and far wall with its tobacco-coloured stucco, had been

Peevo's for thirty years. Maybe forty. Peevo had once been the security man at Dave's. Now he sat and sipped, almost invisible in his lair, a urinous gleam from the glass in his fist. Peevo drank draft Bud. Maybe fifty glasses a day. Last week Juan had found himself next to the Pole in the Men's, watching him unstrapping his denim dungarees, observing him piss the colourless beer back into the bowl, one minute, two, a man venting from the white balloon of his body, three minutes of voiding himself until the next cold glass. A fat man, Peevo, an enormous sluglike man who had once held troublemakers by their lapels and tossed them on to the avenue. Yes, a swollen ghost Peevo, in his ammonia-crotched Wrangler's. Part of the furniture, Peevo, who wrapped himself close in the fog of the bar.

Mary Mack had deserted her post. She was watching the film, a bowl of Prairie City doughnuts and yellow Jell-O on the table before her. But sometimes she zapped to the television for sleeping draught ads. So many adverts, Juan noted, to put people to sleep.

Wanna sleep? Mary would shout. Buy our bourbon.

Then she'd switch back to Midnight Cowboy.

It was always Cowboy at Dave's. Jon Voight and Dustin Hoffman becoming Joe Buck and Ratso. The hustler, the conman. And always Mary with the remote, replaying the scene when the bus comes out of the tunnel and the big blond Joe Buck finds himself in Manhattan for the first time. Joe Buck with his buckskin fringe aswing, aiming to put the man into Manhattan, rolling up the tunnel in a black Stetson.

And what does my beautiful Joe see? Mary Mack would cackle. Little ole us. Us good people at Dave's. Oh we were here in 1969 when that fillum was out. Oh yes we were here. Dave himself was here, as I live and breathe.

Mary Mack played Midnight Cowboy every day. Now she switched back to the ads.

Juan took over. This was the best time. He was the bus driver now. He was the patron, gazing round, taking in the glint of the mirror tiles, the empty booths down the wall, the tables with their wood-pattern formica.

Hey, he said to the Pole.

Peevo peered across. She's getting her place next week, Peevo said.

That's good.

She's getting her place next week.

Yeah, good.

Juan refilled the fat man's glass.

Two Sams, said a kid down the bar. His friend loitered behind.

Sam's off, said Juan. Got Bud.

Shit, said the kid. Give us two Turkeys.

Got ID?

The students showed their cards.

Two Wild Turkeys, smiled Juan.

The boys were looking round. Told you, whispered one. This is the real deal. None of that Shooters glitzy crap here. You seen the jukebox? Awesome.

Juan refilled Mary's cup. She was fast forwarding.

It's coming up, she nodded at the screen. Here it is.

Dustin Hoffman and Jon Voight were on a Greyhound. They were going through the tunnel on the way to Florida. Then Voight was getting off at a mall stop and buying two summer shirts.

Real fancy Florida duds, hissed Mary Mack.

The placard man was in now. He had left his boards at the

door. They said 'Sin, when it is finished, bringeth forth Death'.

The Lemon Man was next. He asked for a quarter lemon. Juan passed it over and the man left. He would return two minutes later, asking for a cup of hot water. Juan would also pass that over. This happened every day but only happened because it had always happened. The Lemon Man was another Pole. Sometimes he spoke Polish to Peevo but Peevo only said that she was getting her place next week.

Juan glanced at the film. Dustin Hoffman had died on the bus, just like that passenger up in Canada. So who cleaned up after that greasy little Ratso pissed his pants? In the script they laughed it off. Called it an unscheduled rest stop. But, like Mary, Juan loved the movie. How those boys shivered on the streets, in the burning floes of cold that blew off the Hudson. How they scraped a life, from Broadway's iron kerb to the Bronx brownstones where they might blag a bed.

Juan had long realised that hunger was this city's pimp. And winter its enforcer. Voight had to let that pervy kid suck the jelly out of him. But the kid was broke. Not a dime for the dick. That's where chasing cooter had got Jon Voight.

How quickly after he came out of the tunnel, out of its black tube, it had gone wrong for Joe Buck. As to Ratso, he had been coughing from the start. There was blood on his vest like ketchup on the crackers. Everyone in that movie was cursed by their own dream.

Ratso and Joe Buck? Mary Mack would announce. Of course they came in here. They were my best regulars. They had a drink here before getting on the bus. Dave remembered they was always scrounging peanuts off the bar. Then they was going down in the dark, down with their bundles to where the Greyhound was waiting, waiting to go through the tunnel, all the way down that tunnel and into the light.

The first chords of Europe's 'The Final Countdown' crashed out of the jukebox. Right on time, Jesus arrived. Juan poured Jesus a macadam-black coffee. They would have spoken their Spanishes but Mary Mack didn't hold with language. Jesus worked in the tunnel, picking up garbage. Soda bottles, shredded tyres like crows' wings.

The students were discussing whether Europe was an American or Swedish band.

Hey fellahs, hollered Mary. What youse think of the place? Grand's the word. You know that Tom's Diner? Tom's up on Hundred and Twelve? They say they filmed Seinfeld there. Kind of a comedy show, they say. But this is the place to be. What you call authentic. Take a booth, boys. You like meatloaf?

Meatloaf's off, said Juan.

Bat Outta Hell, said one of the students. It's on next.

Mary went back to the sleeping pill ads.

Recently she had asked Juan where he came from.

Salta, he had said.

Where the fook's that?

Argentina.

Why you washed up here then?

Money, he said. Banks. The politicians changed the money. No, they murdered the money. And they killed me.

Mary Mack girned at him. Oh yes, those politicians, she hissed. Anybody ever say you look like that Barack Obama? Only like, whiter. How old are you?

Forty, Juan had said. He couldn't believe it then. He couldn't now. He was forty. A man of forty looking out of a dirty window. At the black snow. At the mouths of the tunnel, the three open mouths. On his wall was a picture of somewhere that wasn't

Salta. One of the hawk's wing feathers, a foot long, barred brown and black at the tip, stood in a glass.

In Salta, Juan used to go up the street until he was almost out of town. But there was the house. It was the house they held at the *Peña*, a labyrinth of rooms where couples gazed into one another's eyes. He'd make his way through the chambers until he came to the garden. The *parrilla* would be glowing, the coals reddening as two cooks turned the spits, prepared the *chorizo*, the *lomo*. How that roasting meat scented the air. And the guitarists would be crooning their songs, the poets their rhymes. He would slip in. Nobody stopped him. Men and women danced in candlelight, the waiters hurried past with jugs of wine. One of the cooks might pass him a piece of *cabrito* and Juan would laugh, knowing the goat fat oiled his chin.

The twenty bucks was folded stamp-size in his pocket. For my *Peña*, he thought. Might a *Peña* work here? It could work here. Real charcoal grill. Grease on the chin and a guitarist's cries as the diners unwrapped, like his special presents to them, the corn leaves of their *humida*.

Dead man in the tunnel, said Jesus. But we didn't stop traffic. Oh no.

She's getting her place next week, said Peevo.

Mary Mack was asleep with the zapper in her hand.

Peña – traditional music and song.

Parrilla – grill or barbecue restaurant

Chorizo – one of the first meat courses at an Argentine parrilla.

Lomo – fillet steak

Humida – corn (maize) paste served in corn leaves.

The boy with the rock 'n' roll gene

1

The children Fabien knew lived near the bus station at Tiete. That's where they'd go before and after school, running round the Santa Ritas coming in from the suburbs, the thousands disembarking, the thousands waiting to get on.

At first, it never occurred to him to ask where these people were going. But by the time he was twelve, he'd often watch the cometas loading up for the outlandish places beyond his city, the other cities of his country, his country which the teachers said was bigger than all the other countries, his country with its jungles and waterfalls and all that wild *cerrado*.

And as Fabien watched he wondered. Step on, he learned, and in three days he might step out in Brasilia. Wasn't that the new capital where no one had ever been? Or he might go to Rio. Rio with its white sand. He knew a rhyme about Rio, its thieving cariocas who wore sparkling wedding dresses. How long was the road to Rio?

The passengers would look at their bundles. Then they doubtfully proffered them to the luggage handlers and pressed coins on those perspiring men who used pikes to push their possessions into different compartments. Once a woman brought two cockerels fighting in a Panasonic cardboard box. He grinned as the handler slid the box into the darkness under the bus and both birds grew quiet.

Fabien learned the bus companies' liveries. They reminded him of the city's football teams. Fabien's team was Corinthians although he had never seen a game. There were ancient buses with turnstiles and tickets on clicking wheels, while a modern coach, hot from Buenos Aires, purred like an aeroplane. He watched a couple emerge from its smoked glass, blinking in the dawn. After forty hours their journey had ended. Now they must start again.

Yes, what a place was the bus station. That's where he saw men cry, women cast themselves in despair to the ground. A bus had departed too soon. Someone had not arrived. Once a petrol-blue macaw walked around the Curitiba cometa, as if checking its suitability. Such a bird. It was as tall as his chest. Squinting up at him, it said, *Oi, oi*. Then *Oi, oi* once again. Behind the macaw came a humpbacked man who carried its cage and a dangling leather strap.

When the police chased the children off he'd walk along the banks of the Rio Tiete and regard the sewage floes already glittering in the heat. Sometimes he'd see whole families of capybaras emerge from the water or the undergrowth of the shores, dusky sows, grave and circumspect, the piglets behind in single file as they minced through the rubbish, the city's traffic stalled five yards away on the highway.

But always the boy and his gang would drift back to the bus station and pool their money and buy coconut or sherbet at one of the barracas. People said it was the biggest bus station in the country. That meant maybe the whole planet. How he loved to breathe the sweet exhaust that hung over the station, feel the uncertainty of the travellers as the children danced around the bays. No fear there for him. No treasure of his tied up in a dirty blanket and wedged between an old woman's shoes. This was where he came from. This was the centre of the world.

One morning he arrived and stood still. A face had appeared in the bus station, an enormous face on the outside wall of the east side waiting room. He looked up at the face and shivered. Such a face, the pale face of a man crowned with dark hair. And on the head of this man a cap like a soldier might wear, or maybe an engineer. A working man's cap. Maybe even a bus driver's cap. But this was no ordinary man. This was Bono. Bono was coming to the city to play a concert, Bono with his devil's ears, his torturer's grin. Bono had saved the world and now everyone was celebrating. And even though Bono was wearing his working man's uniform, Bono was a lord, one of the great *senhors*, his teeth strong as a goat's, his songs an electric wind that blew around the world.

The boy had heard 'In the Name of Love' on the radio and now it was in his head forever. Love was what Bono sang about. Love love love. And here was Bono in the city. Ready to sing for them about love. How hugely he loomed, above the people who clutched *Il Globo* and their little travelling altars, above the man who rested an alabaster madonna like a rifle on his shoulder.

2

When he was fourteen his mother moved the family across the city. Olimpio was his barrio now, Olimpio where the Santa Ritas ran, but not the great coaches with their silver fuselages and names of cities lost in the rainforest. There was a rat in their new apartment, and sometimes a hummingbird came in down the passageway to drink at mother's hibiscus.

Olimpio was a long street crossed by flyways and bridges. His mother didn't need to tell him to take the bridges instead of the subways, but that's what she did every day. The subways scared Fabien, but he still ventured there. Men lay on cardboard in their own piss. Druggies begged for change. You could see the bones in their faces, the scorched silver paper.

At night he'd walk out on Olimpio and watch the lightning in the southern sky amongst the skyscrapers. Every night it seemed that lightning soldered the south and the rains came down.

Fabien was fourteen now and quite the young man. He wasn't tall but he was lean, his body tawny whipcord. He watched the schoolkids doing the lambada, the hot rains on their skin and the moths coming out of the dusk to float around their hair.

Sometimes they'd all kiss one another, and he'd pass a peppermint from his mouth into the mouth of a trembling girl. Even when the girls were taller than Fabien they stood on tiptoe when they kissed him. He could feel their bodies straining, his hands upon their tiny waists.

A few of the girls were dyed blonde now. There were gang tattoos on their arms. Fabien was also in a gang but he never thought about it. He carried a knife and he never thought about that either. Olimpio was not such a bad place. He danced along the street whistling his songs. There was music in his head, rhythms from the street, from the radios playing in the lanchonetes, a rhythm different from the thunder. *Hey Fabio!* the Paulistas would shout as he danced past. And he would smile his big smile.

Because Fabien was happy. That's what his mother said. The

weather was stifling, the city was loud and her son was happy. Life wasn't so bad. Even when acne erupted on his face, Fabien kept smiling his fabulous smile and soon those scars were healed and he was as smooth-cheeked as before. Sometimes his mother would stroke his chin and ask him when he was going to start shaving. Like a real man. Fabien would shrug and smile. Who needs to shave? he'd ask. It only slows you down.

Eventually there was a line of dark hair on his lip. But no bristles. His cheeks stayed silky and his mother would embrace him and kiss her son until he laughed and struggled away. Like a snake, she'd think. A snake in the sugarcane.

His older brother had left home now, his sisters too. It was only Fabien and his mother left on Olimpio, the traffic flying overhead, the old men sitting on the streets with their lottery tickets. Fabien knew them all.

Then one day he came around the corner and he saw it. He saw the shop. He had passed that second-hand clothes shop a thousand times but today he went in, right to the back. The shirt hung there, on the last rail.

All the clothes were second-hand on that part of Olimpio were Fabien lived. The boutiques were in a different barrio. Sometimes he and his friends made expeditions there and crowded in, but the security guys only gave them a minute before they moved the gang on.

He paid for the shirt in soiled royals. It was Fabien's shirt now. From the back rail's motley. The shopkeeper whispered 'bless you'.

The shirt would look good on him. Entirely plausible its ivory sequins, the wild jabot. Fabien shot the cuffs and admired their blacker stitching. He had never seen a blacker shirt. *100% algodao* it said on the label. *Made in Brasil.*

Well bless you too, Senhor, thought Fabien. And bless the boy who must have sold the shirt to you, the skinny boy who first owned this shirt, tight as a toreador's waistcoat. Yes a black bolero, this shirt. From the inside rail.

3

Fabien decided to keep the shirt a whole year until he might wear it in public. He had a plan, a delicious plan. Fabien shivered in bed when he thought of his plan, and he shivered when he stood on the Olimpio bridges and watched the lightning and the existence of the plan returned to him like the memory of the most marvellous thing in the world.

Lightning was like an idea, he decided. An idea coming into his mind. And once the idea had arrived, his mind could never be the same. No, no, never the same.

Lots of ideas occurred to Fabien now. He owned a guitar and had learned a ballad of the city that the old men sang in the bars. The old men sang of love and rum and death and rum and tears and rum. Which was stupid really. But the ballad gave him more ideas.

He played the guitar so hard his nails bled. He started to write verses into an exercise book. He made lists of all the songs he would write and the order of those songs on the CDs he would release. Lists were important. Lists were an art. Some songs, he knew, belonged together. And some needed to be kept apart. He thought about the teachers placing children in the classroom. He had sat by Maria but maybe they hadn't belonged side by side.

Anyway, that was over. Since leaving school he had helped in a lanchonette in the Praca da Republica. His mother thought it too far across the city, but an uncle had found the job and good jobs were scarce.

In that bar he learned how to make coffee on the Belle Epoque with its nozzles and spouts. He learned how to bang the milk jugs on the counter to make best use of the froth. He laid out cups and glasses in the morning and cleaned the microwaves. He went to the supermarkets to buy rolls and the little squares of cheese and ham in plastic packets. He also learned where to stock the Brahma beer and where the golden Antarctica. Behind him at the counter he gradually came to sense where lay the Fernet bottle and every crusted *cachaca*. One man always ordered *Johnnie Walker Black Label.* The boss warned him to pour it carefully. Every drop was precious. The drinker let Fabien keep the change and said he had a beautiful smile.

In his breaks he'd wander around the square and listen to the fortune tellers. Once or twice he would enter the cathedral. It was peaceful there after the crush of Republica. Candles burned and women prayed in the candlelight. More ideas came into his mind, just like the candlelight seeping through the gloom. His friend Mauricio came with him once and they sat in the middle of a pew. Mauricio's girl was pregnant and Mauricio was planning his escape. They ate sandwiches from the lanchonette and watched the candles, the hundreds of candles, a reef of candlelight in the south transept. Write to me, said Fabien. Tell me where you are.

Then they had gravely kissed in the cathedral and Mauricio went off to pack his bag and Fabien to taking Antarcticas out of the fridge to wait under the counter in their circles of dew.

4

At last it was time. He wriggled in the looking glass. Maria had come round and she was helping him prepare. Fabien didn't think the shirt looked right. Not as it must have looked on the boy who had first owned the shirt. The rightful owner.

He wondered where that boy was now. Probably out tonight as Fabien himself would be. He could see him clearly. There he sways, thought Fabien, amidst the sweat and the *sucos* and the sinners on the Santa Rita, its rattling silver through the slums, that other boy strap-hanging down Olimpio, disguised for destiny.

Only a bus, the Santa Rita, thought Fabien. But if I took that ride I wonder where my soul would sit. And then Fabien thought of the child who worked till midnight stitching his mysterious shirt.

Fabien also wore a belt fastened with a silver snakehead. His jeans were black and shone like oil, his black winklepickers were from another booth on Olimpio. Maria was to come with him, Maria who was not cool or cute or anyone's idea of a rock chick. Maria was plump and floral. But Fabien was grateful. Fabien was scared.

He popped a pill. Maria refused one. Then out into the street they went, the traffic flying overhead. He carried his guitar in its canvas case, Maria already trying to keep up.

The two bus journeys took an hour. A short walk, and then they came to the revolving door. Maria wanted to catch her breath but Fabien walked into the foyer and joined a line for one of the elevators. There was a deskman watching a screen. The buildings in Manhattan were collapsing over and over again.

But no one stopped him. No one looked at him. The lift was a glass cube. Fabien could see the back of his own head, the glossy comb marks. On the thirty-second floor they emerged with another couple, the woman with her hair spun like candyfloss. And then, at last, the Bar Unique.

Fabien headed for the bar itself. Again, nobody stopped him. One minute later he and Maria sat on high stools watching a man mix their *mojitos*. After a while, he began to look around. And what he saw was what he expected to see in a place like that. Women like roses in cellophane. Men absorbed by other men. Behind them the city spread its pinnacles. Fabien could see helicopter lights, a neon newspaper title.

He knew where these people came from. Turn uphill off Olimpio and walk a straight kilometre. The gang had done it often. He remembered one Sunday morning. How he had laughed to himself. There were the ancient rich in their paranoid paradise. There were the edificios with their gates and guards, the yellow butterflies and the pekingese turds. There were men with dark glasses and radios watching the drawbridges come down. There were the laughing parakeets, laughing especially at one old man who had bought a newspaper so bulky, Fabien thought it might take him the rest of his life to reach the Corinthians match report.

Plastic surgeons, whispered Fabien to Maria. The finest dentists of the age. But there were others too. And when Fabien sang, it was for these younger drinkers. Those were the ones he serenaded. Fabien began to sing 'Yesterday'. Wasn't McCartney in the city, his face rising like Gulliver over the sides of buildings, the ruined cherub on his greatest tour, the DVDs of previous concerts playing in the malls?

So far away, sang Fabien. So far away. He was standing above the city as the Bar Unique revolved. Its own planet, the Bar Unique, the city lights exploding behind him, the police helicopters moving between the towers, and behind the towers the forests ghostly in rainsmoke.

5

He waited with his pack and guitar in a room he used to run through, whooping, whooping. There were electronic boards there now and he studied the city names. So many places south and west he had never been. He knew he would never go there. Because it was north he was travelling. The great *El Norte*.

He sat in the room until it was dark. Children tore around him. Of course, what arrives with the darkness is lightning. Fabien was the great connoisseur of lightning. That night its incendiaries raced out of a sky the colour of a tattooist's inks. It flashed as he stowed his bag and as he entered the cool cometa.

Fabien travelled all night and the only sign of human life was firelight struck in oil drums and bodies prone around each dying blaze. Ahead swung the meniscus of the new moon, pale as a palmito.

His seat was next to the coffee machine. The cometa coffee was black and hot and so sweet he shivered the first time he tasted it trembling with the saccharine rush. But soon he held his cup with both hands as if refusing to let go while the land dried out, the forests changed, the savannah stars burned huge and indecipherable, and gauchos rode with him a moment out of the barbarous thorn.

At dawn Fabien glimpsed a pool of herons, and there were the herds and there the stars' junta, for still there were more stars than steers. And as he gazed at the roots of the day, flocks of parrots passed overhead, their voices full of stones.

A day later, outside Salvador, Fabien thought he might have reached Africa. It's all too much, he decided. There are so many rides. And the timetables don't work.

In the dirt, by a barraca made from drinks cans hammered flat, thatched with banana leaves, he asked how to get to the airport. This he knew was a very stupid question, but it seemed one more risk wouldn't matter.

The taxi driver was playing a CD of voodoo drummers. It bored Fabien immediately. He'd heard all that *Macumba* mumbo back home. Why should he be superstitious? Slavery was over. It's over, over, he hummed to himself.

Hey, that will be a line, he said to himself. That will be one of his great lines in one of his great songs. Yes, he smiled, a song in the key of A. Because A was freedom's key and A was childhood's key. And wasn't A the sunshine on his hairless face when he had strolled the barrio?

6

He slept on Venice beach. At dawn the kelp was cold and lay in swathes along the shore. He could hear a siren. Fabien showered at the pipe before the dogwalkers arrived and then he stepped into the city. Two hours later he had a job.

He had passed a café and turned a corner. There was a police car up the street so he glanced into a shop front, paused and went back. The café was painted purple and there was a name written so curiously it was difficult to read. Maybe the place was called The Purple Palm.

Coffee, yes? he asked.

Okay, said a harassed man behind the counter. We're just opening.

Fabien looked round. Last night's glasses had not been cleaned up. There seemed hundreds of them.

You have a toilet? asked Fabien.

The man shrugged. Through there, he gestured.

It was dark in the corridor and Fabien slapped the wall until he found the switch. He pushed a door, the striplight ticking.

Around him the walls and ceiling were covered with coloured laminates. The pictures were of men, men golden and men black, and no daylight between them.

These men seemed to be devouring one another. Above Fabien and below, the fresco filled the room and its cubicles. Yes, a feast, he thought. For the starving. Because the bodies he saw were ravenous. But the men here were only part men and the best part of them had been taken away. These men were only thighs and shoulders and the orchid-coloured cocks that erupted from their loins. These men seemed armoured by their own flesh.

Iron, thought Fabien. Scrapyard iron, weeping rust. Or statues of warriors released from their plinths, flinty statues that rubbed sparks from other statues. Statues that dreamed of fire. Or desperate men imprisoned in stone.

Was there an eye to look into? A face to understand? Fabien saw not one. But he laughed as he wandered the bathroom and laughed as he shat in a Kleenex-strewn stall and laughed as he gazed at the taut and electric skin of these men golden, these men black. He thought of the cathedral in Republica. There was a cupola there painted with angels wrestling with demons. How cumbersome these figures seemed in comparison. There was no lightness in them, and Fabien understood that lightness was all.

His coffee waited on the counter but the bar was empty. He wandered round and came to a framed text. Fabien composed himself and recited it to the room:

The first time I became famous I was too young to understand.
The second time I became famous it was over too quickly.
The third time I became famous I was preoccupied with the jealousy of my contemporaries.
The fourth time I became famous I was addicted to laxatives and painkillers.
The fifth time I became famous I urged others to save the planet.
The sixth time I became famous my image rights were stolen by aliens.
The seventh time I became famous I vanished in a vortex of vodka and cocaine.
The eighth time I became famous the contents of my dustbins were sold on eBay.
The ninth time I became famous I was arrested for shoplifting. My attorney said it was a cry for help.
But the next time I become famous I will retire undefeated. Because now I know how to do it.

When the man came back, Fabien was ready.

Your coffee's bad, he said.

I know, said the man. Sorry.

You want help? asked Fabien.

The man gestured. One of the boys quit last night, he said.

I make good coffee, said Fabien.

The man regarded him. You know what this place is? he asked.

Yes, said Fabien.

7

Sometimes Fabien thought he had been too lucky. Venice was full of cafés and bars. There were markets and music and always the cries of street theatre. There was work everywhere. Perhaps he should have been choosy. But when he wasn't making coffee or cleaning up, they let him play his guitar and sing songs, his new songs and the ballads of his own city. A few times he tried *choro* rhythms, Paulista style. That was when he wore the black shirt, and although no one stopped talking or drinking when he sang, his boss seemed pleased.

And they gave him a room above the café. This was great good fortune. It was really a stockroom, but he shifted the boxes and they found him a couch. He wrote to his mother and to Maria proud of his new address.

Gradually he came to know the district. There were musicians aplenty and poets who declaimed to the street. Crowds gathered in the coffee shops, everyone shopped for organics. On TV, politicians talked about the war and a need for surveillance. Even the bar had a camera installed.

Late afternoons were quiet times. Fabien was sometimes the only one working. A banker or realtor would come in, put their case on a seat, and adopt the bar identity, which Fabien knew was something they never used outside. In The Purple Palm they could be melodramatic, either mad or sad, and Fabien would have to ask them about the latest crisis, smiling his smile as he used his gang knife to take the plastic off the neck of another bottle of zinfandel.

One day, he was pulling the dead fronds from the palm tree. This palm grew in a purple pot and was the centrepiece of the bar. Years earlier someone had brought in a seed from the beach. People thought it was a coconut. Eventually it was planted but nothing happened and it was forgotten. Then, ages later, as the legend had it, shoots appeared. Now there it was, The Purple Palm's palm tree. Dependent on Fabien's husbandry.

Hey, said one guy, his jacket on the seat. You seen the news?

No, said Fabien.

They found this tribe in Brazil. Living in the forest, about fifty of them. There's this clip of them waving their spears. You know, stone age types, never contacted by white men before.

There was a silence.

Oh yeah, grinned Fabien. Those white guys.

And he laughed. And when Fabien laughed it was a certainty that everyone else would laugh, the realtor in his cufflinks, the Citibank youth, pale, frail, whose first day this was at The Purple Palm. He sat under the poem and observed the protocol of laughter. So did the other stranger who coughed from a barstool, briefcase between his feet.

Hey, I'm a comedian already? announced the realtor, beaming around the room. What I say?

8

Sometimes the police came in and joked self-consciously. Fabien didn't have a work permit. The boss had never asked and the police had never asked. Once, a patrolman enquired where he came from, but it was part of a conversation with some of the regulars, and Fabien had his answers well rehearsed. In Venice, everyone came from somewhere else, and if he didn't deal drugs he guessed the law would leave him alone.

One Tuesday afternoon, Fabien was playing a set. There might have been twenty in, chatting, listening.

I like you, said a man to Fabien. He looked mid sixties. I can see it in you. Boy, it's there.

What's there?

The gene, son. You got the rock 'n' roll gene. I'd like to put you on.

A gig? asked Fabien.

Sure a gig. Plenty of gigs. You're the Jean Genie, son. And look at this.

The man shook a tiny silver box.

Got the whole act right there, he said. Sound and vision. We'll put it out on the street as a bootleg. YouTube, you name it. Get some important people talking about you. You know, I just don't think you understand how good you look.

The man paused. Hey, is there anywhere we could go to talk about all this?

Upstairs in his stock room Fabien looked at the man's grey pony tail, his parboiled hams. In his right hand the guy's balls felt like soap. He squeezed and the man burst into tears and buried his face in Fabien's hair, his black hair oiled and glossy as a grackle, his hair that was longer now and tied with a black ribbon.

Sorry, kid, said the man, zipping up his leather pants and wiping his face. You don't need this. Maybe I owe you one.

Downstairs the boss shook his head in mock disbelief and poured Fabien a decent Napa Valley.

Well for Chrissakes, the boss said. There's an awful lot of coffee in Brazil. Play 'Yesterday', quick. It'll do us all good.

Fabien shrugged and grimaced and forgot about it. He was becoming good at forgetting. He rarely thought about Olimpio now. Life was changing for him. He'd put on weight and he didn't wear the shirt any more.

At times he imagined he'd like to get married and take his kids to the beach for them to see the sea lions. He'd go to the beach deliberately after the bar closed at 4 a.m. And listen.

Two hours before dawn a sea lion would start barking. Fabien would look at it slumped over the crosstrees of the pier. Its voice seemed black and made of rubber. For Fabien, the sea lion voice was a stress ball clenched in the night.

Sometimes he imagined that the ocean came almost to the door of his room, all night its pulse alive in his sleep but a lullaby he could not trust, the seep of a black sea through the crazed beachfront cement of the street.

He would crouch in the sand. Soon all the sea lions would be squeezing their voices out of the corals of California. The black rain would lie agleam on the deck, like a torrent of bottles tipped into a bin by some bar worker such as Fabien himself, a glass avalanche one hour before dawn, the streetlight broken into cullet, armfuls of *Sierra Nevadas* slithering into the return bin. The sea lions under the pier would roll like lobes of mercury, fat as jeroboams, while the pier neon printed itself further out in the kelp and shale-coloured shoals.

For Fabien, the sea didn't seem to move. But he knew it slid like broken glass, this sea in its cisterns and in its fireboxes, the Pacific that flung itself at his feet and smelled like a damp attic room thirty minutes before dawn. He'd wander through mist and through salt, and outside his window the palms would be black snowflakes against first light. Fabien had never seen snowflakes. Yet that's what he thought. When he looked from the pier he thought he might glimpse lightning. But lightning was rarer now.

Occasionally he felt he was being observed. In the gloom of

Ocean Park he'd stop and the echo of his footfall would stop. Then Fabien would turn around to see nothing. Who watches the watchman? he sang to himself. That could be a tune. Yes. The music would sound mysterious and his voice would merely breathe the words of that slow and smoky song. One day he'd write that song.

9

Phil, the boss, was good to him. Fabien ate his meals at the Palm, found all his drinks there. He sipped red wine now, from lunchtime on. Phil needed a drinking partner, and introduced him to the indigo malbecs he bought at a local importer, the staple merlots.

You know what I like about you, Fabby? the boss would sometimes ask. You're fastidious. You see, so many guys your age are out there screwing like cockroaches. They're led through life by their dicks. And you got a fan club here, make no mistake. But you don't give it away, do you? People sense that. They can tell there's a something else about you. A something almost special. Compared to these airhead bodybuilders and roller-skating assholes that have taken over the shore, you got a little bit of mystery in you.

Fabien was eating a baguette. He picked his teeth. He had started to feel he needed a bigger room.

Then, one afternoon, the pony tail guy walked back into The Purple Palm.

Hey presto, the man said. All right, it's not a world tour. But there's a day of local talent at this place I know. Just up the coast in Santa Barbara. You're part of it.

That's a long way, said Fabien. What about the Venice Theatre?

Believe in me, said the man. Look, who introduced Jim Morrison to Ray Manzarek? Who told Jim about the Doors of Perception?

Yeah, said Phil, red in his goblet. And who gave Morrison his first leather pants?

You want it, it's yours, said the man. Okay?

I'm thinking about it, said Fabien, holding his glass as Phil poured.

10

There were two thousand graves on the beach at Santa Barbara. 'Veterans for Peace' had erected this 'Arlington West' for Veterans' Day, a national holiday.

Happy Veterans' Day, someone said to Fabien. He didn't know how to respond. A sign said the two thousand crosses represented the American dead in Iraq.

A crowd with go-cups had gathered to listen to the veterans' speeches. Fabien tried to peel a persimmon. The demo did not simply involve an antiwar group of those with first-hand experience. Veterans for Peace linked 'the Iraq resource war' with 'the twilight of worldwide petroleum reserves and climate stability'. You gotta connect terror and oil and all these hurricanes, bellowed a man with a megaphone.

The persimmon was the sweetest fruit Fabien had tasted in California. It was sweeter than the Rees's chocolate and peanut butter blocks which he bought in the Korean store next to the Palm. People in the crowd cheered, a few cursed under their breaths, and the vets played rock music and read poems. Some had a barbecue going and were offering wings and ribs.

The yellow fruit dissolved in Fabien's mouth. His lips went numb as he knew they would. Then his tongue. But beach volleyball had restarted and the sea ached blue. Five miles out, the oil rigs were almost invisible in the haze. Fabien tried to order a beer but couldn't speak. A man put a *Sierra Nevada* into his hand and waived the charge.

An hour later he was sitting in the Lobero Theatre, waiting his turn. The sound check for the rock groups had been endless and Fabien was bored. Pony tail kept dropping by, asking how he felt. They had driven up together that morning, the older man playing *Ventura Highway* on the CD.

This is it, kid, he kept saying of the road. America was a great band and that's their finest song. And we're right on top of it all. Yeah, this is Ventura. Feel its fabled curves.

In his theatre seat, Fabien shrugged and waited for the pill to kick in. There was no space for him in the dressing rooms, full as they were of men and guitars.

By the time he played, the show was running an hour late. The crowd kept coming in and out and there was a racket back stage. He'd spoken to the boy at the mixing desk who was doing his best, but through the open theatre doors he could see the sky turning white over the boulevard and hear the sirens, the constant sirens, worse than Olimpio these days, he caught himself thinking, distracted and mid song.

You did good, said Pony Tail in the bar afterwards. But the Lobero's not your scene. It's like a fucking opera house in there. As to Santa Barbara, maybe I was wrong. Money's killed it. Those vets on the beach are getting a hard time. Look, here's some cash. Take the Surf Rider back to LA, it's a great trip.

Get me a glass of wine, said Fabien, slumped. *Cabernet.*

Whatever the pill was doing, it wasn't what the pill should do. Fabien was starting to feel far away. So far away.

The dead-letter men

It's white bread from the shop in Fort William. No seeds in it, only a yellow crust. And soft as snow. Just how I like it. But the meat is dark, dark red sausage meat marbled with fat. Cheap, nasty meat, Alice would have said. Alice would also have said it's mechanically recovered spare parts from the slaughter house floor. Well too bad. I'm starving. I cut a slice with my penknife and make a sandwich. John has a sachet of mustard and I squeeze that in. Then I sit and sigh with my back against the pine tree. It's not comfortable but the food puts things into perspective. As food will.

After another sandwich, concentrating on tearing bread, slicing meat, drinking this isotronic orange cola whatsit stuff from a plastic bottle, I'm able to relax and look around.

We are on a forested hillside and the way leads north and up. Or so John says, John the map reader and expedition leader. But, as he keeps reminding me, we might be there already. The Mecca, he says. The ultimate. So keep your eyes peeled.

As if I need telling. That's John's trouble. Stating the obvious. Am I stupid or something? I might be boring but I'm not stupid. You bet my eyes are open. Because I'm looking. I'm listening. There had been a treecreeper on one of the pines back there and I'd watched it for a while. But John paid no attention. We're after something else, aren't we? Something more important. At least for John.

I watch him peel his apple. Bloody John and his fruit. His five, his eight a day. We'd bought the apples with the other food. The last three in the box, bruised and yellow grannies, going soft. But why peel them? Surely if there was any goodness left, it was in the skin. John has a bigger knife than mine and it's much sharper. Good blade. How quickly the peel lies in one piece, its curls in the pine dust. But who the hell peels apples now?

And, wait for it, I think to myself. Now comes the other blade for the next operation. The coring. One twist, and there it is. Little pale embryo, black seeds intact.

Meticulously neat, that's John. But not as mad as you might think. Some of the others are extremists. Utter obsessives. There's this chap, Tim. Dotty about dotterels. That's all he looks for. Maybe a kentish plover. But, fair play, John has another life. In fact, I've always thought he has his hands full.

There's his mother, to begin with. And John's job. John's a mail sorter at the Mount Pleasant depot. Working nights, he has plenty of time for his other profession. That's what he calls it. Now some of those types, the bachelors still at home, you never get to see where they live. The kind of time warp they inhabit. The sad squalor. But John is relaxed about me coming to his flat. It's upstairs in a street over in Archway. Near the Drum and Monkey, a pub he's never been in. It's a bit Irish round there and for historical and employment reasons John doesn't like the Irish. He's lived in that flat all his life.

John's mum's a queer old stick, I suppose. But not bedridden or anything like that. Her legs are thick and inflamed, but she hasn't suffocated him, as I might have expected. The flat's her palace.

Ooh, he'll be out in a jiff, she'll say to me. He's just doing his books. Have a cup of tea, love.

Whenever I come round, John is doing his books. But then he'll emerge from his bedroom and she'll waddle off into the kitchen, which isn't a kitchen, just part of the front room. Tight fit that nest. Two big eggs. After she serves the tea, in china cups, lump sugar with a tongs, she'll retreat to her bedroom and the telly will start. A quiz or something. She does crosswords too. And read? John is proud of his mum's reading. Biographies of the stars. You know, the newsreader type stars. Glamorous weathergirls. Breakfast show bints.

I remember once recently, I called round and John was working on his Gambia sightings. Ledger XLV1, to give it the full title. Some people use photographic records but not John. It's not the look of birds that pleases him. It's not the colours. Some people even record songs, but you have to draw the line somewhere. No, it's the very act of seeing that's important. Important to John, that is. The observation itself. Not the appearance of whatever's observed. And then the logging, the listing in the ledger. The listing's as important as the sighting.

It's a special kind of imagination that works like that. But John is his own man. He doesn't need photographs to prove to anyone else what he's seen. He hates those types who put everything on a website. Because if the Gambia ledger states that John has seen some sunbird or a sulphur-breasted bushshrike, then that's enough. He trusts his own eyes and what those eyes see is added to the ledger's columns. The ledgers are his chronicles. His Domesday Book.

He's commandeered those ledgers during his turns at the dead-letter office in Mount Pleasant. Apparently that is a trusted role. The Post Office doesn't let just any common or garden sorter loose in there. You see, John by now is a senior sorter. They give him the difficult stuff to decipher. No, not Santa Claus letters, but the mysterious parcels and envelopes. The indecipherables. The incxplicables. Sometimes they have to be opened and that again is a responsibility. Everything's tiered in the Post Office, see. And John's up there. Well, that's what he implies.

John also tells me he gives advice on anything suspicious. That's all he says. But suspicious is a serious word. You might think that he means nutters. Blokes with a grievance against any one of our glorious bureaucracies. Which probably means all of us. You know, the oddball who might send a letter bomb to the taxman or the speed camera people. But, really, it could also be terrorists. Anything suspicious, John says. So follow the logic. I asked him once. He just tapped his nose. Experience, see. He's out on his own is John.

Anyway, John has transferred all his earlier birding records to the ledgers. Even his schoolboy stuff, because he started this lark when he was ten. Names in Latin and English, locations, dates, times. All done with fountain pen and Indian ink. The sunbird and the bushshrike, by the way, were recorded in John's hotel grounds in The Gambia. Sixty big ones, he told me.

If John was impressed, then it was, shall we say, significant. A big one is his term for a completely new species. A first. They were in the bloody gardens, he hissed. Sixty! He even said the bloke with him never left the hotel. Didn't need to. A week in The Gambia and the chap was in his element. UK Gold on telly, English grub, and sulphur-breasted bushshrikes on the pitch-and-putt. For a lot of the men I've met in this game, that's a version of paradise. Couple of bottles of Julbrew beer – the Export comes in at 5.7 alcohol according to John – and you've got yourself sorted. Then three hours of *The Sweeney* while you're writing it up. Birder's heaven. Though not John's cup of tea of course. He did the jungle trip, the river trip. Got another bundle of big ones. Including, nice one this, the western banded snake eagle, which is always hard to spot. Or so everyone says.

It's not bad under this tree. John says it's a Scots pine. The food's finished and I'm looking round. There's a shaft of light on the pine needles and the pine cones and the orange flakes of bark around us. Everything is sparkling. But the forest gets darker in all directions.

No, it's not bad. But not great. I've never been in a forest before. A real forest, that is. Where you can't see the edges. Must be three in the afternoon now. But don't they say it stays lighter in Scotland? Closer to the North Pole? You know, the northern lights. Maybe that's only in summer, but I'm not going to bring it up and show my ignorance. Not worth it with John. After all, he's the traveller, I'm not. Though after this trip, that may change. Alice wanted to go on the Eurostar to Paris but I didn't fancy it. Too pricey.

But travelling's hard work. It's Sunday and we're supposed to be driving back tonight, which is crazy. It's six hundred miles and the van has to be on the forecourt tomorrow at nine. I work at a car hire place see, New Jersey Road Wheels. We do all the Fiat models and it can be busy. People like Fiats. Nippy and cheap. Spare on the juice too, which means everything these days. The boss said I could borrow a Punto. Seeing I've been there twenty years, that's the kind of perk I expect.

But it was tough driving. The M40 was a giant car park. I don't know how much longer we can go on like this, forty tonners going past from Romania, Slovakia. That's where they make the cars now, John said. Slovakia. They say it's booming.

That's interesting, I said. But, fair play to yours truly, this has been my longest drive. Ever. A New Jersey customer had left Abba *Gold* in the CD player, so I kept putting it on. Got it all by heart now, from track one, 'Dancing Queen', to track nineteen, Waterloo. Can you hear the drums Fernando? became our catch phrase. Going north was hard work. John decided we had to be driving north west of London. But past Brum then Manc, it was 'Fernando' all the way.

After the umpteenth play, John put it off. It's rubbish, he said. Those horrible rhythms are rotting my brain. That's the trouble with Abba, he said. No soul. No personality. Not real is it? Typical Swedish flatpack crap. It's Ikea music.

We kept going and soon I was further up than I'd ever been. The smell was different. There were all these old mills that had become apartment blocks. Cottages with stone roofs. Fields full of black sheep. By the way, I've always liked that song, 'Life in a Northern Town'. Pity we didn't bring it. After a while we stopped for food at the Rheged Centre near Penrith. John said there's a Penrith Road in N15 and a Penrith Street, with your associated closes and suchlike, in SW16. The guy's a genius.

We had extra coffee to keep us going, then a quick tour of the exhibitions. Rheged was all wars. Warriors with dirty great swords. God, isn't England great? I said. Why do people fly abroad when they could be exploring their own country? But John had his mouth full of Cumberland sausage and soon we were bombing on.

What are we looking for? I kept asking. But all he would say, till he told me in the pub last night, was it will be an honour. An honour for any British birder to see what we were going to see. Just the two of us, he said. On an expedition. It's time you came on an expedition. And this is best there is. Stuff the Gambia.

Well I'm not stupid. I can get a motor, can't I. So I'm on the team. We slept in the Punto last night, by this lake just north of Glasgow. Had to knock ourselves out with a bottle of scotch. We've both stiffened up. Before then we'd been in the Bay Horse in West Nile Street from about 8 p.m., and I was bushed. But proud of myself. That's a haul.

The pub was serving these great pies. Traditional fayre, as they say. We had two each. Pity about the Bay Horse. They're going to demolish it, and that really outraged John.

Look around, he said. It's perfect. All these mirrors with the optics reflected and names like Ballantyne's and Dewar's in gold in the glass. Even a whisky-drinking competition going on. Group of blokes, and a woman too, not throwing it back but tasting the different blends. Holding their glasses almost daintily, glasses that looked like little pots of honey. Which is not something you'd think would happen in a Glasgow drinking den. Sipping, then writing things down. And this long bar with a footrail and stained glass diamonds winking in the windows. It was almost a church in there. But the Bay Horse is going to the knacker's yard

Well it must have been a good pub because John is a hard man to impress. As I've said, he's meticulous. I might have said scrupulous but there are too many ways to interpret that. He is also a bit of a veteran. It's his fiftieth, his mum told me. My John is fifty. That was five years ago. A lean man. Yes, wiry. That's the word for John. His hair has thinned but there's not a spare pound on him. In my experience, blokes who live with mum tend to turn podgy. Soft and cuddly like golden labs. But John's sinewy. As if he's a deliverer, a real postie, not a sorter, not an investigator. Because that's how John sees himself.

I patrol a unique territory, he informed me once. (Yes, John informs you of things.) That border country between the missive's existence as a live entity, and its possible fate as dead letter. Or worse.

God, I used to sneer, silently of course, at that word. *Missive*. John used it a lot. Missive in action was one of his quips. And John's a good quipper, fair play. Come to think of it, *quipper* could be a bird's name. Because there's babblers aren't there? Yes indeed. So, northern quipper? Or just quip. Smew, twite, scaup, quip. One of those species named after its cry. Plausible.

But missive I don't like. Yet when John talks about the dead-letter office, I listen. And what's worse than a dead letter? I've thought about that a lot. Like there's a mysterious category of mail that only John knows about. A secret state of being. A state within a state maybe. Yes, I find it almost thrilling. A dead letter? How is a letter dead? And why? It has something of John le Carré about it, don't you think? Rainy Berlin streets and espionage in black and white. A chess match against the Stasi. I picture John writing codes into a book, a lamp with a green shade on his desk.

Code is the crucial word here. Codes are codswallop to me but there's something of the code cracker about John. Or, if he's not an actual code breaker he's a believer in numerological systems. Hidden secrets and ancient wisdoms. Reading the runes in the dead-letter office. Which he tells me is a subterranean hall with a chained library of atlases and dictionaries. No windows. A pinging strip light and entry vetted by an ancient crone. John has a pass, he tells me. Unfortunately he can't bring it out on civvy street. Sacking offence. Like he's in the military.

But it's all going to the dogs, he tells me. And after forty years he must know. Sorting's an art, says John, when we meet at the Junction Café of a Saturday morning. That's become a routine.

Suits me. Excellent fry-up. And cheap? You bet. It's John's one extravagance, the Junction. Proves to me he's still human. So he gets extra black pudding while I have two side orders of toast. White, always. Can't abide brown toast. Big brown pot of tea between us. Gets refilled twice.

Yes, an art, he says. You learn an art. You study that art. Then you practise that art. But the people I'm working with now, they're clueless. They think sorting's a step on the way to somewhere else.

Now our Christmas sorters, he'll continue, I've no problem there. University students. You can talk to them. Some even know a bit about birds. And travel? Oh boy, they're the RyanAir generation. Nowhere they haven't been. Lucky sods. But these others spend all night asking me where's this go? Albanians, Nigerians, coming up and sticking an envelope in my face. Mr John, they say, where, where? So it slows me up, doesn't it? If I'm not interrupted I can reach one hundred and twenty items of mail per minute. But not now. Oh no. So I look at the envelope. *Clackmannanshire* it'll say. *Bourton-on-the Water*, it'll say. Goes there, I say. Put it there, I say. Two minutes later it'll be Mr John, please Mr John. Where this go? That's Brixham I have to tell them. Not Brixton. And Henley's not Hackney. Strewth.

Look, John will tell me, constructing a bacon sarnie with tomato sauce. (It's always the red by the way. Counts as one of your five fruit or veg, he tells me.) Some of them, he'll say, more quietly, can't read English. Illiterate, see. Or as good as. Your first, your most basic requisite in the Post Office is competency in the English language. It's the Royal Mail, remember. Have a look at the stamp. So don't tell me if you've just come on the bus from Heathrow with your worldly goods tied up in a blanket and you're sharing a room down the Southall Broadway, that you know where a Clackmannanshire letter goes.

There's sixty-four boxes in front of you where that letter might end up, says John. But there's only one where it belongs. Where it has always belonged as far as I can remember, and no one in that office has done a bigger stint than me. So it's no guessing game. It's all based on history. Our history.

At least it's not raining. And John's in a good mood. Kind of euphoric. Because we're here at last. Ancient Caledonia, he calls this place. It's pristine, he says. The way it's always been. John likes the Scots, see. He says they're different from the Irish. John's told me that the sorting office was a dangerous place when the IRA were on the boil. The front line, is how he describes it. And yes, when you think about it, he's right. John was on the front line. You never knew, he says, you never knew if the next letter was going to be your last. John's been around.

So I'm listening hard. But there's nothing. It's completely silent amongst these pines. We've been here five hours now, trekking up, down. Woke at six because I couldn't stand it any longer. Had to wait while John did his callisthenics, but there were these clouds of midges, getting into everything. So we drove off.

Since meeting John I've looked at people on the underground and the buses in a different way. Those Senegalese men selling sunglasses? They're dressed like kings. And what about the Slavic girls, Lithuanians maybe? Skinny as gymnasts. And their eyes staring right through you, blue as lupins. They're haughty bitches. Are they working down the sorting office driving John spare? Can they even read this country's language? They certainly know how to suck its tit.

You know, I'm pretty tolerant. I've never bothered with politics. But I've started to think. What's going on? In your own country you write a letter. To someone else in your own country. You post that letter. It's collected. Tipped up onto the conveyor. Then it's sorted by hand. And that's where the trouble starts. The sorter can't read. Thinks Luton is Leyton. That Lee is Lea. It's as if the England around you is dissolving. Getting murky like an old film.

So I make up tests for those people on the trains. Passes the time. It's like liquorice all-sorts down there these days. Chipping Sodbury? That would fool a few. Rhosllanerchrugog? Cop a load of that. Went on holiday there once. Oh Mr John, Mr John! they'd cry. Help me! What this terrible place?

Because I think John's correct. The sorting office is a proving ground. He says if you're incapable of working there you can't qualify for citizenship. That this citizen exam they give them now is bollocks. And I'm sure that's right. Spot on.

Yes, it was five years ago I met John. Seems longer. Sometimes it feels like I've known him all my life. That was a bad time for me. I'd been married two years and thought everything was fine. Didn't have any money but the flat we rented seemed good enough.

It was a Saturday morning. As per usual I was in bed with Alice and I was just waking up. We'd met online and everything clicked. Same age, same everything. Hunky dory I thought. So I was all dreamy because I knew it was Saturday. No work. Nothing to do. Luxury I thought. Nice lie in. Get *The Times* for the sport. Takes all morning to read it but brilliant footie coverage. Real analysis. But Alice was sitting up and she was looking at me. After a while I thought it a bit odd.

What's wrong? I asked.

Oh well, Lloyd, I was considering, she said.

Considering? I said. She didn't say thinking. She said

considering. Kind of ominous, that word. And she was using my name. For some reason she never used my name.

Considering what?

Last night, Lloyd, she said. Friday night. What did we do?

Watched telly, I said. *Big Brother*.

And last Friday night? What did we do?

Can't remember, I said.

We watched *Big Brother*, Lloyd, she said. What happened in it?

Christ knows, I said. Search me.

That's right, said Alice. I can't remember either. You know why?

She was looking down at me. I felt I was trapped in bed.

Why? I asked.

Because nothing happened.

Yeah, I said, sort of relieved. It's crap.

No, she said. It's not that *Big Brother* is crap.

Well, it's okay, I said. I was still coming round.

No, she said again. I don't mean that.

What is it then?

You want to know? she asked.

Yes, I want to know, I said.

Well, it's you, Lloyd, she said.

Me? I said.

There was a fire drill in my head now.

What about me? I said.

You're boring, she said.

I'm what? I said.

I've been looking at you sleeping, she said. And now I know for certain.

Know what for certain? I asked.

That you're boring, Lloyd.

You what? I said, struggling up. I'm not boring.

Yes you are, she said. You're boring. And that's why I'm leaving you.

What? I said. You what?

But she never answered. That day, that luxurious Saturday with nothing to do, she had it all planned. In the evening, after packing, she would go to a friend's. I lay in bed late. Like the *Big Brother* people did.

Eventually I called down the stairs.

We could go to my mother's, I said. Take her a cake.

Five minutes later she brought me a cuppa.

You don't get it, do you? she said, pulling the suitcase off the wardrobe.

Boring? I said.

Yes, boring.

I felt weird. Boring? I asked myself. Boring? That was below the belt.

Which is why it was a bad time for me. But after a while I started to understand what Alice had meant. Because what does it mean, being boring? Not a crime, is it? Not a sin? But I thought and thought. I thought for two weeks. Then I rang her.

Okay, I understand now, I said. You mean we should do things together.

That's part of it, she said.

Interesting things, I said.

That's right, she said.

Well, I said. What about bird watching?

She put the phone down.

Look, it's not as if I was in the football chatrooms all night, or bloody Youtubing it. I didn't go drinking. Much. And taking your wife to a pub always feels a bit strange. Like you're being sized up by other blokes. Has he pulled a looker, is what they're thinking. Well Alice is no looker, okay? Bit plump. Homely. Nice eyes though. So why was I boring?

Yes, birding was an out of the blue idea to Alice. It was even new to me. It happened like this. I'd caught the Brighton train, but got off after Haywards Heath. Suburbia with bits of grass. I used to live there for a while when I was little and I hoped it would be a good place to consider stuff. I was on this rise, mooching about.

Alice had always noticed that about me. You're a moocher, she used to laugh. I'm sure she found it endearing. With your shoulders hunched, your hands in your pockets, she said. Mooching about. All moochy, aren't you, Mr Moochy? And she'd pinch my bum.

So there I was, minding my own business. No one about, gorse bushes on the hill, and these big rocks with yellow lichen like egg yolk spilled everywhere. Then I see three people coming up the path. Cameras, pagers, the lot. Two passed me with dirty looks. The third man was wearing a woolly hat.

Thanks, he said. Very sarky, like.

What's up? I asked.

You see a little brown bird up here? he asked. Not a sparrow, mind. Grey on it.

Um, I said. No. Why?

The others had gone but this bloke stopped. He was holding a book, not a camera.

It's rare, he said. A red lister. And you've scared it away.

Hey, sorry mate, I said. I'm just on the public path.

Well, he said, it's supposed to be here. We've been tipped off.

What is it? I asked.

You won't have heard of it.

Try me, I said. I had the feeling here was somebody else who thought I was boring. That he picked up an aura of boredom around me. That I radiated boredom.

But, speaking personally, I wasn't bored, was I? Well, not much. Alice said that I bored her. Which, for a husband, fair play, is not good. But hardly inexcusable. Not grounds for bleeding divorce. She had looked at me in my sleep. Well everyone is boring when they're asleep. Aren't they? Now here was this bloody birdwatcher implying it.

Wryneck, he said. In England we're down to a single breeding pair. But this is a September migrant. Hard to spot but not exactly an LBJ.

Oh, I said. What's that?

Little brown job.

Look, I said. I'm interested in birds. Course I am.

Well come and spot this one for us, he said.

Yeah, I said, looking round. Seems like I owe you one.

We never found the wryneck. Maybe it was there or maybe it was a false alarm. They're so elusive, the guy with the woolly hat told me later in a caff. That guy was John.

I learned quickly that birders have this incredible network of communication. Soon there had been other groups tramping over the hill. I was amazed. Could have been a hundred twitchers. Some chaps had walkie-talkies. Bloody laptops too.

There's this pub where they meet up in Norfolk, John explained. Used to be the Red Lion. But so many birders called it the Parliament of Fowls that the pub changed its name.

He looked at me then as if he wanted a reaction.

That's nice, I said.

So when I rang Alice I thought birding was the solution. Here was something we could do together. Saturdays in Osterley Park.

We could walk down the Grand Union and watch the ducks. Take sarnies. I'd already bought *The Observer's Book of British Birds* and started scanning the RSPB website. It was an *enthusiasm*. That was her word. She always said I lacked enthusiasms. But birds for Alice were out from the start. A real no-no. So in a way it was the wryneck that put the mockers on my marriage. And not many people can say that. Bastard LBJ.

But I've come up here, haven't I? The Caledonian Forest, smack bang in the wilds of Scotland. John has a map spread out on the pine dust and is looking at it with a magnifying glass. John doesn't wear specs or contacts. Seems he's made it a point of principle. Which surprises me. How does he read all those addresses, then? I've looked at the map and it's difficult. All these names of hills and streams, like they've been misspelled. Just lines of Scrabble. There's houses up here literally miles from the road. You wonder what goes on there. Spooky.

Yes, he says, finally. Keep your eyes peeled. Let's keep looking and listening. They'll be coming in to roost about now.

The van must be two miles from here, parked on a gravel track. But I'm not sure of my bearings any more. And I'm hungry again. John's map is bloody empty. Just a mass of tree symbols and those Scottish words with the letters jumbled up. To tell the truth, neither of us could understand a word in the Bay Horse either. There's even different money in Glasgow, which was news to me.

It was funny too in the shop in Fort William, buying our provisions. Nice-looking kid behind the till but I had my suspicions before I spoke to her. She's not a local, I thought. Can you hear the drums Fernando? I said to her. She just kept chewing her gum.

There was this poster for a Shinty game. What the hell is

Shinty? The shop had different foods too. I didn't know if they were Scottish or not. Black bread on offer, with all these seeds in it. And that meat I bought. It didn't look normal but I thought I'd try it. Perhaps it's haggis. Pretty cheap for right up here in the sticks, where there are more bloody crows than people. In fact, there are no people. Just hills and moors going on for miles. It's spooky all right.

And now it's three o' clock and dark in the forest. John's out of sight, gone up the hill. There's not even a path, just a stream bed with flat stones and a trickle of water. That's all I hear, the stream flowing. But I think if I crouch down, if I'm really unobtrusive, and if John has our bearings right, then I'll see one. Or at least I'll hear one. Which will be fantastic. Because I've my own ledger now. John took it from the sorting office. Says there's a stash of them going to waste. Beautiful books, superseded by technology. I can imagine myself tomorrow night, or more likely Tuesday, ledger on the kitchen table, writing it all down. Even bought my own fountain pen, a Parker Vector, first since school.

Loxia Scotica, I'll be writing. The Scottish crossbill. September 11, 3.10 p.m.

And, although you're not supposed to do this, I'll do it anyway. I'll add:

The Scottish crossbill is the only bird indigenous to the British Isles. This means it is found nowhere else in the world. Thus it is unique. The breeding population is static and its habitat has not changed since the last ice age. The Scottish crossbill is highly endangered.

But this is where the problem comes in. My book doesn't mention the Scottish crossbill. Must be too rare. And even John says that there is only one way to determine it from the two other crossbills that come to Britain. Now *determine* is a typical birder's word. It feels scientific to me. Authoritative. But with all three crossbills, the male is red and the missus is green.

Apparently those others can irrupt anywhere in the country. Another birder's world that. *Irrupt.* Sounds sudden and dangerous. Like they are Vikings or something, come here to pillage. These foreign crossbills fly over from the continent when there's a shortage of food. They fancy our pine cones and nick them off the natives.

So, there is only one way to determine our unique bird. That is the song of the crossbill. Not size, not plumage. Officially, the Scottish crossbill has a Scottish accent.

John says he'll be able to tell *Loxica Scotica* immediately. Well, he wasn't so good in the pub last night. *Pint of heavy*? he had to ask. Heavy? Excuse me, what's that?

The young barman looked at him and said something that could have been in Icelandic. Whatever it was, this woman sitting at the counter nearly choked. Charming. But I watched John in the mirror. He looked old and small in his woolly hat, peering over that polished mahogany. Almost uncertain of himself. There were posters on the wall where we were sitting. One was the band, Texas, with that Charleen Spitieri. Now there's a looker for you. Sorry Alice. The other showed Mel Gibson in *Braveheart*. He was painted blue and looking well pissed off.

Take it easy, I said to John. You'd be grumpy too if your head was about to be separated from your body.

Fucking Picts, John said. But under his breath. He drank more than I've ever seen him last night. Snored like a badger.

But anyway, I better wait here. It's roosting time. There ought to be a chattering, a chittering all over. Before he disappeared into the trees, John talked about *territories of song*. Listen out, he told me, for a kind of guttural warbling.

Och aye, I said. John says the Scottish crossbill may be observed individually or in small flocks. Well, I'm bloody looking. I'm bloody listening. But there's nothing. John says the name of this place is Glen Affric, and that all that's happened here in the last ten thousand years is that real British animals like the lynx and the bear have died out. But landowners want to bring them back for tourists.

It's crazy, John says. They'd have to find the skeleton of a British lynx. Then somehow extract its DNA. That's the only way to bring back a proper British lynx. You can't just whip them over from Norway.

Hear hear. But I'm thinking about something else. You see, apart from John's mum, no one knows we're here. Up in Scotland, John told her. Brilliant. Gives a search party a lot to go on.

It's darker now and still there's absolute silence. When you work on the Jersey Road, this sort of silence is weird. Everything's hollow. It's ringing in my ears. But the stream bed's my reference point and I'll stay here till John comes back. Tell you the truth, I might be going off this ornithology business. But you know what? I think Alice would be proud of me.

El Aziz: some pages from his notebooks

Even for that season it was hot. I went west along the coast and found myself in Nerja, everything shivering like cellophane in the haze.

I saw they had built a palace where the dunes had been. Once the dune pools held egrets. They had reminded me of home. Creeping close I could glimpse the birds' reflections in the water. Now there were fountains, but the fountains were turned off, and the swimming pools empty. After the first palace was a castle. After that castle another castle. Or palace. Each castle was fifty apartments piled on top of one another. Towers and minarets, but all empty. No cars in the parking places and the dune grass like wire breaking through the tar. And everywhere the signs; some *Se Vende*, some *For Sale*. But the English have stopped coming. Suddenly there are no English.

At last I saw a man and I asked him about a job. A watchman's job. A caretaker.

I'm going to Madrid, he said. My cousin has a tapas bar. The polytunnels are for the Africans.

I was in Madrid once and saw the living statues in Plaza Mayor. It crossed my mind. Who would I be? I thought of Picasso. They named the airport in Malaga after him. Then I thought of Lorca. I saw a plaque for him in Benal Madena. I looked up from the street and there it was. But how does a poet dress?

Then I thought of Clint Eastwood, the man with no name, the thin cigarillo between thin lips. Who would dare refuse him money? A fistful of dollars? But I would have to stand on a box. No men are tall where I come from. Even in this place, they call me *Lazarillo*. The little Lazarus.

I turned a corner and war had been declared. There were the Rangers supporters and there were the police. Grown men were vomiting in the street. There were police horses with white eyes, men with helmets and shields. The warriors are called The Gers, a Glasweigian tribe half naked and painted blue, singing outside GMex and The Thistle. I trod the broken glass around the Briton's Protection Hotel. A gallon of Grunt, an eight pack of indigo SuperT. Bellies brimming with gold. I thought of the desert I had once crossed – all that ash as if the world had burned. Goat herders in their cinder-coloured rags.

I used to sell the *Big Issue* near Woolworths. I used to tell the people who I was and that I had come here for a better life. Across the road outside Streets night club, a woman older than my mother would play the accordion, its white teeth brown as nicotine. She knew only one tune. Then Woolworths closed. Then the night club closed. Some boys took her accordion and stepped on it. How it groaned in terror. I heard its protest and went to help. The boys were gone and I was glad. Those boys in their hoods, their trackwear, glancing at their screens.

Today I have been cutting cloth. When he gave me the job, the man didn't ask my name. The bale of silk was cold as river water in my hands and upon my chest. We might have been anywhere. But there was a newspaper, the *Manchester Evening News*, and packets of teabags. After a few days I knew where I was. We were working in a warehouse on an estate off the Salford Road. There were two English women who smoked when the bosses weren't looking. One burned a hole in the fabric and they had to hide it.

There are no windows in our building, and the strip light hums. Our toilet is at the end of the corridor. How the women sigh when they see it. They bring their own soap, their own paper, and there is a bootmark on the door.

Have a break, the man said yesterday. We were all surprised, but we couldn't go anywhere. There is a yard with puddles and piebald ice, and the german shepherd on a chain keeps the people out, keeps the people in.

When I woke this morning it was dark, darker even than the Euphrates where I once rolled at night in its velvet bed.

I found the costume outside the Piccadilly hotel. Somebody had been sick on it but I sponged it down with hot water and Lenor in the laundry room.

This evening I walked into the Woodlands lounge. There were a good group of the residents there. Two or three saw me at once, then all turned their heads. The men cheered. Then everyone clapped. It was December 28 and I was Santa Claus, a green Santa Claus in a green Santa costume, a green Santa hat. Only the boots were missing. I have a pair of trainers from the sale they have at St Michael's every Saturday. My other shoes have come to pieces.

Bit late aren't you, Laz? called one of the men. Or do your lot have Christmas on a different date?

*

My room at Woodlands is small and next to the boiler. Sometimes I hear the pipes grumbling, like an accordion. The manager said it's not ideal but she needs people to stay overnight.

I understand that. Night nurses are expensive. Roisin said they used to have schoolgirls and they slept in the lounge. But they were bad. They were wicked girls. They took the box of Yellowtail wine from the cupboard and lay on the floor and drank from its tap.

Now they have me. At night I walk the corridors. I stand in the kitchen reading the rotas, the tickets on the fire extinguishers. I open the freezers and their doors rise with a sigh and the cold smokes. And there is tomorrow, foretold within the freezers. There are our burgers, our frozen fairycakes. There are all tomorrow's parties. All in their icy envelopes, an industrial ice the colour of old women's skin.

I look around the kitchen. How still it is. Like a photograph of itself, I think.

There is a cockroach on the floor. I listen to the sound it makes, an electrical sound, a tickering of a watch. I once shared a room up a flight of steps in Malaga. We were watching television in the afternoon and I had poured orange juice. When I picked up the plastic cup there was a cockroach in it. We all gathered round to watch it swim. All seven of us, making bets on whether cockroaches drown.

There are only mugs here so I make a mug of tea and take it to the lounge. Three a.m. I put the television on, very low, and flick through the seventy-two channels. There are always more channels now. Like books and magazines. Like cockroaches. Sometimes I play the DVDs the residents' families bring. I have watched *Titanic* and listened to the real ice rise in its cliffs, its cordilleras. I have watched *Descent* and seen the women lost in the dark caves.

What a strange film, I think, to bring your mother, your grandmother. Women lost in the dark, their torches dimming, almost out. And I have settled back and listened to the silence.

At 4 a.m. there was a good show. The British are pure, it said. Eighty per cent of the British have common DNA. It can be traced back 12,000 years to hunters who followed the reindeer to Britain. Not so many, those hunters. A few hundred. There was a picture of people in skins, children wrapped in furs. They trudged the frosty ground, past stunted trees. Then on the news there were more demonstrations. British jobs for British workers, the banners said. Yes, I said. Yes I understand.

But do they understand, I wonder, the old people here? Understand that it's only me tonight? The manager away, Roisin away, everyone else away. Only me on duty tonight, only me in my green Santa suit.

I. Me. Their only guard. Me in the silence. Not even a clock tickering. All the clocks digital here, and all around me the Christmas food. Boxes of liqueurs, mince pies in biscuit tins. And chocolate money in gold, in silver foil.

I collect the chocolate money and look at it. My treasure. These coins I can see in the dark, a glint from the coins, a glimmering. Maud who knits, Magdalena who knits, gone to their beds whilst here in the darkness are their fortunes abandoned. String bags of coins as a miser would hoard. A miser from the fairytales.

Those tales make misers miserable but I have always believed misers the happiest of people. It's not what money might buy that makes the misers happy. No, it is the metal of the money itself. Its chinking coin, its smell of other hands, its coolness on the skin. And such a pillow those coins make. For the head or for the heart.

I bite into a chocolate liqueur. Its dark green taste is a mouthful of the night river. I steal the chocolate, I who was once the night swimmer, I who kept the key to the city of Babylon on a cord around my neck.

I had seen Woodlands when delivering leaflets in Slaughter Street. The Alpha Interiors leaflet was orange and said all blinds were 10 per cent off, plus free home consultation. The leather sofa people were offering 50 per cent off the Relaxo Recliner, and more for the Ritzy. Happy Dreamz was half price too, all their beds unbeatable bargains.

I remember that often in Babylon Aadam's car wouldn't start, which meant we couldn't get home to sleep. Business was always bad in Babylon when I was there. Not that I stayed long. There were only Russian tourists then, and few of them. Sometimes a bus would come with retired doctors and teachers from the city. But it was usually quiet. Aadam sat and smoked like a grand vizier while I took the entrance money, sold postcards and maps, water and dates. When his Nissan couldn't go we would lock the gate and wander around.

I sat with him once in the Street of Processions, the car pushed under the wall, and listened to his stories. Aadam, with his yellow skin, his camphorated clothes, knew all of our history. His father or his grandfather had fought the English in the 1930s. Now there are jobs in the English graveyard, he told me. Cutting grass, keeping the children out. Steady work. Above our heads, carved in the stone, I knew there were creatures not from this world.

One night we sat in the weeds beside the black lion. The masters of stone had carved the lion devouring a foreigner, some enemy of our city.

Look, said Aadam, pointing up. That is Mars.

The planet was bright as a spark from his cigarette. Then Aadam asked me what I would do. Where I would go.

A friend is in Spain, I said. Good prospects.

It was so hot that sleeping out was no problem. Sometimes I eased myself into the river and allowed my body to be wrapped in its green sheets. And many times I lay under the palms and listened to that river sliding by. Slow as blood. I could hear its echo in the ground, the current breathing in my ear.

I also heard another sound. Two lovers crept into the grove. They paused and whispered, embraced and lay down, whispered and laughed. Then went their way. I could see the stars through the trees. Silverfish, I thought, on mother's pantry stone. Mars was lower now and red as myrrh. It seemed to be coming nearer.

No one in Slaughter Street would ever buy a new leather sofa. I could have told them that. But I delivered the leaflets anyway. When I came back I sat on the wall of the Mount Joy Club. Tanya would be singing there next Tuesday, followed by karaoke. I watched the taxis pass. Every one was driven by a Pakistani. In town, the people selling the *Big Issue* were now Romanians. I sometimes see them go behind Boots and speak on their mobile phones. A beautiful language, I have come to think. But all the morning I looked at Woodlands.

One day I remember I call the good day. I turned down Evening Street, which was a redbrick terraced street. Once I had delivered leaflets here. Now it was morning and people had gone to work. There was a milk carton on the step of the first house. I took it. Halfway down Evening Street was a packet of two Sheldon soft white batons on a doorstep. I took it. At the end of Evening Street was a wall with a bramble growing over it. Snagged on the thorns was the green string of a purple balloon. Attached to the string was a card from the Salvation Army. I read the card. It said come to our hostel. Our army hostel.

Two streets later was a park behind railings. I sat on a bench there and ate the bread and drank the milk. The bread stuck to the roof of my mouth in a paste but I finished every crumb. I watched a woman put a Tesco plastic bag over her hand and pick up her dog's shit. She placed the shit and the bag in another Tesco plastic bag and tied the bag's mouth. The woman looked at me. Then she spoke to her dog.

On the next bench was a postman. He was wearing blue shorts and had orange flashes on his pouch. I looked at his pouch and it was bursting with envelopes. Every pocket in that pouch bursting with envelopes. What a good man, I thought. Such a solemn duty. Delivering letters to the world. The world's news. Like me, he was drinking from a milk carton. Cheers mate, he said.

Bins and beds, the woman in Woodlands had said. That's easy to remember, isn't it?

Yes it is, I thought, because I am a quick learner. Bins and beds. I take the black plastic bags that the residents leave in a place they call the scullery and put them in the wheelies outside. The wheelies are emptied on Monday and Thursday mornings.

There are forty residents, and I thought that would mean

many bags. But these old people don't waste much. They are careful people, they have always been frugal.

The beds are stripped every week, the sheets, the duvet covers, the pillow cases. We also have the residents' clothes for their weekly wash. Mostly, their strange underwear.

How we laugh, Roisin and I, at the underwear of every Lady Ga Ga. Zhao Si never laughs because he is a real launderer. How sad it is, that underwear. Revealing their last secrets. The last secrets of their lives. When Roisin says 'gussets' we know when to laugh. It is our codeword. A detonator.

And it will never end. When someone leaves, a room is not long empty. Another woman arrives, frail, tearful, making the best of it, her family around her, soon glad to get out. Up or down in the lift they go and out into the rain, across the road to the Mount Joy Club car park, over to Slaughter Street. Back in the rain to their Ford Fiestas, the husband and wife, the son or the daughter. Crying. Sighing with relief.

I opened the lounge door, closed it carefully, and crossed the grass. The wall is only one metre high and then I was on the petrol station forecourt. Then another wall, then the slip road and I was within the Tesco car park. Trains of trolleys in their bays, one car in all the frozen field, frost on its windscreen like a grey eggshell. An egret's dirty egg.

Inside I walk the aisles. Such a strange light. A dead light, I think, yet bright. Deathly bright. A camera follows me, then another, and a security man stands at the end of the aisle, watching, arms folded. Then he moves. But not far. I pass the avocados, I pass the butternut squash. Like bells, I think, the squash. I pass the toothpaste, I pass the place where people buy Caribbean holidays and insurance for their silver cars.

Tesco is open twenty-four again. Life is returning to normal. I put the chocolate money in my basket. They are half-price now, the golden coins. I go through the bin with its cut-price DVDs. Here is one, *Day of the Dead*. I put it in my basket. So many movies now about the dead, the dead people who cannot die.

Maud broke her hip today. She slipped and the ambulance took her away. We know she will not come back, that she has taken the last step but one. Maud's knitting is on her chair in the lounge but I am thinking instead about Roisin in the laundry, where she showed us her own underwear.

Enough of these, she laughed. These crappy keks. Cop this, Lazza.

And she unzipped her jeans and there was her red thong. Red fur within the squash. No, I thought. Cleft of a peach. An Andalusian peach. I stood in the street eating a peach, its juice dribbling on my chin and I looked up and saw Lorca's plaque. So many poets.

I used to stand under the statue of the poet outside the Baghdad museum. At five, the girls would pass, in their dark glasses, their red lipstick, hurrying from the Ministry of Information.

Now that's what I call underwear, Roisin said. Even Zhao Si laughed and leered, who never laughs but leers as a lizard will in its cold blood. I remember the wall lizards at home. They smiled like old men. Never trust the old men, my mother said. Do not go with them.

At the checkout the man looked hard at me. Then smiled.

Bargains, he said. Lots of bargains now. Bit late for that, isn't it? he asked, and brushed his fingers on the sleeve of my green suit. A gentle touch, I thought. But a dismissal.

Outside, the Fiesta was still there. I tried to scrape the ice on the driver's side but it was too thick. I wanted to look within, I don't know why. Such a winter. I remember Malaga's yellow steps, the peaches piled in pyramids on the market stalls.

It was 3 a.m. and I crossed the car park with my Tesco bag. I pictured myself in the stony light of the camera screen. When I paused the camera paused. When I passed the camera followed.

Roisin has often asked how old I am. She knows I am older than I look.

We were in the Tesco cafe where we meet two other Iraqis. And the Albanian. We go there because Roisin says it is good to get out. To see friends. Roisin says she is going mad, surrounded by all the old women. All she can think of, she says, are the tea stains on their blouses, the old women's tights like seaweed flung over the Donegal rocks.

But the Tesco girls are kind to us. One teabag and one lemon slice costs me one pound sterling. But there are free refills.

We should plan a night out, Roisin says. Go across to the Mount Joy. The Albanian boy smiles and smiles. The Iraqi boys smile and smile. Everyone loves Roisin.

I think of the couple under the palm trees, lying upon the crackling fronds. Aadam once told me there were crocodiles in the river and not to swim there. He said it was in the Christian bible, in the Book of Isaiah. All the children who went missing, Aadam insisted, were eaten by the crocodiles.

So I pointed towards the palace on its hill. To the ziggurat where we were never supposed to point. I said to Aadam, yes, of course. And is the great crocodile himself at home today? If so, from which of his six hundred rooms is the great crocodile spying on us?

Aadam laughed and rolled his eyes. Not so loud, he said. Not so loud.

That day in the Plaza Mayor, I had looked at the human statues. No, not a poet. No, not Clint Eastwood. Instead, a terrible thought had entered my head. I gasped at myself. I reeled at the impact of such a thought.

Why couldn't I be the crocodile? The crocodile dressed as one of the Bedouin still dress, in the black jalabiya of Badiet esh Sham. Those desert-coloured robes. Yes I could be the crocodile. The crocodile with his fierce moustache. His hand held up in peace.

Hey Lazza, said Roisin, reaching out to touch me. It was as if she woke me from a dream. When are you going to tell us what door your key opens?

The wild strawberries

June 17

Dear Kazia

Hey, I did it. I knocked on the door and asked if the warden was there. I told him I wanted to visit the castle.

When?

Is now convenient, please? I said.

Fair enough, he said, and pulled out an iron key from a drawer in the hat stand in his hall. We crossed the green and he opened that door, the one with the studs and bolts. And I was in and he just left me there. Alone. No history lecture, no nothing. Went back to his telly. I had the castle to myself. I was the queen.

So you cross the lawn and go up the steps and through the *portal*. I love that word. It felt like a ship. Above the portal is a broken wheel in stone, an arc, an arch, an enormous ammonite in a stone whiter than the rest of the walls. Those are rubble, not blocks like I'd imagined. I could go up the staircases to the windows and look out. Holding the bars of course. A damsel. A wimp in her wimple. Keep up, Kazia! And views in every direction, over the houses and the fields up to the mountains and down to the river and all over this town.

But iron key or not, the kids had got in. Might have been the previous night, there were about twenty Strongbow cans scattered around. The black and the gold. And the plastic bottles of White Lightning and the takeaway trays. What a place for a party if you can scramble over the wall. If you can steal the money to give to strangers to buy the booze for you. Remember the bushes outside the Jagiellonian and the vodka oranges?

Anyway, I can see those children now, lighting their fire on the lawn, more excited than by anything else in their lives, the pages of their magazines blackening and rising up, the burning tits and arses flying away over the town. Those kids sharing the spliffs and the whizz and running around screaming their heads off or lying back and saying things that are deeply wise and which they'll never remember. Then wondering who's going with whom. Yes, whom. Who's going to be selected. And who's not. The best times ever. Awesome.

And I bet they were doing the same eight hundred years ago. Looking down through the darkness from the firelight. Looking down at this frontier town because yes, that's what it was then. That's why they built the castle. And it still is a frontier, of course. It's taken me all this time, ten months, to understand, because you never see it in the papers or the TV programmes they are making about this place. We're famous, Kazia. You see people in the street with DV cams. All these journalists looking for a good hotel. An expense-account meal. But none mentions the frontier. And if you'd realised that Kazia, perhaps you would have stayed too instead of scarpering back to good old Krakow.

I had my sandwiches on the lawn, *Krakowska* from the *sklep*. You'd have been proud of me. Then I put the litter in the bin. Inside were three aerosols of Palmolive Soft and Gentle anti-stress deodorant. These children like to sniff. And all those golden cans. It was Strongbow Super, Kaz. That's 7.5 per cent alcohol. It could rot your pants.

Hey, you can come back any time, the warden said. He's a lazy type, I can tell straight off. But I will be back. It's one of the best places I've found around here and you know how I collect placcs.

Love, Zuzanna

June 21

Look, Kazia, longest day!

Yesterday was Sunday and I took the bus to the seaside. Loads of people got off at the amusement park entrance, so I did too. There's a swimming pool, a cinema, shops and a bar with a sign that says it can hold 1400 people. They have a signpost in the middle of the pub – on it is London 200 miles, New York 3150 miles, Paris 325 miles. I thought that strange. It's like asking the people why they're not somewhere else. Somewhere that's bound to be better. By the way, it doesn't mention Sosnowiec. Funny that.

The fairground was best because it was hot weather and I bought real candyfloss off a man called Pat who was doing good business. Then I picked up courage and went on a ride called All Around the World.

But you don't do anything. You just sit. So I sat in a carriage on a rail that went past the Taj Mahal and the Pyramids and ended beside a red double decker in Trafalgar Square. The painted people on the bus wore bowler hats. Like, come on.

Anyway, the boys working the rides were from all over. I

heard two speaking Lithuanian.

Labbas ritas, I said, and they stared open mouthed and then shrugged, as if to say, hey look, we made it. We said we would and now we have.

But it's no fun on your own so I kept walking. Soon I was at the wall they've built around the camp. And I could see the beach and behind the beach these huge sand dunes. So you know me, Kazia. Me and my places. Maybe there's a place for me up there, I thought. So I walked on, remembering landmarks like a green lifeguards' shed, and keeping the sea on my right, staying on the path.

It's hard work too, travelling in sand. But gradually the track grassed over and turned inland to the dunes. An hour later, Kazia, I was at the top. And how high I was, with the greatest view you could ever imagine. The town was hidden on my right, the funfair with its huge wheels somewhere over there too. But the sea was bigger than anything I expected. Blue, blue and such a blue. A blue that invaded you. I wanted to drink that blue but it felt like the blue was drinking you. Me. And where I stood was a hill of flowers. There were so many I had to tread on them. Stars in the grass. Yellow spears taller than I am. And roses, Kazia. Everywhere roses growing out of the sand.

I should be a botanist, I thought then. Maybe teaching Charles Dickens to thugs and dimwits, going to the bars in Kazimierz on a Friday night with the gang isn't so ambitious. But flowers are like challenges. What do they mean? Up on that ridge the flowers seemed more alive than some of the people we know. And a lot more mysterious. Because it was wild, Kazia. How could that be? Because I could almost see Burger King.

Ten more minutes, I thought. Then I'll turn round. It was only 3 p.m. but so hot. Sometimes it gets hotter here than we thought it would. I was burned, I knew. Red and bitten and burned. But indefatigable, Kazia. You know me. (Look it up, you lazy trollop. You can always call me a termagant, remember.)

So I walked out on to the ridge. It was like a spine, the land falling away into a wood at one side, the plain on the other. That's when I saw them. I crouched down to see what these red things were. And they were strawberries, Kazia. Wild strawberries. First there was one, then two. When I looked again there were a hundred. All along that ridge, a thousand strawberries, maybe a million. Strawberries the size of my thumbnail. And no one else in all the world had seen them or knew about wild strawberries.

I've told you about the prices here, haven't I? Mad cabbages. Insane beans. And how expensive the strawberries are, the Californian strawberries like cows' hearts we used to see in the butcher's. But these were the real thing. These were prehistoric strawberries. What all the strawberries since must have been bred from. Oh, it made me laugh, Kazia.

Here was I, on top of the world, filling my handkerchief with strawberries, filling my mouth and my bag with strawberries sweetened by the sun and the sea air, strawberry juice on the knees of my jeans and running down my chin. And there are Anna and Petr and all the others, I thought, picking strawberries in polytunnels somewhere, ludicrous strawberries, grotesque and tasteless, weighing them, getting paid. Getting paid money for picking strawberries. Learning to hate strawberries.

If only they could see me, I thought. On top of the ridge, the bees around me, the yellow spears. The sky was that weird white, like the sheet they put over my father's coffin. And that soundtrack in my head that I couldn't forget, the song they played at All Around the World. Andrea True Connection singing 'More, More, More'. You remember, Kazia, they always play it in the students' bar. Wow, Andrea's had a life, Kazia. She only made that record because she was trapped by a volcano on a Caribbean island. Can a porn star be a role model? Well, Andrea can.

Love from Zuzanna (not a porn star. Yet.)

June 25

Kazia, guess what? Another one's happened. Though now it doesn't take much guessing. And this one is different. This boy had gone missing about a year ago, months before we arrived. Nothing unusual in that. He was 22. Off to London, they thought. Find a new scene. But somebody discovered him in sheds behind the fairground. Where I was this week. Apparently it's all derelict there. They call it the Backs. They've been going to knock the sheds down for years but nothing gets done. He was there. In that horrible place. Only rats, Kazia. And broken glass. Old carriages from the funfair rides. A carousel horse with the name 'Nathaniel' painted on it.

He'd been there all that time and nobody had the wit to look, despite the missing person posters and the newspaper articles. So although he's the latest, which makes him the twentieth, they're calling him one of the first. The first to do it. He'd hanged himself like most of the others and now it's on the television. His famous face on all the big programmes. And he looks so lonely in that picture they use of him. His hair shaved in swirls, with this silly tuft on his forehead, dyed red. His eyes bewildered.

But when I watch those shows I can't help but laugh. The journalists are always struggling to describe this area. Industrial. No, ex-industrial. Or unlovely. Or unremarkable. Always ex or un. Something that it's not. Defined by what it isn't. Even undiscovered. Yes, that's what one of the TV people said it was. One of the undiscovered parts of the country. Because nobody famous comes from here. Nobody anyone's ever heard of. And there's despair here. And hopelessness. And it rains. And there's cheap drugs. And everything's unpronounceable anyway so let's not bother. Maybe they should try Soznowiec. So here I am, Kazia, wandering about the same place, keeping my eyes open, and to me it's obvious. It's like, blinding. *There once lived, in a sequestered part of the country of…* Ha ha, Kazia. Keep up.

After work yesterday I caught the bus to the Odeon in the retail park. Took my pizza to the usual seat where we went that time, right at the edge where you can look down the glass wall into the atrium and watch the kids messing about. Some of the girls were off their heads, but from up there you can tell how they take care of each other. Motherly protocols. It's all ritualised.

The Mutant Crew they call themselves. I think it's ironic. Some programme last year asked if we're creating a new species of young person. Anyway, I couldn't really understand what the girls were saying because they all seem to use text language to one another. And all their ring tones were going at once. But, as soon you get over how loud they are, they're quite sweet. Easy to see their priorities. Straight out of school, get the rhinestones and slap on. Then down the centre and pretend to be bored. Pretend to be bored when really you're terrified. And you're terrified because you don't understand how it all works yet but you're there to learn. Even if the north wind is blowing down the crack of your arse and Red Square vodka tastes like cat litter and makes you puke. You are determined to learn. Because there's no alternative.

Sorry, yes, there is an alternative. The alternative is not to survive in this unplace. This explace. Everyone else has already written you off, but you're determined to prove them wrong. So you scream at nothing. You text crap. You eat junk. You drink poison. And then you paint each other perfectly in heartbreaking L'Oreal. Foundation, concealer. Block up every pore. And you learn, Kazia. You learn down there amongst the plastic palm trees and the takeaway kebab trays. I call it *mall-ediction*. I call it *mall-ancholy*. Tell me you get it, Kazia.

But I'm learning too. I'm learning up here with a margarita slice and a coffee with as many sugars as will dissolve in it. Writing my letter to you, Kazia, but about to pay half price for *Into the Wild*, which should be good because Sean Penn directed. It's about this silly, sweet kid, Christopher McCandless, who drove away from everything. Pulled the plug on the world. With the inevitable result.

Maybe he should have met the girls down there, with their silver belts from Primark and their denim shreds. Uniforms for the front line. Maybe if he had found an interpreter they might have taught him something. Because there they are in the life class, all of them down there, determined to graduate, bawling under these huge pieces of polystyrene fruit. A five-metre long banana. An orange bigger than a chillout room. I think it's part of the healthy eating campaign, Kazia.

Love from your maddening friend, ZuziX

July 3

It's Saturday night, Kazia, and there's a war going on. I just came down the hill from the railway station. I'd been to see another film, *Once*, which is pretty good if you believe in fairy stories. Which I do, so it was great.

But back to reality. There were hundreds of police in the station. Well, about ten. A boy's been killed. They kicked him to death, someone said. This stupid gang. But they were older men so not so stupid. Just brain dead. Desolate souls. They came out of the hotel and the fight went on all the way back up the hill. Skirmishing they call it. And one boy was cornered and they kicked him down. He was trying to escape. He was crying. But they stamped on his head. That's what this man was saying who saw it all. How nonchalant he seemed. Or perhaps he's given up caring. They jumped on the boy's head, he said, like it was a burst football. You could see the brands of their trainers on the boy's face.

All this is one hundred yards away from the flat, Kazia. Under my window they're still coming out of the clubs, Marilyn's, The Matrix, Sacha's. Some are lying in the street even though it's misty and cold. That's men for you. I can't understand them. Why can't I understand men, Kaz? Next year I might want to marry one. Or next week. Seems bizarre now but you never know how your hormones are going to betray you. Because your totalitarian genes want to reproduce themselves. Like moss does. Like mildew. Everything demanding another chance of perfection. Imperatives of the slime mould.

The streets are pedestrianised here, so at 2 a.m. the girls are swinging on the flower baskets and pissing in the doorways. Men are fighting but not properly. They're too drunk. So why don't

I understand men? Or the men down there on the precinct. Like negatives of themselves in the orange streetlights. Ghosts in gold chains and designer vests. Ghosts with their heads shaved like stormtroopers.

Remember that football crowd we saw in Warsaw? We were at a café table outside, and there was a grumbling sound. I thought it was thunder. Then everybody started to get up and leave and around the corner came the supporters. Good word, that. Supporters. What do they support, exactly? With their flags and their boots and a thousand broken bottles under their boots. In their white tee shirts their mothers had washed. So clean and well scrubbed. I smelled that crowd, Kazia, and it smelt of aftershave. Of deodorant. A chemical garden. But such a sound. Like it was coming out of the earth. Out of the sewers. Drum 'n' bass shaking the room.

There's no one like that here, really. They're all too drunk to be organised. But what I notice is the men are hard on each other. They don't help each other out like the girls. Where were that boy's friends, the one whose head was split? On Bebo and the other sites you look at the faces of the boys who've topped themselves, and you think, maybe they hated this. The fighting. The glassing. Maybe they hated the hatred.

Note that word. *Top*. As in to *top yourself*. A kind of phrasal verb. Your favourite. Yes this is the perfect place to live, Kazia. For now, and for someone like me, it's good. The flat's like a theatre seat but of course I'm only peeping. You know, between the peeling wall and the tatty curtain. I love nooks and crannies. Remember the art room? I could work there because I had that tiny space in the corner, surrounded on three sides. That's why I love Alchemia. But if they saw me looking down there'd be trouble. Yes there is a war, Kazia, but I think there always has been a war. *Or else we have fallen upon strange times, and Heaven only knows the end of them.* Get it Kaz? Sorry.

Now the boys are sitting around the plastic flowerbed that was put there last week. A token to the summer. Most are half-naked and their tattoos are black in the sodium lights. They're all the colour of those Strongbow cans. How perfect the steroids have made them seem. And now one is lying on the pissed-on concrete. He's down to his jock strap, Kazia. In the streetlight he's like a golden altar. Not the sacrificial calf but the cold stone itself. Perhaps he's dead too.

These might be the Roid Boys. Locally notorious, if you believe the newspapers. Their headquarters is the Station Hotel. I looked in once but deemed it prudent not to linger. Ha ha. There were three of them playing pool. The biceps of bison, Kazia. But the drugs shrink their funny little scrotums. Their dicks become babies' dummies, apparently. And their brains go to blubber. But nobody cares about that. I bet they still smell gorgeous, Kazia, the boys out there. Of manly roses. Of masculine violets. How I want to breathe in their magnificent perfumes. Do you remember the Spartans, my darling? Always combing their hair?

L.Z.Xxx

July 5

Kazia! You say it's always about me. But it's not. About me. Not always. I'm not one of those idiots who put my travel diaries on a blog. I could have blogged the sand dunes here that nobody seems to know. But I didn't. And I'm still finding sand in my shoes.

I remember my grandfather telling me a story about when he was a boy. There was a potato field behind their house. Their hut. Well, my grandfather and my father used to go out at night and steal the potatoes. Because no matter how well harvested a potato field is, he said there would always be potatoes still there. It was impossible to get all the potatoes out. And they would sprout the next year. So my father and his father went out stealing. At night of course. Scavenging for potatoes because everyone was poor and some people were starving.

They would dig in the frosted earth. Sometimes the ground was frozen, he told me, hard as concrete. But it didn't stop them. They dug with bare hands or trowels or knives or spades. And my father was the one who always found at least one potato. Sometimes a bag full, but always at least one potato to take back to my grandmother. My father was the best potato thief there was. Potatoes with the frozen soil on them. Potatoes that were icy inside, which was bad news, because they rotted. And grandmother would roast the potatoes. Or boil them. Or make chips with the black fat they used, which was part coal powder and part old oil and part offal. They'd have a fire of sticks and wood shavings and stolen coal from the sidings. Once he told me they even boiled potatoes in a kettle over a candle flame. Imagine how long that would take. Would the potatoes boil before the candle burned out? But it was food. Their food. As good as if they'd grown the potatoes themselves. Better, because sometimes it's harder to steal food than to make it.

And they tasted wonderful, my grandfather would say. There's nothing like a mouth full of hot potato. And there was my father, waiting for the potato to be passed round, his hands still in their filthy mittens, his fingernails broken by the frost.

You know, I was thinking about us, Kazia. About being

friends. Remember two winters ago when we said, hey, let's go to Oswiecim? Just like that. Two little Goths with our black nail varnish. So we caught the bus to the village and walked in the frost. How cold it was, your breath like a scarf. I was wearing your brother's leather jacket, remember. With the Harley badges. We laughed because there was a condom in the pocket. And we were the first people in the cafeteria and had cabbage and dumplings, and boy, it tasted like the best food ever.

That cheery waitress said you look famished, girls. So she heaped our plates out of the steaming vats. The first portions that day, she said. There was an old man in, drinking coffee. She said he was there every day, winter, summer, even when it was crammed with tourists. Drinking his coffee. He always took his coffee there.

What was his story? we asked. She said she didn't want to know his story. Anyway, it was obvious what his story was. Everybody had a story. There were millions of stories about that place. And each one of them was the worst story in the world.

But you didn't want to be inside, or in the huts. Being in the huts on our own would have been too much. I always prefer it when there are schoolkids there. Lovers holding on to one another. Some moron with an iPod. So we hitched with the electricity man over to Brzezinka. His leg touching yours. How electric was that? And it was better, you said, because we were outside in the clean air. Absolutely no people, and the ground rumpled and broken as if they'd mined coal. Everything crooked and falling down. Pulverised and frozen into strange shapes. A derelict factory with iron coming out of the ground. The broken ovens. All that abandoned space.

And we walked around and you found the plover, Kazia. A golden plover.

It had been caught in a snare. Or at least a piece of wire coming from the earth. It was dead and perfect. You spread out its wings and there it was. A bishop, I said, but you said no. An angel. It's like a fallen angel, you said, with his wings spread out on the ice.

The grass was white as needles but you were smoking like you were on fire. I thought there was a fire inside you that day. A flame burning in your blood. And we stood there and looked at the plover. How big it was. A bubble of ice at its beak, its leg twisted. It came down on the moor looking for food and it never flew away. The white moor of Brzezinka. We both had our cameras but we didn't take a shot, and we both knew why.

Before we went you freed the plover's leg and we left it there. Because what else could we do, what else but study where the gold of its feathers met the black. Then walk away. There was only us, remember. And the crows hunched up in their overcoats. We walked away and you said you were never going back, even though you live so close. We walked away in the dead of winter and everybody on the bus was too cold to talk.

So you see, Kazia, it's not about me. Truly it's not. It's about you too and about everything. It's about your randy brother and his girlfriends, and the man with his coffee, who is there now in the canteen, I know it, even as I write. Sitting there on his own and sipping that horrible coffee every day of his life. Which is his way of telling his story. It's about him too. And the potatoes. It has to be.

Love from Zuzanna

July 8

Kazia, I'm playing Andrea, over and over. More more more. It's a really true connection tonight. You know she's a therapist now? In Florida? And yes, I confess, I'm drinking. Red Square vodka like the mutant crew. I like the mutant crew. They came through town tonight and they were the only people on the streets. Nobody older than fifteen the whole evening. So this is an SOS. What does SOS mean? Save our Souls? Save our Shit, more like. I just don't trust it. Don't trust vodka. But it's only water, after all. Only water. But we should have tried. To trust water. But we never did. So it's out there now. Coming our way. Black. Black and white. Black and white and no colour at all. Roaring. Whispering. Speaking its own language. And coming our way. Coming out of the ground. Coming out of the air. Made in the clouds. Made in the sea. Coming out of me, Kazia. I can even smell it coming out of me. Strong as battery acid. Stinking. Like the brakes on a train. But it's made in us. We're making it. Cell by cell. Making itself in us. And it's coming. It's coming all right. After everything we've done to it. After everything we've done to ourselves. Damned it. Dirtied it. Denied it. Derided it. We should have blessed it. But we blasphemed it. We bastardised it. We belittled it. We should have worshipped it. But we worsted it. We should have worshipped water. Because water's a god. No. Water's the only god. But it's too late now. Because water's coming. It's angry at last. So water's coming. Black water. White water. Black water and white water and water no colour at all. Retribution they'll call this one day. Or justice. The justice of water. Maybe we should pray. What else is there? There's nothing else. Because where can we run when it's in us already. So I'll pray. I'd better pray. But what

does praying sound like? A river running? A typhoon turning? Or maybe praying is quieter than that. Like a tap running? Quieter than that. Or a woman crying. Quieter than that. Or vodka over ice. That kind of crackle. Quieter than that. Then maybe it's like a hailstone. A hailstone dissolving. On the tip of your tongue. As quiet as that? Maybe. Yes maybe that's the prayer that's going to save my soul.
Indefatigably, Zzzzzz

July 10

Sorry about the last one, Kazia. I think I'm catching whatever's wrong with this place. But you know me. I like to experiment with my head. And Meryl, the landlady, remember her, was scrubbing the pavement outside with her bleach bombs and the hosepipe straight through to the kitchen. There's a leak in it and she flooded the passageway and called me to help but I pretended to be ill. Somebody had puked on the steps outside and somebody thrown curry sauce around. The usual. Filthy little swine, she was saying. Little swine.

And, as if you couldn't guess, there's another one. Another boy. He's hung himself in a wood. Why do they always hang themselves? Don't they know what that means? Sometimes I think they don't understand what it is to be dead. Now coming from where we do, that's no problem. At least that mystery has been solved. For once and for all. But these boys are children. Which doesn't stop them having their own children, by the way. They're fathers. But I'm still sure they don't understand. That it's oblivion. That it's annihilation.

Last week I passed a place where people had left flowers. Pink carnations in their cellophane. And teddy bears and photographs of Manchester United or the rugby team. Soon it's just compost, like the pizza boxes and kebabs. And don't they know what happens when you hang yourself? You don't just look like a rag doll. All sweet and floppy. No. Your head comes off. The skin of your neck stretches like elastoplast. Maybe you shit yourself. But they don't put that in the paper. All you see are the obituaries and that sexy word, tragedy. You never see the truth of it. The body gnawed by fairground rats.

This latest boy's photo is in the paper today, Kazia. Of course he looks a normal boy. Not a corpse. If you get on to Bebo and the other sites you can read the tributes. All written in baby language. Seems one of his friends did it three months ago. Another friend last year.

So Meryl comes up with tea and toast and asked if I was better. I felt so bad about not helping, I said I'd go to chapel with her. To help clean it. Meryl likes cleaning things and I'm starting to see why.

Boy, was she pleased. It's only two streets away, and called Ruhamah. And Kazia, it's huge inside, you could get hundreds of people in. She told me normally there's eighteen. So there she is with this old rag mop which looks like a rag doll, with J cloths and disinfectant. Meryl said she uses a litre of bleach every week, squirting it round the pavement cracks outside the house so the dandelions don't get a hold. No microbe is safe.

There's this gravel area she's proud of. Where nothing must grow. Absolutely verboten. The eleventh commandment. Not a leaf. If God has a smell, it must be pine-scented disinfectant. Or maybe God is the genie in the toilet duck.

But I had a shock. In the vestry as we went in was a pair of long boots.

Jackboots? I asked. Trying to laugh.

Galoshes, Meryl said.

And they were still wet. Apparently there's a tank in the chapel where they baptise people. In holy water. The minister holds them down. It's total immersion. There'd been a special service and there were his wellingtons, his galoshes, still wet. And this dirty mac behind the door.

ZX

July 14

Now Kazia, what with cleaning Ruhamah and helping marvellous Meryl, please don't think I'm getting religious. But there happen to be a lot of old churches around here. Yesterday I went into one near the sea. It's called St John's, and there's sand in the graveyard. The door was open and in I went. You know me. Well, it was all very old but stark. A plain beauty. Ho hum.

But then I saw the pulpit and I had to laugh. And you know how I laugh, Kazia. Like a cat being sick. Or that's what the comedian in Alchemia told me. Right in front of the whole audience.

But this leaflet, which I didn't pay for, claims the pulpit was the work of a medieval artist. Yet I could tell immediately what the artist had done. He, or maybe she, Kazia, but probably he, had carved Jesus being beaten by two men. You know, the flagellation. Yes, keep up girl! All three figures were based on local people who must have been around this area seven hundred years ago. They must because they're so distinctive. Little, shrunken, mean people. Badly nourished. Mall nourished, ha ha. Christ is the good one of course and the other two the baddies. But they're all like weasels. How the locals must have laughed when they saw it. A really good joke. It's a seaside church and it looks like Jesus is being beaten with ship's ropes. Or stinging nettles. These days it would be a FCUK tie. But the figures seem so real. There's a pub next door to the church and I bet you can see the three of them in there any day. I bet Jesus is in there now with a glass of white wine and a salad sandwich.

And I thought then, yes, I want to do that. I want to be a sculptor. And move around, selling my work but never signing it. Staying anonymous. An artist going from church to church, adding an angel here, a demon there. There are wonderful demons on the churches here, Kazia. Perhaps they're the ones who've cursed this country.

Indisputably yours, Z!

July 16

Kazia, it's your turn, you know it is. But here I go again. Because this evening I went swimming. Not to the pool with its greasy scumline. All the oldies go there. No, the sea, I went into the sea.

You know where I picked the strawberries? Down that track but don't turn inland. Keep going along the beach until it's all sand and no rocks. Yes, I've been exploring again. Courtesy of this huge map I've bought which is up on my wall.

It was after work, about six. The bus takes only quarter of

an hour, but there was nobody else there. I couldn't believe it. Not a soul on the sand. Not a speck. The tide was miles out and I walked through the rockpools. All I did was take a bag, a towel, wear shorts under my jeans, put the jeans, tee shirt and sandals on a rock, and hide my card and ticket nearby. No phone, no camera. And there I am. Up to my ankles. Up to my knees. Black shorts and that old grey bra you hate. Up to my waist and it was so cold at first I peed myself. But not colder than the pool in the Vistula.

It took me ten minutes to pick up the courage. To go under.

But when I did I thought I could hear a bell beneath the waves. It was my heart of course. My blood pounding, telling me I was alive. And I laughed. I laughed because I was alive in a foreign country with a foreign ocean knotting its dirty silk around my legs. And birds low overhead in the blinding light. Eight white birds with only inches between them. Like a silver kite.

So don't tell me off. I wasn't murdered. I wasn't raped. The sand was bubbling as I walked back and I could smell the weed and the salt on me. What a gorgeous smell that is. All I did was float, Kazia, listening to the waves rustling. They sounded like the jackpot from a slot machine. Waves coming in, lifting me up, putting me down. And all the time I was thinking, *mother of pearl, mother of pearl*. If I was a painter I'd paint a huge canvas called Mother of Pearl. Violet and rose at the top, merging slowly into silver, into grey. So slowly you never see the change. Yes, that would be my masterpiece.

Because I found an oystershell and I'm stroking the inside of it right now. I'm going to sip some Red Square out of it tonight. Taste a dangerous pearl. And I'll see you soon, my darling. One month's time and we'll be back in Alchemia's candlelight with the others, spilling our beer. Me in my old grey bra with sand in it. You with Mr Right. How is Viktor, by the way? I didn't mean to be rude that time, I keep telling you. But oral hygienist, Kazia? Open wide my bonny bride? Come on.

You see, Kazia, I think I could live here. Because even if this place is an unplace or an explace it might still make me do things. Make me make things. It has a jagged edge. Listen to this. *But now, when he thought how regularly things went on, from day to day, in the same unvarying round; how youth and beauty died, and ugly griping age lived tottering on…* I might read that to the Roid Boys. Walk into the Station Hotel where they play pool with their shirts off, and say it aloud.

Er, don't worry. You know me. I'm only doing what I always do, which is reporting from the frontier. Either I'm looking down from the castle or out from my room. And right now I'm stirring my coffee. Got the strawberries as a screensaver and the light switched off. I'm just waiting for the skirmishing to start.

Love from Zuzi X

I say a little prayer

It's dark now and the Greyhound station is out of town. I sit in the waiting room with the Mennonites in their black bonnets and cloaks. These Mennonite men have square beards like Abraham Lincoln. The Mennonite children seem sad. I wink at one of the girls who looks away and then glances back. I smile at her. She looks away. A little girl, head to toe in black. We're all waiting for the circular.

I used to know a poet who wrote about bus stations. Did a gig with him and he read a doleful piece. We are in it together, he read, until the last buses go out. In it together. He had looked around a bus station and seen Pakistani and Chinese people and he wondered what they were doing. In Bridgend. And what he was doing there. I kissed him on his stubbly mouth and he whispered he was in love with me.

Buy me a drink first, he said. Then we'll run away together.

But not all Mennonites wear uniforms. Years ago, me and my guitarist were booked into the students union of a Mennonite college, way out in rural Indiana. We arrived early, checked out the PA, ordered a beer.

We don't do beverages, miss, was the response from this big black bursar in the refectory.

No way, I thought. So we asked a student about the closest

bar. Hey, I'll take you, he said. Fancy a walk?

What a walk. Along these narrow roads in the cornfields, the maize ten feet high, the cobs in their purple sheaths still closed against the stems. And us trudging like pilgrims through the Mennonite corn. After two miles we came to a crossroads. And there was a bar there. Right there. The Country it was called. Well we had a good old chinwag about music, and then took some Moosehead back with us and sat in the woods in the college grounds. Drank out of bottles which we kept in brown paper bags. Very respectful. It was a quiet gig. As I remember, some of the women there wore black. But not the men.

That was just after I'd met Amir, and he did the booking. Now Amir, he always says I talk too much. Which is true. But there is a flickering home movie in my head, starring Amir himself and my parents and characters from *Seinfeld* and *Bleak House*, and the Bible, and 'Polythene Pam' and the 'Girl from the North Country', and everyone who has never existed anywhere but my mind.

They're all there. In Barry Island and Inwood and imaginary places that are real to me. So if all that's playing non-stop, I have to talk about it. Yeah, too much. But my mind's an exchequer of dreams. Okay, I had that line ready. I've fitted it into a song and sing it about every third gig.

There's this other song too that I've been trying to write, called '37 Cents'. That's what Stephen Foster had in his pocket when he died. Don't tell me you've never heard of Stephen Foster? Best American songwriter ever. 'Beautiful Dreamer'? Boy, he was far ahead. He just wasn't made for those times. He died in 1864 and his last address was 30, The Bowery, at the North American Hotel.

I went down there once to look around because I was doing

this unplugged thing at the Bowery Poetry Club. I told the club owner he should do a Stephen Foster tribute night. He said it was a great idea. I looked at him and spoke a verse.

Gorgeous, he said. So I sang it that night as part of my set, and I've done it ever since. And you know what? People simply love it. God bless you, Stephen Foster. And I'm not joking when I say you belong in the Rock and Roll Hall of Fame. These days it's full of crap like Aerosmith. No class.

It's Tuesday I think. But who knows where the time goes? Last Tuesday it was raining. Icy veils were blowing off the Hudson. I had nothing much on so I took the train to meet Amir at JFK. All the way down on the 1 from 207 to 59, then the A out to Howard Beach, then the airport shuttle to Terminal 4. Now, that's fourteen dollars return. Wasted. But I wanted to surprise him. Yet it was me who was shocked.

Amir had been in Amman for two weeks to see his parents. I waited at arrivals long after everyone else had come through. Then I asked at Royal Jordanian. Amir was still at customs. Correction. Amir had been detained by Immigration. Correction. Amir was being interviewed by Homeland Security. They were putting him on the next flight back.

But this is his home, I said. He lives in the city. He's a US passport holder.

Did no good. I kept ringing but his phone was off. Cell phone? The words give me the creeps. But there was nothing to do but go back to Inwood. That night the phone rang and it was Amir. Before he said a word I recited our little joke. 'If ye cannot bring good news, then don't bring any.' That's what we always said to one another. It was a philosophy. Courtesy of the wicked messenger.

Amir was still stunned. Denied entry, he said. Even with a

US passport they put their fingers up his ass. He's back in Amman.

I could see him there. I'd visited with Amir, about ten years previously. We'd just met. Of course his parents thought I was *the one*. Amir's intended. Made me feel a little queasy because Amir's gay as a lark. In New York, before he found our Inwood studio, we often slept together. But only out of necessity. I'd tease him by kissing his neck but he never came on to me. He had these freckles like cappuccino chocolate on his back and black fur on his belly. Dark little cock like a dufflecoat toggle. Sweet and unthreatening. Now I could picture him on the land line in his father's house, the desert dawn streaming through.

One evening we were eating supper there, flatbreads and humus with lemon and thyme. I looked up and saw a lizard on the ceiling. Then Amir's dad caught my eye and everything went crazy. They found an aerosol and a stepladder and started squirting that lizard till the room stank of pine forests.

Amir's mother was hard work. Grievously melancholic. She had sold her business, a nursery school, and now was missing the routine. The new owners were making a success of it and she felt she had nothing. So Amir became even more important to her. She treated me like the betrothed. The special one. She never once asked my age, but I was over thirty-five then, five years older than Amir. Okay, I'm forty-eight. And dealing with it.

I had my own bedroom. At night you could feel the tension. The parents were waiting for Amir to sneak in. I could hear them listening. A man must make his move.

But it never occurred to him. I think they were disappointed. But one of his brothers, a fat kid with a moustache, tried it. Came into my boudoir. By mistake. I told him to leave or I'd tell daddy. So what we did on that visit was to sit around the TV and watch the Bill Clinton impeachment interviews. It was hard for me to credit. I was in Amman and we had satellite TV and Amir's brothers were lying on the floor, sniggering at stories about blowjobs. The most powerful man on the planet, humiliated. Silver hair. Red cheeks. I thought the world was ending. How could they treat a president like that?

What we gonna do? I asked Amir on the phone.

You do the gigs, he said. I'll talk to the US embassy. It's just the usual paranoia.

I like Inwood. It's cheap. Two coffees and two English muffins in the Capital restaurant for four dollars. But it's being discovered, just like Williamsburg. Sometimes we walk up to The Cloisters where Sting did that lute concert and look at the jays and those incredible incarnadine cardinals in the bushes. Yeah, *Macbeth* rocks. We call that path our Blue Jay Way. Once we decided to trek all down Broadway. Now that's a hike. Went through Harlem and this gang of black kids were jeering 'Sugar Hill, Sugar Hill' at us. Thought we were dissing them. But we kept going, past Colombia where Dylan used to serenade the students, and came to the Broadway Dive on 101. We'd walked over one hundred blocks.

End of the road, Amir said. We went in, had Guinness and french fries, put Aretha on the jukebox, and just sang along. Forever, forever, you'll… whatever. Then we took the train back.

So I've begun the tour that Amir had organised. Started yesterday morning. After that call he hasn't rung again, but I have all the contacts. The six gigs are guaranteed. The PA is guaranteed. The amps are there. All I have to do is turn up and tune the Tanglewood.

Normally, Amir would drive. But driving over here is a challenge for me. So I caught a noon Trailways from the Port Authority, reckoning to be in Binghamton by five. The Brandywine Bowl would be just over the road, as would the motel.

What can I say? It's only rock and roll but I like it. Only I don't. What do you see when you hear the word Bowl? That's Bowl with a capital B. I see the Rose Bowl. I even see the Hollywood Bowl. I thought the Brandywine Bowl would be a modest concert arena. But it's not.

It's a bowling alley. Amir had booked me into the café of a bowling alley in the boondocks. Christ, Binghamton has seen better days. Derelict buildings, grey snow. Men in plaid shirts and ball caps. Everything like a bleached-out video. But I survived the Brandywine Bowl. *Hallelujah*, as Leonard Cohen would say. And I spent the fee on a bus ride.

One of my stranger gigs. I did three twenty minute sets, all interspersed with the skittles flying and the bowling balls crashing along the gutters. No, not skittles. Pins. And dorks ordering pizza in the café and just chit chit chattering. Like starlings. I did 'Days' by The Kinks, which went down well. I sang that once at a crematorium for a friend who OD'd. Twelve of us there in a concrete box in the rain. At the Bowl I also tried out Radiohead's 'Creep', which was maybe ambitious. I haven't enough chords to make it as weird as it should be, and a bowling alley is no place for a tune like that. That's right. I like slow songs. Sometimes Amir tells me to rock it up but songs are poetry. And I'm not Motorhead.

I sold twelve of my 'On the Brink' CDs. Afterwards the manager took me out to dinner. Ravioli with a cream sauce. Real all American glop. Earlier on, I'd changed in his office and he saw me in my bra. So he gets protective. Which quickly becomes proprietorial. Doesn't it girls?

I googled you, he said. Was a teensy bit disappointed.

Why? I asked.

Thought there'd be more stuff about you, he said. And your site's down.

But he liked the YouTube songs, 'Beautiful Dreamer' done extra dreamily, and 'Island Girl'. No, not the Elton song or the Beach Boys song. My own song. About Barry Island. Redbrink Crescent to be exact. That's where I was brought up. I was always on the brink – well that's what people think is the chorus. My ever plaintive side. Then he bought me a cocktail. It was blue. I'd have preferred a Guinness.

You got nice hair, he said.

I just laughed. No I don't, I said.

I was tired. My mouth felt like I was getting a cold sore. He walked me to my room and put his hand on my elbow. Kind of steering me.

Hey, I laughed, I'm not that ancient. And I locked the door.

Creep. No. Just a kid. A kid doing well at the Brandywine Bowl, and maybe the only person duking it out in Binghamton.

I took a long soak. I could see the telly in the next room and Sons of Anarchy was on, about middle-aged Hells Angels who probably come from this part of the world. Utica, with its Vietnamese triads. Or Albany. But the room's not bad. I've poured all the shower gel into the water and it's like a Hollywood bubble bath. But the site's down. That's grievous.

Amir's spent a lot of time rebuilding my site, including new pictures. I told him to keep the gypsies. He can't understand that but had to agree. We took that shot in a suq in Amman, when we were finally sick of watching Clinton squirm in his blue suit. There was a couple selling tea out of a silver pot, all dented and blackened. Amir spoke Arabic to them but he said they weren't Palestinian. Gypsies, he supposed. The woman had the moon and stars embroidered on her skirt. The man smiled like a goat. And you know, they spoke some English to me, this couple serving us tea. English in that ancient place.

So speak some of your own language, I said. But they wouldn't. They sort of withdrew then. Amir said their language was the dark language. Only for the clan. A private speech that wasn't Arabic. I suppose I have my own dark language too. But I never got round to learning it.

You know the most Welsh I ever felt? I was about sixteen and me and two friends had a free double period. We left school and went walking in the lanes. It was cold and under the hedgerows were these scarves of frost. Ice in the hoof prints. But roses were flowering too. Haggard but still there. We drifted on, all in our uniforms, me and Jane and Michael.

And we came to Barry Zoo. We'd never been that way before. But there, as usual, was the tiger in his cage, standing on his concrete floor. The tiger that would never look at us. In his shame he couldn't meet our eyes. A tiger in the frost standing on this piss-stained concrete. Surrounded by slaughterhouse bones. We mooched around a bit and went back through the fields. Then a man passed us. In that lonely place. There was no one else about.

Bore da, the man said.

He startled us.

Bore da, said Jane.

And then I did too. I spoke the dark language. Or it spoke me. *Bore da*, said the dark language.

Michael just giggled. Wanker, he whispered.

Jane and Michael had an argument and I joined in. Because for the first time in my life, I mean outside the classroom, I had spoken another language. But I was really thinking about the manky tiger. His feet were the colour of those roses in the frost.

I'd already taken the gypsies' pictures on the Sony digital Amir had bought. And it's on the site, this couple squinting through the steam, the woman with a red scarf, the man bareheaded. I still think it's one of my best. I wrote about them, of course. A song called 'Lost Tribe', and I'm doing it on this tour. Tonight, in fact. At the Blue Tusk.

Good tea, I had said. The woman laughed and looked me up and down, while the man grinned with his big tobacco-coloured teeth. Hey, gyp. Long may you run.

I slept well. And on the dot of ten Mr Manager Man knocked on the door. He was taking me for breakfast, and then to the Greyhound stop which he claimed was not a good place.

Binghamton is sort of depressed, I said, over the Special, which was eggs, bacon, sausage, hashbrowns, orange juice and endless coffee. And me a vegetarian. Yeah, breakfast in America. You can't beat it. Then I told mein host about the UK, to make him feel better.

I was travelling with this band, The Dodgems, in a van on the M62. Say, two years ago. We'd just done the Upper George in Halifax together and the boys were giving me a lift south. But there'd been an accident and we had to leave the motorway and head into Manchester. It was wet and misty and the driver didn't have a clue. So we're amongst these redbrick streets. I was riding shotgun and could feel it getting dodgy. Well moody.

Women in burkhas, old men with their devout beards. Yeah, I pity the poor immigrant. Then it changed. There were groups of boys on the corners. Not Muslims, these boys were white.

White as corpses they looked to me. In their Adidas uniforms. Their murder clothes. Then this one street had a sofa in the middle, like a throne, with a black kid sitting on it, his weapons on display around him. Including, I shit you not, a sword.

Around us now were burned-out shops and houses with metal frames over the windows. That country's children were just one vicious sect after another. Real gang land. How it's going to be everywhere when the banks finally collapse.

So what does the driver do? The driver is the drummer, so what can you expect? The driver stops and asks how we get to the M6. Immediately there's a hammering on the sides of the van. Sound of breaking glass.

Christ, shouts the singer in the back, just get the hell out. And so we're haring through this maze and I stick 'Milk and Alcohol' on the CD player. Doctor Feelgood were the best road band ever and Wilko Johnson is still my favourite R&B guitarist. And we're all singing along to the track and laughing and generally pissing ourselves, and I even sang Memphis Minnie's 'Me and my Chauffeur' for the drummer. Those boys had never heard it before. They thought it was a driving song. Bless their hearts.

What a strange brew on the Greyhound. Old codgers, Chinese girls. All gone to look for America. We were driving past these dismal swamps, and sometimes I could see hunters in orange jackets out in the trees. But people were rare. All around us were these reeds in the wall-eyed ice. I saw a programme about how those reeds are invading the country. I think they're Chinese, and they're tall and pale and everywhere. The reeds that are burying America. Then I glimpsed a hawk on a fence post, hunched like one of those hoodies in the Manchester rain.

About 4 p.m. we swung into a Burger King. I bought a coffee and studied the men at the next table. Six old geezers, all looking eighty plus. And I thought, Jesus Christ, this must be their local pub. They meet here every Tuesday afternoon because there's nowhere else. Polystyrene cups and garbage on telly. They should be around a real fire with glasses of Saranac or tots of bourbon, telling tales of brave Ulysses. But when I listened in, it was all about rheumatism.

And the TV? It's a never-ending epitaph for this country. I did an unkind thing once. Woke up one day and Tom Jones was on *Good Morning America.* Live at 9 a.m. and still belting it out. Christ, I thought. Won't that man ever stop? So I wrote these words as a joke. Called the song 'Past It' and took the tune from Lennon's 'Crippled Inside', which I usually jump on my iPod. Slowed it down a shade. Yeah, I slow everything down. First verse was *Used to say about Tom / He was a real sex bomb /But since women's lib / He's been a damp squib.*

I did it in the KGB Club in the East Village. Some people laughed. At the end of the set this guy sidles up.

Liked the Tom Jones thing, he said.

Great, I said.

But I gotta question. What's that damp squid line all about?

Some things don't travel. Language doesn't always travel. They've never heard of a damp squib over here. Killed it as far as I'm concerned. So it's the UK only for that mother.

The Blue Tusk is going to be another nightmare. What was Amir playing at? It's a big bar in downtown Syracuse, boasting about its real ales and rare wines and whiskies. But it's a strange U shape without a proper stage. Not as bad as the Bowl but still a poor venue for someone like me. I need intimacy. Which I'll get in spades, but I mean tolerant intimacy. I know Amir's losing interest in the whole music business. It's film now. That's where the excitement is. Film it yourself, edit it yourself, be in control.

Better than the same old songs done for drunks talking trash.

But seeing those old timers made me think of Dad. I'll try to ring him tomorrow. You see, I live with him. With my dad. I'm forty-eight, he's sixty-eight. And he's a heroin addict. When he's up for it he drives a shop rider around Asda. Like a demon. Got banned once and it was on the news. He was flying the skull and crossbones and blasting out 'I Wanna be Your Dog' by Iggy and the Stooges. He's been on the methadone but now he favours codeine in lemonade.

It was the drugs that made Mum leave. They'd been classic hippies, following the music from school, living in a commune. Mum had money from her parents so anything was possible. But Dad got in too deep. Did acid, then brown. Now he's a victim, a rock-and-roll suicide, who needs a carer. Usually me. He's sixty-eight and he's wasted.

Anyway, when I'm gigging, and it's not as often these days, the council takes over. As to Mum, she met this retired fellah, Brian. He had sold his building business and bought a house in – get this – 'the most southerly street in Wales', on the coast at Rhoose Point. She lives there most of the time. They've got the Bentley, the golf club membership, the apartment in Marbella whilst me and Dad are in a flat in Topaz Street, Cardiff.

Sometimes we go down to the Millennium Stadium, him on the shop rider, or over to the Roath Cottage or The Canadian. I once did a set in the Cottage, especially for Dad. My 'Blues for Johnny Owen' always makes him cry. *Never been kissed, Johnny. Never been kissed*. And I looked at Dad and his eyes were alive for once. In that shrunken face. *And now you'll never know what it was you missed.*

Once or twice I take him to Spiller's to look at the records. But it's getting strange down there. All those apartments they've built block the light. Cardiff used to have this wonderful maritime glow. But it's lost. Cardiff has sold its soul. Like New York.

I showed Dad Bob Dylan's 'Bootleg Series: Volume 8, Rare and Unreleased'. You know what he said? Not really, he said. I know what he means. Everything comes in a boxed set these days. All the mystery's gone. We never used to think about what was hidden in the vaults. Never used to bother. Or if we did, it was with this thrill of unknowing. Because little known is best known. The mystery was a mystery because it was a fucking mystery. Never demystify life. At least I've learned that. Now every muso's so self aware they're hoarding their own shit and thinking it's gold bars.

I had dinner with Mum and her new hubby when I was last over. Really heavy cutlery but chicken from the house of pain. Free range was the least I expected. Christ, she used to be a vegan. I've changed, she hissed. And so should you.

We'd both had a drink. At least that stays the same. The house is on a promontory and the sea was filling the room. We held each other and looked into the spray coming over the cliff. We're like sisters really. There was a piano there and I plinked out a couple of tunes. Just stay in C, girl, and you can't go wrong. I did 'Imagine'. Yes, imagine that. And Mum sang along. She sang along with a crystal goblet in her hand and this hideous jewellery all over her beautiful skin. And we cried. We both cried. Brian stood there bewildered. With his brickie's hands. His redbrick face.

He wants to take her on cruises with retired bankers. The bankers who have destroyed the world. I went to the downstairs bathroom. There was a bidet there they wouldn't know how to use. A whirlpool bath with gold taps. Christ, Mum used to like the Incredible String Band. Time to grow up, Rhiannon, she hissed, when Brian went to get more Valpolicella. Time to grow up, girl.

Yes, Rhiannon. I was about fourteen when the song came out. Stevie Nicks and the reincarnated Fleetwood Mac. Just a gorgeous tune. Mum and Dad used to sing it at me. Not to me. And of course I pretended to hate it. But it's been part of my set for years, a slower tempo, just me and the guitar. Some people at gigs think I wrote it.

Tonight I was going to do 'I Would Rather Go Blind', that Christine Perfect thing. Just listen to her sing it and you can tell it's real. A woman's perfect pain. But the chords need to be sustained, like with an organ, so it's out. But it's a real bus station song. And I might do that Duffy tune, 'Warwick Avenue'. Christ, where did that chick come from? Newest kid on the block. And there are so many of them now. The bluesy girls. The winsome girls. Yes, here come the girls.

Maybe the world's trying to tell me something. My visa's up in three months and one of my front teeth is loose. So I eat with a limp. Proclivity they call my problem. Teeth are Dad's problem too. They're down to nasty brown stubs. The junkie's giveaway.

You know why he takes codeine? And all that H? To take away the feeling. The feeling of life. He lies on his bed, comfortably, unutterably numb, while the world slinks past on the Jeremy Kyle Show. His bed's in the front room of our downstairs flat. The shop rider is parked in the hall. Peer through the lace curtain and you'll see him, spark out most of the time. But dreaming. I'm sure he's still dreaming.

In front of me in the queue for the circular the little Mennonite girl looks round. She takes in my guitar case, then my leather jacket. I whisper *Beautiful dreamer, wake unto me, Starlight and dewdrops are waiting for thee.*

That kid's got a hard face. Kind of flat. The words don't seem to register, but she goes on looking, keeps peeking at me from under her black bonnet, the hem of her cloak dragging in the wet. Such a serious child. Aw, honey. It's too early for you to be in mourning for the world.

No matter how much I know I know I know nothing

In our back yard on West End Avenue was a porcelainberry vine. I loved the colours of its fruit, their turquoise enamels shining through the fall. Those heartbreaking falls. The berries were like the Navajo jewellery I saw a man selling in the street, where West End joined Eleventh. The earrings and bracelets were pinned to a blanket.

Long ways from Flagstaff, he said to me.

I looked around. Are we? I asked.

I was at Iwo Jima, he said. My brother too. Left him there. I used to help him with his English.

The man's face was dark. Skin like earth.

All he cared about was horses, the Navajo man said.

So why do I remember that? Why do I remember anything?

And now they tell me the porcelainberry is banned in New York. It's apparently a pest. They root it out, use poison spray. Ah well, I think. Ah well.

Our housekeeper would tell us that Mr Rachmaninov used to stay at 502, West End Avenue. Not far from where we lived later on. And yes, there I was, the girl from Dove Street and Kazimerz, become an Upper West Side lady. Well, that's where they told me I come from.

As to West End, I always thought later it was a melancholic avenue. It runs parallel to Broadway and is Broadway's quiet, no, tongue-tied, cousin. West End somehow thinks it might be grand. But really it's relieved to be dark and away from the burlesque. A European street, everybody said.

Yes, it was all mansions, sometimes with faces at high windows. I imagine the composer's face, white, haggard. Another concert that night for the great Rachmaninov. Great Christ, another concert. Surely that's what he would think. His shinyassed tuxedo on its hanger. Or the hateful tails. Like a man dressed for his own funeral. Then downstairs the limousine waiting, the big Phaeton ready to take him to Carnegie, the chauffeur in his purple livery smoking a Lucky on the sidewalk.

Poor Rach. All that concert nonsense when music was simply firelight on snow. The colours of the porcelainberries. And for him, the tunes not coming. The riffs, the grooves as they say on the radio. The ideas. Rach on the wrack. How he longed to get down to it, the housekeeper told me. Down to proper work. Sleeves rolled up, a shirt and dangling braces, the score like a white sheaf exploded around the Bechstein. Yet the music uncatchable in his head.

Yes, I used to imagine the composer. In the front bay. A face up there. A genius made performing flea at 502 on the West End. Such a doleful district I came to think, strong with the smell of exiles. Or that's what people said. So what was that smell? Mothballs and damp astrakhan. Chainsmokers lighting up. And the usual sight? Why, rich Jews of course, and rich Nazis too, standing together, watching their pekes lift their tiny legs to piss against the iron kerb.

Meanwhile, I was listening to the radio. It was fantastic. Little Anthony and the Imperials were always on. A neighbour here in Zichron told me they are still going strong, fifty years later. Don't be ridiculous, I said. How strange is that? And The Excellents. I liked their 'Coney Island Baby' because I liked Coney Island. Maybe it was there we went on the carousel. Or maybe the carousel was out on Broadway on a Sunday, or in the park. I'm confused.

But then, I've always thought time ran a crooked line. Like a river meandering, so it seems to run backward or even parallel with itself. The green Vistula with the ice in it? No, I can't remember the Vistula. But that's how I imagine it when they talk to me of Krakow. Or the Hudson's dirty sleeve.

In school, I liked geography better than anything except English. I liked the ideas of cliffs and rivers and whole oceans changing their shape. I liked to picture a river that flows both ways, like an underground train. And yes, my own river, the Hudson, too close to home, was such a river. Yes, it flows both ways. I loved that.

So high school was fine. My friend there was Millie. Her address was 3960 Broadway and we'd go to her bedroom with its Keep Out! sign and play her doo-wap records and eat crackers with peanut butter and jelly. Once she took me to 126 Street and we saw the crowds for the Apollo Theatre. It was late afternoon and I still had my school bag but the people were there already to catch a glimpse of Buddy Holly and the Crickets. Who were white. So it was a big deal. Some of the crowd didn't like it, and a few of the women hissed at me, the gawky girl from the Upper West Side. But Millie said it was all right. I was with Millie and Millie was a celebrity on that stretch of Broadway, a cool street cat in her tight red trews and hair piled high with a red barrette.

I could see the men looking at Millie but she never glanced

back. Not even once. She was an eel wriggling through the crowds and I had to follow as best I could. And Millie would turn to look for me and say don't get lost, and suddenly we were at the back of the theatre and Millie pushed a door and we were in a corridor and then we stepped out into the auditorium. Not a soul about.

All I remember is the smell. Women's perfume. And that lemony stuff the men used. The dance floor was like a lake of black ice. Millie wiggled her hips and spun round on her bottom on the polished blocks. Her ass was just a perfect red heart. So I held my bag like I thought you might hold a boy. Then I hugged it and smooched it, and Millie hooted and then a man chased us back down the passageway and I went home on the 1 Train.

And, yes, I remember the little cabbages. They grew on the sidewalk at West End. Ornamental cabbages with dainty leaves, green going mauve. Cabbages for show? How peculiar. The Kazimerz cabbages would have been eaten, every one. Or so they tell me. Cabbage *zupy* with dark green and pale green shreds. Stinky cabbage soup in every kitchen. I think that's what I'm supposed to remember. But I don't remember. I don't remember the attics where I was kept, or the ocean liner that brought me to New York. No, the first things I remember are the West End cabbages. And the elevator in our building. It had a mirror in it with a gold frame. That's how I came to know what I looked like. Going up. Coming down. A man polished it every day and sometimes I helped.

In 1961 when David asked me to marry him I didn't understand. I was twenty-one, and he was David. I had lived with him for fourteen years in the big apartment. Yes, I came from Krakow. Yes, I was concealed. Smuggled like a parcel from roof to roof. But I thought David was my brother now. David who had never kissed me. His older sister, who was my sister, lived with us on West End too. And their mother, who was my mother. And now he wanted to marry me.

David was exactly my age and at twenty he had started going downtown every day to the bank. With his briefcase, his umbrella. Careful David, his sandy hair already sparse, his wire glasses pebble-lensed.

The week before our wedding he moved out to the Hotel Wales, over on Madison. Sometimes we had all gone there for brunch or Sunday recitals, the whole family. They wheeled the palm trees round on castors. So David was comfortable. I stayed there too on the wedding night, and then we took the train to Los Angeles.

That way I saw America. The highways, the swamps with their night herons. Then the deserts, and one evening a herd of horses running beside the train, wild white eyes and streaming tails outside our window until they veered off. Like stars, I thought, the lather on their flanks. Soon even their dust was gone. Or maybe that was a dream, like everything else. Dream horses in a dream life, the dream horses that go round and round on their carousel, Rachel and David and Nathaniel. Where had I seen that carousel and the horses' names? On the cobbles of Kazimerz? Maybe Coney Island where we went twice a year, I think.

During our train journey there was a sign. Flagstaff it said, and I remembered the Navajo. How small the town was. But the train kept on through the parched land, the red dream desert racing away as we followed the line to Union Station. When I stepped on to the platform I stumbled. Perhaps I fainted. Our sleeping carriage had been so small. We were much too close.

But instead of taking me in his arms, David called a porter to give assistance. David wringing his hands. David my brother, David my father. David my husband in his white nightshirt, his spectacles gleaming, his jars of wintergreen and goosegrease upon our sleeping car's *cabinet de toilette*. Yes, my David. Skinny with a pot belly. Once I wetted my forefinger and traced the vein in his cock. Just like my forefinger on page after page of the atlas, following the railways, the roads, the great blue rivers. But he tut tutted and pulled down a handful of hem.

After we returned we stayed on in West End. We had the third floor to ourselves. His sister loved him, his mother needed him, loved and needed David who went downtown every day, a rolled *Times*, a furled umbrella, David who worked for Sachs until his seventieth birthday, and then said, yes, we must go. To Israel. We must go. It's all arranged.

The apartment was sold quickly, his sister provided with a place hidden away near the Nicholas Roerich Museum. West side again, on 107. Another dreary street. More cabbages behind the railings.

Now I sit outside, under the olive tree. David is comfortable in the cool room, the cedar shade over the window. The young man has hoisted him from bed to chair. A young woman will put him back this evening. David will drool, David will murmur and I will spoon him bread and milk. Sometimes I damp his lips with the local wine. Diluted of course. The Baron's wine they call it here, the best wine in Israel. I often take it myself and sit and talk to myself as I always have. And then I will read to David from the English newspaper.

No, we never really spoke, David and I. We were husband and wife, so he saw no need. As to children, there was never a sign. Never a flutter under my heart.

Yes, David spoke in announcements. There have been many great announcements in our life together. David was retiring. We were departing for Israel. But the first, and greatest, of course, was that David and I were to be married. But since his stroke it's impossible for him to say very much. So I read to him. David seems old now, a ghost in his nightshirt and diaper. Without the bright pebbles upon his eyes he looks like a blind man.

Sometimes I think it must be now that he tells me what he has to tell. It must be now. Time is very short. I don't know what he did at Sachs, but he had the same secretary for many years. Perhaps I should have spoken to her. When I looked up at him from the platform in Los Angeles he seemed lost. But if Israel was his dream he never explained it. After we bought this house in Zichron Ya'akov he used to walk out under the olives and look over the ridge to the Mediterranean. How blue it was. Like new laundry.

And then the catastrophe. Which has killed David and has not killed him. So he lies in the shadow and I sit in the shade, watching the hooded crows in their grubby frocks. Listening to the olives drop.

After we were married I always did my best. David collected things, and his favourites were matchboxes. So I helped him. Because that's what I thought a wife must do. In the mornings I would walk in Central Park and pick up the interesting boxes. I knew David liked the Dutch varieties, made by Vlinders. They had pretty pictures of the stars, like Chubby Checker and Natalie Wood. Yes, I thought. These people are even famous in Holland. And I used to think about all the Dutch people coming to New York and walking around Central Park and striking matches and lighting their cigarettes and throwing the empty matchboxes away. Sometimes I searched on Broadway or Seventh Avenue, and yes, there were Vlinders boxes there too. Or maybe, I thought, maybe it's the same man who is dropping all these matchboxes. Boy, he smokes a lot. And I made myself laugh so much I had to sit down on one of those granite boulders in the park and wipe the tears from my eyes. Oh David, I thought. David who is my David. With your albums. Your albums of matchbox labels in their little plastic wallets. Sorted by year, by country. Thank you so much, Mr Dutchman. Thank you Natalie Wood. You have made my David happy.

As I said, David communicated in announcements. One morning he informed me we were moving to Florida. Somewhere near Tampa. Sachs wanted experienced staff because Florida was exploding. The markets were exploding. Yes, that was the word he used to me. Then he left for the bank.

All I knew about Florida was the state's shape on the map. A peninsula, a dangling penis, big and sliced like David's. Florida was hot and green. There might be hurricanes. So, why not Florida? I asked myself. Anyway, it was already happening, like everything else was already happening. Florida was part of everything else, waiting for me to catch up.

We lived on a long straight road in, or near, Seminole Heights. Were we in or were we near? It was hard to tell. The houses were big and some had swimming pools. The garden lawns were being laid, trees cut down and other trees planted. I can remember walking along the road to my friend's house. When it rained, the earth smelled of ginger. The wild ginger grew everywhere, and the big raindrops rolled down the leaves of the papaya trees. David left for the bank every morning in the Impala. Then I would have more coffee and walk out to see Robin.

Yes, my friend Robin. She lived a mile away. I would step out through the wet air and the long cars would pass and the ginger smell ooze out of the ground and the raindrops would sparkle on the eucalyptus leaves and I would think: yes, this is me. This is Florida. This is my life.

Robin was my first friend since Millie, and she was the last. She taught me about daiquiris and manhattans and we would take our glasses into the pool in her garden. The hummingbirds would crowd the feeder, and Robin would fix another drink, and maybe another, and we would take off our costumes and stand together in the water, our breasts touching, our breath tasting of peppermint or strawberry or whatever Robin had put in the pitcher. David never liked any of that schmutzy stuff, as he called it, and Robin told me that if I had a problem, that was it. The schmutzy stuff.

Then Robin would make a salad and a papaya shake. She grew fruits in her yard but there were so many they shrivelled up. Or just lay on the earth. I used to wander the garden touching the mangoes, the oranges. Once I saw a snake under a tree. Striped, thin as a whip. After lunch Robin would drive us into town to the American Picture House. Sometimes we were the only ones in the theatre, shivering together in the aircon. Even for *Apocalypse Now*, we were almost on our own. I thought the napalm was all around us. I couldn't look.

And yes, I remember once, after a movie, we were across the street having coffee. Or maybe Robin was drinking a martini. Usually we sat at a sidewalk table but Robin preferred to be inside the dark saloon, out of the glare. How mysterious it was in the bar. The shapes of men came looming out at us. Once, I asked her who the Seminoles were.

Hey, honey, Robin laughed. Better watch out.

For the Seminoles?

Sure, she said. You're living on their land.

But they're gone.

Oh yeah? From Seminole Heights maybe. But honey, we're still at war.

War?

Yeah, war. With the Seminoles. They never surrendered. Or at least they never signed a treaty.

Aren't they dead? I whispered.

Well, most of them, I guess. We did a pretty thorough job. But they're still hanging around, out there in the Glades.

Then, Robin winked. You'd be surprised, she said, who's living in the swamps. What's left of them.

I thought of the old Navajo again, his face the colour of the red rocks David and I passed on the train in Arizona.

Then Robin was laughing. She was always teasing, especially when she was tipsy. She wore coral pink lipstick. Even in the pool. Her mouth was like a hibiscus flower. Oh Robin was beautiful, and yes, now I see she was my best friend. Robin could hold her breath so long underwater, I'd get frightened.

Woosh, Robin would gasp, coming up at last. Hey chicken, fix me another.

I was always listening to the radio. It played in the kitchen when I was getting David's dinner ready. Robin would drop me home and I'd have to wipe her lipstick off, and I'd do meatballs and mashed potato, and sometimes 'On a Carousel' would play. By The Hollies. I'd bought the single in New York, years earlier, in its Imperial sleeve. It was Top Ten on Billboard. Round and round and round and round and round and round and round and round, the singer sang in his odd voice, and my head would be spinning too, and I'd think of the horses, dream horses,

David and Rachel and Nathaniel, the carousel blue, the horses dappled grey with their names in gold, the poles that held the horses polished by all the children's hands, the top of the carousel like an emperor's crown in a fairytale, and the singer singing about changing horses. Then the Impala lights would swing into the driveway and I'd put the skinny green beans to steam. They needed only three minutes but David liked them soft. So five minutes. David always said give them at least five.

Coming back from Florida was the last long journey we made. Until, that is, David said we were coming here to Zichron. So when we were back in New York, I would walk across the park to the museum to see the dioramas. These were huge paintings on glass showing all the American landscapes. I'd seen some country from the honeymoon train, the wetlands, the deserts, but in the museum I was close up. Some days I would stand staring for hours. There were eagles and bison, grizzlies and chickadees, with real autumn leaves and poison ivy. There was the red wolf too, that lived in New York before it became New York. I gazed into its eye and saw myself.

At first I asked David to come to see the dioramas on the weekend, but those were his album days when he'd trawl through the catalogues. And mother was ill and he'd be on call, he said. And sister might need him, our sister Rebecca who played the piano in her room and combed her hair and cried. Yes, we were a quiet family.

But once we went to Washington DC. Once we stayed at the Carlton Hotel. After that I started to dream. I didn't dream every night but when I dreamed it was the same dream and in every dream I spoke. I spoke what I heard on the soundtrack to the film they showed. This is what I said in the dream.

Visiting the Holocaust Museum is profoundly moving and enlightening. At the Carlton Hotel we can also make it comfortable and convenient. We will secure your tickets in advance, arrange for late check-out on day of departure, and do whatever we can to accommodate your wishes.
The Carlton Hotel is conveniently located near the museum, the White House and other historic sites. Our accommodations are elegant; our services impeccable. Our restaurant, Allegro, is one of the city's finest. Weekend Museum packages are available at $185 per night and include deluxe accommodations, two tickets to the Holocaust Museum and Sunday brunch. For reservations, call your travel planner or the hotel direct and ask for the museum package.

And in the dream I would go on speaking.

In Kazimerz the mist's a mere where I mistake the moon for a mattock. And such mist. It rises from the Vistula and rolls over the brass founder's and the vulcaniser's, the tenements and the pasture.

At dawn I watch that mist rising in the streetlight. It sweeps the ground like a peacock's tail. But now the traffic unfreezes and my driver makes up time and soon I am in the queue for coffee with condensed milk, and there are Doktor Mengele's twins ahead of me, white as wishbones, both now at the counter with plates of dumplings and sauerkraut, ladled from the vats by an apple-cheeked peasant girl.

Next I walk under the gate. Arbeit Macht Frei *it says. Strange that the people who made this place chose those words. Because, in a way, they were right. Work makes you free. Yes only work, the right work, makes a human being free.*

Then, I begin to count.

Ten thousand shaving brushes. Two thousand kilos of women's hair, fifty pfenigs a kilo. The bookkeepers' pride means every monocle and magnifying glass still exists. All the better to see them with. Such clerical diligence. The bookkeepers' ink the barbed wire where corpses hang.

Now what's this? The starvation cell. I look through the spyhole. After sixty years, Father Klobe is still praying. And here? The suffocation chamber. Then here? This is the room where darkness itself has been imprisoned. When I listen closely I can hear darkness pacing the floor. In the dusk the latrines are a cabinet of blown eggs. And there in the corner? That's the nightsoil bucket fog has filled.

Yes, maybe it's night. Somehow. The moon a scythe rising. Head in a hood I hold a hand before my face and watch it dissolve. On Dove Street I disappear from myself, am translated into different dust. No matter how much I know, I know I know nothing.

What this fog means is I go where there's no going. There's no flow in this field. A folkless film has fallen on the world. Yes, the fog's an agony on this field. The huts have their unhutting, the chimneys are iron corkscrews trying to pull the earth out of the earth. Ten thousand shaving brushes will not sweep this fog away.

Now the next day. Time's speeding up. A sun is rising in an irrigation ditch. That sun a spool of copperwire. Out of the mist the bald faces of the corncrows.

Hsst! Here's the Sonnokommando. On the double or we're for it.
And yes, the Doktor's twins are singing in my head. There at the counter with their rations, identical twins and identical portions. They sing:

You will not hear the dog,
nor the trambell in the frost.
You will not taste the white borsht.
Your ribbon will be lost.
But when you step from the ramp
you will live forever.

Strange broth indeed. Teeth in a gold crucible. Blood in the yolk. I know I know nothing no matter how much I know. Outside, the floes of fog groan in the grass.

Ah fog, I think. Old friend. You're the Führer, fog. How we need the good old fog. The strongman who stands on his eyelashes.

And the dream has stayed with me. Since the Carlton Hotel I've dreamed it all my life. No one left alive knows my history. But there are those who would create it for me. David said he was taking me home. To the olive trees and the Baron's wine. That's all he knew, he said.

As to mother, she told me I was safe. Safe at last. Wash your face, child, she said. Wash your face.

And Rebecca? She would play me her tiny tunes. But where in my life have I heard a trambell? And what has become of Nathaniel?

Fellow Travellers

Mic

August 13, 5 a.m. Hackney, London

He awoke. For some reason he had been dreaming of the bushes, the piss-smelling bushes near Skanderbeg Square. People camped there, hung their wet clothes on the branches, shat right outside their bivouacs. Because there was nowhere else.

Once Mic and one of the men on the demolition crew had been drinking arak. It wasn't Mic's idea, he normally hated the stuff. Homemade arak could blind you. But something bad had happened, the boss had shouted and sworn, and his friend had led the way to an underground bar near the Hotel Tirana, a cellar with a few tables and dirty glasses. How they had cursed fate, cursed bosses. There was cement dust on Mic's hands and the seams of his clothes. This had been one of his worst jobs.

Mic had woken up in the bushes, not knowing where he was. And tonight he had been dreaming, dreaming again of Skanderbeg, its statues and invisible beggars, the bushes where the lost people lived.

God, thought Mic. His mouth tasted of arak. He had been dreaming about sleeping and waking and now he had woken up. There was a pain in his head. Which was the pain of the dream. And a noise somewhere. Which was not part of the dream. It was the hostel noise. But a different noise.

In the hostel dormitory there was always someone getting up, coming back, snoring, weeping.

Once Mic had tried to read by the light of a tea candle, but the protests were too much. He thought of a torch under the sheet but had no torch.

And it was hot. It was London hot, the air unmoving in the room, the windows painted shut. The heat was coming out of the walls, out of the London clay. For two days there had been thunder from a white sky. But no rain. 'Close' was the word the English people used. 'Bloody close,' they cursed, as they trudged through the suffocating streets, disappeared into holes in the ground.

The hostel windows were illegal but no one would care. The hostel was temporary. It had been temporary ever since it became a hostel. What had it been? Some kind of school. The men slept in one of the classrooms, women and children in another. In Mic's room there was a blackboard still on the wall, words written upon it they didn't teach in school. But you learned them there anyway.

One of the Roma had brought in chalks and had drawn a woman, a white and yellow woman, voluptuous and cruel, a woman with a mane of yellow hair, belisha breasts, a swollen vermilion vulva like the London Underground sign. The sign said *Mind the Gap*.

This woman leered above Mic's bed which was pushed against the wall. Mic hated the drawing but dared not rub it off. The woman was holding the Union Jack, flying it above her head. Beside her was a man, a huge man who also brandished the flag, a giant warrior who served the woman, a giant who held a gun, his cock a gun barrel too, his body tattooed with English words. Love and hate. That's what his body announced. Love and hate.

Mic looked up at the pair in the gloom. Soon it would be dawn. He needed to piss but couldn't make the effort to get up, go out of the room, go down the corridor to the boys' toilet, the urinals with their green beards, the cubicles with smashed doors and more drawings, more love, more hate, other monstrous women, other warriors with guns and missiles and swollen cocks.

When Li failed to turn up at St Pancras he had waited for two hours, abandoning the Champagne Bar to lean against a pillar outside, watching the entrance. By midday, he knew she wasn't coming. So he decided.

Mic walked to where Li lived, a terrace off Junction Road in Archway. Of course, he knew the way. Often he had stood in Bickerton Road and watched her door, the men entering, emerging, the English men, the Nigerians, the little Chinese workmen, neat as shuttlecocks. They came from the supermarkets and the restaurants and the laundries, these Chinese men, some in uniforms the colour of garlic skin. But Mic had never approached the door.

That day he knocked and was admitted.

Li, he said, showing his money, showing all his money. For Li.

The Chinese man in his Spurs tracksuit, his dark glasses, had laughed.

No Li, he said. New girls now.

And Mic had pushed the bankroll at him and said, No, Li. Li. Then the Chinese man had pushed him back, one hand against Mic's green Neil Young tee shirt, and said new girls now, and Mic had pushed and pushed and then given up. As he knew he would give up, Mic on his heels as the man pushed him out, as he knew the man would, Mic crushing the money back into his own pocket, as he knew he must. And there was Mic standing outside the slammed door, Stanis beside him, hand on Mic's shoulder.

See, said Stanis.

They went home and on the way bought six litres of White Lightning at Costcutter. Then Mic gave Stanis some money and he came back with amphetamines. Stanis had already lost his job. Three days later Mic had not been into work and Greendown told him he was finished.

Mic considered this. It meant no autumn in Hyde Park, no vacuuming up the plane leaves, no watching the lovers unpacking their picnics, or the girls in their school blazers and chicory-blue check dresses. How Mic had loved to watch those girls, those honey-coloured foals, school socks white fetlocks, the joy in them, the black mercury of their limbs as they raced over the grass.

Yes, how he loved the park and its people. He would go back and speak to Obi Wan and Obi Two. They weren't so bad. They knew he was a good worker. One mistake, that's all it was. One black mark on Mic's record.

His head still ached from the dream. But what had that noise been? And where was he now? On a bench in Hyde Park, smelling the cut grass? Under the Skanderbeg bushes, waking up with the arak ache, some angel pissing a golden shaft out of the sun?

It had sounded like breaking glass. Glass breaking as dawn broke. A man asleep on the floor beside him suddenly rose up. The sheet fell away and he stood naked, head to one side, listening. He was a black man, cock quivering. Eyes white.

There were other noises, and voices in the corridor. Then a woman's shriek, far away. Then an explosion.

All the men had woken now. The Roma artist was squashing clothes into a plastic bag, one of the Bulgarians shaking himself like a wet dog. Mic sat up. Mic the dreamer, Mic always the last, Mic who might have married Flutura if she had stayed, Mic who saw his mother folding the dollar bill into that tiny parcel.

It occurred to Mic he was going to die. How strange, he thought. To die in London. The idea made him smile. He saw his mother again. Every spring she had taken him to a wet meadow and told him to pick sprigs of horsemint. Then she wrapped them in damp newspaper and they carried them back to town and sold them in a market. And Mic, still in bed in the dormitory, realised that it was only women who had bought the mint. Never the men. Mic would sit on the street, his fingers smelling of the herb, his hands smudged with wet newsprint. No, never the men. But Mic would have bought the mint. Of course he would. Mic would have given a mint posy to Li, bought her a mojito, minty in a frosted glass.

Now language boiled. The hostel languages, angry and incomprehensible, were tearing at the windows and doors. Someone had called this place *the spike*, this place where people arrived who could not move forward, could not go back. They were speared by that spike. And the languages were melting. They were all melting into one language, and how quickly that language became one word only.

Fire, said all the different words for fire. *Fire*, shouted the Roma artist. *Fire*, whispered the Bulgarian, the Bulgarian who never spoke.

Fire, breathed Mic to himself, Mic who could smell varnish burning, Mic who breathed in smoke, a smoke worse than arak or the bushes where the searchlights never shone, Mic who stood swaying on his own bed, a scrum of men trying to open the dormitory door, the sealed windows breaking, the woman on the blackboard smiling her invitation and waving the Union Jack, the giant beside her strafing the room with the flame-thrower between his legs.

Macsen

August 13, 4 p.m. Old Mint Street, Valletta, Malta

If you look at the map I'm already halfway there. Halfway to where I want to be.

Where I want to be is a lecture theatre with maybe five hundred seats. Expectant atmosphere. And within it is a huge sexy hush.

The screen's already up, the equipment tested. We're ready to roll. My translator is brilliant yet not ostentatious. She is certainly striking, with pale skin and spidery eyelashes. Another one, I'd say, with Iranian blood. Yes, Shiraz and its shining shrines.

What follows is a small delay. We're thirteen minutes late. And then there I am, walking into the auditorium. A good linen suit and appropriate stubble. And, inevitably, granted the publicity, there is applause. Timid at first, then echoing all around, the clapping, the voices of greeting and welcome, the lecture room alive. And the people are standing. Yes, they are standing to welcome me back. After all this time, after the travails of this country and all my foreign travels, it feels as if I'm coming home.

Good evening, ladies and gentlemen, I say. In Arabic, of

course. My translator is smiling. She opens her hands as if to say she has nothing to do. And the audience is gazing down, young women rapt, young men tensed, a phalanx of academics who have brought their best students.

Even now the hall is darkening, the DVD starting. And my film is commencing. There on screen is one searing image. The star-shaped entry point of the first Tomahawk missile in the ferro-concrete of the Amiriya shelter in Baghdad.

That star is the most astounding thing I have ever seen. And yes, you know I have seen astounding things. You must know that by now.

Film there, Nazaar, I said to the cameraman, all those years ago. And I'll remember that direction all my life.

Nazaar, there. There.

I watched Nazaar turn and direct the Sony, watched him flex that steady hand and arm, saw the camera's green light come on, a cat's eye in the murk where we crouched with the scorched and the scarified and the dead.

Umm Ghada herself was just off camera, an inch out of shot. Umm Ghada, in her black, the guardian of Amiriya, was nodding her head at the Sony's faint whir.

Dragonfly wings, I had always thought that Sony sound. A child's breathing. Lost now, that camera. With so much else.

Christ. How long has that image been hidden from the world? Hidden in its film cartridge, hidden in that brown sports bag filled with film cartridges? Then hidden in a drawer, a car boot, hidden in an attic? For so long hidden, the great image that will help the world understand itself. That image is a poem that pulverised concrete, a maqam of Baghdad daylight streaming in to make a pool on the shelter's cement floor. A terrible spotlight.

Yes, that's how my film starts. My film at last re-edited, restored. My masterpiece alive, its fifty-five minutes and thirteen seconds reborn from all the hours of tape, from all those boxes and bags.

And the film ends as it begins. With that ragged white star. With the audience looking out of the Amiriya darkness into the irreproachable day. Just as I did. As Nazaar did. As Umm Ghada did. The three of us gazing from the charnel house into a new morning in Baghdad.

Genius I think, though I say it myself. That image. That edit. As if we are all in the shelter. As if the shelter is the world. The shelter that did not shelter the children that earlier morning as the Tomahawk came down, its nose cone chequered like a clown's trousers.

Yes. I'm halfway there. That lecture theatre is in the National Museum of Iraq. After the screening, the Foreign Minister presents me with the medal. Men shake my hand. Women blush as they come forward. And yes, here is Nazaar. Nazaar is alive after all this time. Yes, here is the real hero. And I hold his arm aloft and the audience salutes the man who cared for the camera as he did his children. But of Umm Ghada there will be no trace.

Yes, that is how it will be in the museum. Next year or the year after. But one day soon.

Melitta is on her roof again. I can see her there from my window. I have the top apartment, Number Five. She is Number Three. Such a colour she is, there on her rug. Milky coffee, I think. And a constellation of moles on her right shoulder. There she drowses with her cup of mint tea and her John Grisham. Perhaps she does not realise I overlook her roof. Perhaps she does. My window is narrow, with a wire gauze nailed over the outside. Perhaps she thinks I cannot see. Perhaps she thinks I can. But there she lies. Naked, oiled. Her hair a cable. Her arse a black crucifix.

Hello, Max, she will say on the stairs, looking at my red hair.

Hello Melitta, I will say.

How is Triq Zekka treating you? she will ask.

It's wonderful, I will say.

And your work?

It goes well, I always smile. Very well.

I'm glad, she will say as she unlatches the door with its iron bolts and she steps into the white light of the morning, or the unearthly mauve of an evening thunderstorm here on the island of lightning.

Triq Zekka is Old Mint Street. I've been here a month. Cheap because the ablutions are not what they might be. Because cockroaches wave their arms from behind the plaster, the plaster that falls and lies white in the webs, grey in my hair.

Cheap but good enough for me. Oh yes. Since I arrived, I'm a new man. Or a man renewed. Because at last I know what I should be doing. Yes this is it and this will be it forever.

I am a writer. I am a film maker. I am an artist. I am all of those. Fifty years it has taken me. Fifty years to find the courage to tell the world what I am.

The film is here. All its hours on a table in a room you might say is my kitchen, my film amongst the teabags and winebottles and heels of yellow bread. I'm doing a paper edit, so the time I buy in the studio isn't wasted. That's my main project. You know that.

But since I arrived, I've met many people. So many *klandestins*, as they call them here. Valletta is their capital and I am writing about them, filming, interviewing. Yes, this is my work too. Every morning I awake and cannot wait to start again. Every night I go to bed and immediately fall asleep.

And such a sleep. I know I dream but what those dreams are is not yet revealed to me. Yet when I wake it is if I am wrenched from a radiance. No, I've never worked like this before. Never slept so deeply.

There she lies. Amongst the lead flashing and the lightning rods. The island girl, girl of Triq Zekka. Melitta grows roses in a bowl, she has herbs in Mr Men pots, a washing line with her knickers pinned up with coloured plastic pegs. All over this city there are roofs like that with girls like that. I think of the fishmongers' stalls in the market, the golden lampuki all laid out.

I know Melitta has her own story to tell. We've talked about the strangers arriving, the Africans who cluster under the olive trees, gazing out to sea.

But now I'm at work. This is what I do. I'm transcribing an interview from last week. Not long ago I hated laptops. Today this one contains my soul. Touching the keys is a holy act. A ritual of love. Here's what I type:

The Soldier's Story

There was a man I sometimes saw at Leone's. We would talk, and one day he told me his story.

Yes, I escaped, he said. Came here in the bottom of a fishing boat. The crew threw me out on the north side of the island, not a crust in my pocket, not a word of the island's language in my head.

For months, maybe years, I had stood in the black land. There were the stars, as thick as leopard fur. And below the stars was our platoon. You could predict each one of us: clown, psycho, clerk, coward. Which was I? Apart from such conscripts there was only one real soldier. The sergeant.

We knew that out there in the desert was the madman's army. We could see their campfires and sometimes the plastic wrappers from their rations blew into our camp. Some of our boys would lick the sugar off the cellophane. But we all understood that their army was as poor as our army, as afraid as our army, as badly equipped as we were, our guns without bullets, our boots without laces. And we knew they were as stupid as we knew we were stupid. And like our army we knew the other army would be full of beggars and boys and pederasts.

It seemed that I was always on guard. But there was nothing to guard. We were guarding the border but the border was a straight line. On one side, a grain of sand. On the other side, another grain. I used to look at the ground where the border was written and try to understand. Surely it should be a special place, a border? Maybe it should be a holy place. So why such straight lines? Were the emperors so bored they required their draftsmen to draw the border through mountains and mosques and grazing land, separating the kid from the goat?

No, they weren't so careless. There was oil in the north. There was oil in the south. But in the middle there was nothing. So the people from the middle stole the oil.

I patrolled the wire. Right, left, up, down. Up and down I looked at Rigel. That star was the left foot of the conqueror and that was a cold light. Right, left I gazed at Betelgeuse. That star was the right shoulder of the conqueror, and I found no comfort in its urn of ash.

Out in the dark there was sometimes laughter, sometimes screaming. Just like our camp. And some nights the sergeant would appear. It had to be in darkness and he came silent as a sniper, creeping along the wire towards me.

Look, sarge, I would say. I'm on your side.

Though he did not reply his mouth would make a bubble. And then he would laugh, a dark man the sergeant, from some southern tribe, black hair on his belly and his billyclub with a bloody ferrule.

Washed was he? Where was the water to wash in the Badiet esh Sham? There was no pool there, no tarn and no tarp to trap the dew. Even in that dry air he smelt like a mule.

Whose side? he would whisper.

And I would look at the whipcord in his cock and see that the border ran even there.

Whose side? he would hiss.

Your side, sarge, I would answer, the wind blowing, the sugar papers trapped on the wire, Orion and the madman's stars almost overhead.

Such a story. And everybody who comes to the island has a story like that. So now their stories are my story. Here on Old Mint Street, on Triq Zekka where I live on sour wine, on bread and honey, here at this stained table I have discovered duty.

And did I tell you? I meant to tell you. Melitta is coming tomorrow. She will be the first one to hear what the soldier said. Then she will sit and sip the Zeppi's prickly pear liqueur I have bought and she will see the laptop screen blossom with one white star. And then I will explain to her everything that lies ahead.

Maria

August 13, 9 a.m. Anthem, Arizona, USA

Anthem is forty miles north. Not so far. But it is a problem today. And maybe a problem tomorrow. But she doubts it. And the day after? There will be no more problems. Because the day after, at least the Honda will be fixed. Jesus has promised her. Two days max. But he will be repairing it in the street because Jesus doesn't have a garage. So Jesus will turn up this morning and get to work on the avenue where she parked, one hundred yards from the apartment. Jesus is her saviour. And unmarried too. Bless him. The car will be almost untouchable today.

Every morning, when Maria walked to the car, she was surprised to see it still there. But the gangs would never take a Honda Civic. A powder-blue Civic with primer patches? No way. A Civic is an invisible car. It speaks of insignificance. Of poverty. Oh yes, Maria had chosen well. Maria had chosen as she had always chosen. Maria knew how to choose.

This is the place they say the bus will stop. Yet to Maria it doesn't look like a bus station. It is a car park with a few bigger spaces crossed by white lines. But there is an office and the woman there with her orange lipstick and orange hair tells her in Spanish, yes, the minibus will come. Soon. Maria had tried to explain that she needs the bus to stop on the highway, that, for mercy's sake, she doesn't want to go all the way to Flagstaff. The woman had shrugged and rolled her eyes.

Maria thought about where she was going. She was going to Anthem, to 509 East Adamanda Court, off North Fifth Street in Anthem. First day at the job, her new job with the Chernowskis at their wonderful home.

Anthem, Jacob Chernowski had told her, is not merely a town. It's a lifestyle. When Larry died, Maria had gone to the service.

You were so good to my father, Chernowski had told her at the Mortensen King's Funeral Center. So good. And Jacob had taken Maria's fingers in his damp fingers, stooping over her, the wurlitzer CD playing as an accompaniment, 'The Breeze and I' leaking out of the sound system like old times.

Three months later Jacob had turned up at the Sunset care home in Black Canyon City. They had sat on the bench under the cottonwood, the Goliath Laundry van come to deliver, the sun dazzling off the Chevron sign.

I'll come to the point, he said, looking down at the dead cottonwood leaves. Mrs Chernowski's not so robust. The new place in Anthem is such a big house. Keeping it as she wishes it to be kept is… arduous.

He seemed pleased with the word.

Yes, arduous.

You want me to…?

Yes, he said. Please. And once again he had taken her hand.

Of course, we can offer a fair salary. Perhaps something better than…

The Sunset's been good to me…

As we would, smiled Jacob. As indeed we would.

In the end, Maria had to scream. The driver didn't want to stop. He said he couldn't stop, that there was nowhere on Highway I-17 he was allowed to stop.

But there is Anthem, Maria shouted. There on the right. And they were passing it. So Maria screamed and the driver braked in a cloud of gravel and the Navistar behind blasted its klaxon, and as soon as Maria's feet touched the road the minibus was moving away, workmen laughing and waving in the back, and she was on a ledge spread with chippings and Wendy's wrappers, and from there it looked a long way down into the as yet unincorporated town of Anthem.

At least she was wearing the right shoes. That was how she saw it. When God gave a woman big feet he made sure she learned about shoes. You give, you take. Maria went sideways down the hill, past a fallen saguaro the colour of bad teeth, over broken kerbstones and piles of cement. The ground was loose. She slid through the goldenbush in a slurry of Heineken bottles. But at the bottom the earth was baked firm.

Maria crossed a culvert where an arroyo might run, yellow plastic tubing coming out of the ground, empty oil drums everywhere. She climbed up the other side of the stream bed, and stood where she hoped a sidewalk might start. But there was only the road. And no road sign.

She looked around and breathed out. It was hot. Maria knew how hot it was. It was 116°F hot. She was usually correct about such things. And she thought about Jacob Chernowski's hands, clammy as the air conditioning at the funeral center.

So, this is Anthem, she smiled to herself. Anthem was completely silent. Not a soul. Above, far above, a hawk was a black cursor in the blue.

You live, she thought. You learn. A lifestyle experience. A lifestyle like the grave.

Maria turned to the right on nothing more than a hunch. Somewhere nearby was 509, East Adamanda Court. The blinds closed, the air cool. Mrs Chernowski would be lying in her bedroom. Soon Mrs Chernowski would require Maria's tomato soup. Yes, soon that soup would be a vermilion shadow on her lip.

And downstairs, Jacob Chernowski would sit at a computer, waiting for his software update. He would come out to the kitchen and enquire about *nopalitos*. There was lots of prickly pear, he would venture, in the back yard. Sometimes he stooped to sniff their pink fruit.

Maria's shoes were dusty but she was humming to herself, humming 'The Breeze and I' and adjusting the grip of her modest overnight bag. Next time she comes there will be no such trouble.

Nerys

August 13, 11 p.m. Theodore's salvage yard, Bridgend, Wales

The Captain says I can burn some of the wood in this oildrum. Those rotten spars, he says. The chapel wainscoting that was already wormy when he pulled it out of Nebo.

So tonight I do it. Chill in the air, summer mist like a spider's web. Soon there's a fire and it's alive in the stained glass, the windows they took from a pub in Cardiff, the Brain's blue diamond flashing indigo at the night, the glass in the yard leaping out at me, yellow these stars, the red almost black, red as that girl's black blood I once saw on the roadside in Chechnya as we marched past.

I melted the dinosaur today. Jason's let me go, he says there's nothing on. So I'm in the fairground full time. Rides, odd jobs, whatever they want. Unscrewed a Sky satellite dish this morning, off the Showman's Motel. Up a ladder so it was hard to get a grip. In the end I had to jemmy the bracket away, and the dish came off in my hands. But so light, it had rusted through. I didn't think they were supposed to do that but the sea air eats anything. Gets behind things, the boys say. Gets inside you. And then we did the dinosaur in the wood.

There used to be a model village there, houses, shops, blue-painted bay. But no one's interested now so we bust it up with mauls and shovelled the tiles into the skip. Over in the trees there was only one dinosaur left. The fairground people used to charge trippers to wander round this prehistoric park, there were even cavemen the boys told me, and the trees like tropical trees. Tall ferns, sharp leaves. But that's mostly gone. Some bigshot's building a house there for his kids.

I looked at this dinosaur. It had eyes like traffic lights. Like these salvaged traffic lights here winking in the firelight around me. Huge thing, that dinosaur. Life size. But made of plastic, so I could pick it up myself. I got the chainsaw, cut its head off and put it in the incinerator. Watched those eyes melt away, the teeth dissolve, the smoke all black and yellow, me coughing, throat stinging. Then those spines on its neck, its armour, then the green-painted belly and then the long tail, the very long tail I sawed into strips like firewood. And apart from the ballast it was hollow inside.

So that was it. The dinosaurs are extinct. Just a pool of plastic left on the firebricks. Somebody came over complaining about the smell till the boys persuaded him to leave. And it was the boys told me about this place. Because although the fair's busy now at peak time, the money's not there. Plenty of people passing through, the boys say, but they're looking, not stopping. One of the rides has been playing 'Money's too tight to Mention', blasting it over town.

There's a last bus out at eleven. I get to this recovery yard by half past. And that's enough for The Captain. He's the owner. Says it's just, just about good enough. Because he's in all hours. So I'm here all night till seven, home by eight, start in the fair at twelve. Four hours sleep if I eat on the job.

Sometimes the Captain's around when I arrive, and then we

sit in his cabin. I love it there, charts on the wall, golden gimbals off a gyroscope spinning on the desk.

He says himself he's out of date. Admits he hasn't a clue anymore what's in the yard. Everything's done cash. So I've told him, look boss, I could put an inventory on a computer for you. First rule of buying and selling, I say, is know your stock.

Where you from? he asks me then. But he always asks me that.

Vilnius, I say.

Oh yes, he says. Docked there once. Nice port.

And I smile and say nothing and he might get his brandy out and we have a tot each, but only a tot, because he has to drive home, he says. Be up and at it all over again in the morning.

There's no room to move in the cabin. There are two glass cases with a stuffed owl and a stuffed magpie from Penyfai Primary School, a moth-eaten hound the Captain says is from the fair. Even Nebo's harmonium with its ivory knobs.

By about 2 a.m. he'll have told me the history of half the junk in the yard and the taxi will be waiting by the padlocked gate. Know him of old, they do, the Captain, the Captain waddling through his alleyways and avenues between the banisters and the newel posts, the graveyard angels with their outspread wings and marble bibles, the big old-fashioned chimney pots like the crowns of pantomime kings.

When he's gone I'm left to it, guarding his empire, the world he's salvaged and stored at the arse-end of an industrial estate. First the stone, the lintels and the gravestones, the cracked kitchen tiles and the immovable farmhouse flags. Then the wood, the rotten gates and rottener window frames, the doors stacked like playing cards. I've seen a school honour board from the 1930s around here somewhere, gold writing on black wood.

Yes, a man's time comes and a man's time goes.

In these light nights and early mornings I've wandered the yard but still don't trust my way. There are aisles I've never explored, rusted dead-ends, caverns under tarpaulins where whatever was precious is now mould and ash. He's tried to protect it all from the weather, but as the boys say, the wet gets behind things. Buckets where nails have rusted together, like sea urchins. Toilet bowls with cushiony moss, a grandfather clock with a pendulum seized at the waist.

But when I sit with him in the cabin I feel relaxed. Yes, maybe I'm home now. In Vilnius they are ripping the old things out, stripping it, selling it on. As if they are cleaning themselves of our dirty history.

Where you from? the Captain asks, and I smile, but Vilnius is vanishing even as I speak. When I wander these lanes at night, between the stone and the wood, the doors and the mirrors, I almost feel I am back in Uzupis, the walls crumbling, the iron street lights crooked across my path.

Maybe I'll keep on at the Captain about the inventory. Better than scraping varnish at Hafan, and the rides have only six weeks left. Virgilijs says he's going home then.

Now in the firelight the angels loom over me, angels of the dead with their empty books. Sometimes I stroke the angel wings, the angel breasts, but they're cold as the gods of Soviet spring. And in the firelight, in this yard, I might be in the forests once again, passing round the birch sap, that sweet, spunk-coloured wine we all drank then, talking about freedom, but never dreaming it would be like this.

Big Little Man

August 13, 7 p.m. Druid, Saskatchewan, Canada

This time he was driving a Cherokee. It made him feel tall, its rusty red the only colour on that prairie. He put it in park and looked at the map again. West of Plenty, east of Superb. Yes, surely, he had arrived. This was journey's end.

The Big Little Man stepped down to the dirt. There was nothing forgiving about this earth. Summer baked it, winter provided an impenetrable exoskeleton. In Huangshan, the earth had been black. Or red, perhaps. Red as the Cherokee. But how soft the earth was at home and how the water buffalo loved to wallow in its pools, the pigs to bury their snouts in its velvet. That was good earth where the tea bushes grew, the tea gardens his parents tended on the hillside, where he crawled under the greenery as the stars came out, staring into mantis eyes.

Here I am, he said to himself, and the Big Little Man touched the demon's face he carried on a cord around his neck, the grinning dragon-demon carved from water buffalo bone, a gift from his sister when he told them he was leaving. Where was that sister now? In Huangshan, selling sunflowers and the loose green tea she picked herself, an old woman still living with the pigs, eating with her fingers from the bowl.

He stretched and scanned the horizon in every direction. Yes, he must have arrived. The map assured him that this was the town of Druid. But of Druid there was no trace. No roadsign or ruin knew Druid now, Druid on its map of silence. True, four hundred yards away a grain elevator broke the skyline. He followed its dazzling azimuth, the prairie on all sides silvered by dust in the irrigation ditches.

Everywhere there were tyre tracks in the dirt, as if men had arrived and waited, waited and chewed gum, waited and spat. And then driven on. Or been taken away. Yes, that was it. Taken.

Very good, the Big Little Man thought.

At last. At last he understood. Druid had vanished. To the final paling. The whole town had been taken. Druid had existed and now Druid did not exist.

And its people? Its horses and pigs, its shock-shot Cherokees and rusted Rancheros, its satellite dishes, its children's bikes? All cleared away.

No, he thought. Not cleaned up. But taken. Their possessions were taken when the people were taken. Everything they owned was taken. So they need not be afraid.

The Big Little Man looked up. The sky was darker now. Soon it would be green-black, with fire within it. There was one star in the north. The star was getting bigger, the star was as great as the Buddha's light his mother had showed him once in the mountains, the misty mountains where the cloud clung to his skin and they stood on a ledge and looked down on an ocean that was not really there, looked down from Heavenly City Peak. Then from Purple Cloud Peak.

Train coming, the Big Little Man said to himself. Train coming with its grilled headlamp, its white ditch lights. And he laughed, the star bigger still, the northern air rushing over the dust.

He thought again about the girl. As he had arrived, the girl had disappeared. On the hourly bulletins he heard of search parties, difficult terrain, a girl in stonewashed jeans and saskatoonberry sweatshirt.

Once, her father had spoken. Everyone was hushed. Her father talked uncertainly, with a trace of hurt, suspicious of the silence he discovered grown about him. He was unable to explain how a twelve year old had dashed away to hide while her sister counted ten, one hundred, ready or not, and kept on hiding.

Maybe a grizzly, someone said, igniting old stories of bears running into the woods, children plucked like pasque flowers from the sweetgrass. Old timers nodded. Child smell. Young meat. They brought bears round.

But all the bears were microchipped, the phone-ins said. And slowly that girl went missing from the news.

It was darker yet. The air rushed by.

Train coming, said the Big Little Man. And closed his eyes.

Juan

August 13, 5 p.m. Roadside outside Cachi, province of Salta, Argentina

They found a room above L'Aquila bar in Cachi. There was no aircon and the town baked. He and the woman lay abed, the woman who had trusted him, the skinny, redheaded woman, lying in her sodden underwear, delirious beside him.

Juan remembered the journey. The land rolling on. Telegraph wires, burned forest, a strawberry sow belly-belted to a tree. He had studied the birds. Doves, parakeets, and, like sentries, those villainous, anvil-headed hawks at the roadside, some glory crushed to grimness within them, a carrion majesty.

After that room another room. Bed, table, a window over the Ninth of July Plaza and its palms. Shoeshiners packing up, waggling their thumbs at each other, those flat and ebonised thumbs. And the fan's engine, the soundtrack to their days, plastic and brass grinding together, impossible to ignore but how quickly he learned to ignore it, turning on the television he would not turn off, despite the woman's protestations, surfing towards the Disaster Channel.

First item. On an interstate a Buick Skylark rear-ended by a Mustang. Again and again the impact, the fireball, and how they blazed in the room, those celebratory blue lights. About suffering we are never wrong. Or satisfied.

Usually he slept. Occasionally sipped from their carafe. But life lay in between, down a corridor where one nightlight burned like a cactus flower and the woman squatted above her blood in the *baños*.

But what was that? What had it been? A flake, a flame, something furred that was flung against her face, the redhead screaming, something flying through the room around her, over the bed and the basin, over the TV which talked of Starbucks in the forbidden city, while all the rest was Mastercard, flying, flighting.

The woman held her red hair in a tight ball, other hand between her legs. Then the something had moved again. The something chased its own reflection out of the mirror and against the walls.

It was a mist. Soft as a mitt. A moth. Only a moth. Yes, but such a moth. He looked at this moth's face. Ghost Aztec. A bishop in his chasuble. What was a moth but an old man buried in his country's flags? A broken toreador? Now there it was above the bed, its blood the dust of tapestries.

How silently this moth moved within the television glow. And how it amazed him, this moth. And terrified the woman. This moth his muse. Its wings two maps of black isotherms. And gone. Christ, where had it gone? she screamed. Where its shoon should be was only a shadow. A dream of dark matter. A moth out of Juan's mouth and mad as a mother.

And the woman's headache came on. In her eyes she said, an insane sun, malbec's violet chaff in the wineglass. She said that her skull was opening. Her head was becoming a TV screen and her bones turning to ferro-concrete, there on the bed beside him, there on the bed her head split wide and grinning, her scream coming out of the screen of her face.

Meanwhile the fan blade swung. Down in the square a shoeshine boy lay under a palm, oxblood in his hands, head on a stolen loaf. It's unbearable, her scream screamed. No one could bear this.

Next item on Disaster had been a Campari bottle beneath Vesuvian ash. Then Icarus tumbled in slomo, again and again, Icarus' fletching aflame, Icarus falling and lying broken, his face erased so they might not identify the dead. And there was Daedalus, rapt, grieving for Icarus his son, born of a slave.

But up had leapt Icarus from the beach, Icarus unfolding himself from the scrunched Kleenex he had become, Icarus' feathers reassembling themselves into wings, so there was Icarus whole again, a hawk in an unblemished sky, as back towards the labyrinth they went, Icarus and his father the terrible engineer, and down again plunged Icarus and up again in resurrection, and once more he dropped, red and ragged, to rise again. Then the woman slept and they checked out in the morning.

You can never go back, Juan says to himself. Never can. But here goes. And he has a good reference. Better than that, it is an impressive testimonial that describes how Juan has managed Dave's Tavern for two years, planned the menu, ordered the wines, and ensured Dave's had become one of the cult places in mid Manhattan. Signed by Mary McIninery, owner. Juan is proud. Of course, he has written it himself. But wasn't that how the world worked?

Ten miles back there'd been roadworks on a bend and an inexplicable delay. In all that desert a red light and one man, one man powerful in his isolation, preventing them moving on. Juan had left the engine run until he saw the temperature dial too high. After thirty minutes the traffic light had turned green and they had moved off, but the damage was done.

Now they are stopped in that high desert, above them the mountains banded copper and bronze, the cacti twenty foot tall, the candelabra cacti that confirmed the woman's nightmares, the condor too a demon she willed to exist, that creature one of many she summons from her nightmares, the cockroaches, the lizards, and now the condor swimming in the oceans between the peaks, the carrion-seeking condor, floating down.

Juan has burned his hand unscrewing the radiator. The steam is rising between them.

He strokes her brow. All the big talk, he thinks. And what is she but just another refugee from the midtown meltdown, a madonna in wraparound shades who wanted her life changed, wanted to write her travel blogs but stay with what she knew.

So here she stands, a skinny creature under the candelabra, its thorns long as hypodermics, its flowers red against a narcotic sky. How quickly her skin has disintegrated, the pieces of her scattered in the desert they had crossed, the ravines.

Cool it, Anna, he keeps saying. This is what you wished for. And we'll be there soon. We'll be there tomorrow.

And Juan describes where they will be. A green swale where the grapes are growing fat in the Andean air. Their first job is to translate the wine labels into English, make them exciting for the connoisseurs. Then the breakfasts for the tourists who will come, the picnic hampers, the evening meals on that wide estancia with its streams and its corn and its orchards.

And Anna sniffs and smiles and nods her head, Anna who had come into Dave's Tavern that day, brave Anna whose restaurant blog was quoted by the press, Anna who had stood beside the denim slab of Peevo, taken off her sunglasses and peered about herself until Juan leaned over the counter and poured an iced water and smiled, Anna who now waits on the hot shales of a world she never dreamed could be so vast, Anna under mountains naked of shade, Anna beneath these cactuses on their plain of crucifixion.

It's going to be wonderful, Juan insists. Trust me.

Fabien

August 13, 9 a.m. University of California, Santa Cruz, USA

Pony Tail didn't show up much now. Yet he did Fabien one good turn. Pony Tail found him a residency. This was at the Dolphin café at the pier's end, Santa Cruz. As far out into the ocean as anyone could walk.

Three evenings a week Fabien would trudge there to set up. Then Darius who worked weekends would bring Fabien coffee and a plate of homefries with tapito hot sauce.

Darius was a young man but his tee shirts always said 'Old Guys Rule'. Fabien knew the brand. Fabien knew the old guys too, he knew that at the end of the pier and everywhere else, The Purple Palm included, the old guys ruled. Old guys like Pony Tail. These same old guys had played with the Grateful Dead when the Grateful Dead were glad to be alive. These same old guys had smoked weed in that alley in Chinatown before it was renamed Jack Kerouac Street. 'The older I get the better I was' was written on one of Darius's Old Guys tee shirts.

Whenever Fabien looked about him he saw the bikers, the surfers, the poets, and they were all old guys. That was the strangest thing about this country. Whether he was in Venice or up here in Santa Cruz, the old guys never died. The old guys hung on and on. The coast was full of them, these old guys. So Fabien sang 'Yesterday', staring at a girl on her own table in the audience. Smiling at the girl. The rest of the crowd were old guys and their fearsome old women.

Yes, he knew the old guys' schtick. Longboards, seventeen-minute drum solos and macrobiotic munchies. Down the pier other old guys lined the railings with their rods and Rizlas. It was these old guys who last year had seen the blue whale that stopped in the bay.

Never a spout like it, they said. Before or since.

Would the old guys never die? he wondered.

Fabien thought of Olimpio's children playing in the gutters' rainwater, of Mauricio trying to ride the capybara in the Tiete undergrowth, and that fat sow squealing and shitting as the Santa Rita passengers urged him on.

When Fabien stopped being a child he had abandoned the city of children. He had left Olimpio behind but knew it was still the same. Only more traffic, more drugs, more knives, more babies, more children, more children splashing in the gutters, more children standing in the fountains made by the Santa Ritas, the red rains of those arroyos soaking the new children of that young country, his country getting younger all the time, although the old guys ruled there too, of course they did, that was the way of the world.

Hey, the girl said. Can I buy you a drink?

Fabien looked at her. Jeans, walking boots, tee shirt that said Audubon Society. More old guys, he decided.

Sure, he smiled. I'm due a mojito anyway.

The next day she was waiting at the bus stop for him. The same clothes, the same scrubbed face. The driver had the radio tuned to KSBW's Action 8 News. Prince Charles and Camilla were talking about visiting an organic farm. Then it was Paul McCartney, starting his tour in San Jose. The girl looked at him and laughed.

The Big Sirs, she said.

Fabien didn't get it but he knew she had made a joke.

The journey took twenty minutes. Then she rose and rang the bell and they stepped off into the middle of nowhere.

I've brought a picnic, she told him.

Good, he said. I'm hungry. It's so early and I'm so hungry.

Her name was Magdalene. She led him down a track towards woodland. Fabien could smell the sea but it was different from the other sea smells. This was a sharp smell. Battery acid, he decided. A smell like the bus station at Tiete. And he smiled at the thought and wondered where Mauricio was at that moment, and Maria, big-hearted Maria who had refused to hurry when Security had escorted them from the Bar Unique, escorted them all the way down in the mirrored elevator. But he had sung three songs. Three songs for high society, the couples applauding politely and never guessing he was not the official cabaret but a boy from Olimpio in a shirt off the back rail.

They walked through the yellow grass and entered the trees. It was gloomy there and very still. Fabien rubbed his eyes.

Okay, he laughed. Where are they?

Take your time, Magdalene whispered. They're all around us.

And they were. They were all around him, but he would never have noticed without the girl showing him, the girl in her hiking boots and green tee shirt, her scrubbed face and black scrunchy.

The monarchs, she whispered.

The thousands of butterflies hung like leaves. They clung

together for security, in shivering hives like red lampshades.

Oh yes, he smiled.

They come all the way up from Mexico, she explained.

Yeah. Like the people.

And they had both laughed. When they found a clearing Magdalene started to unpack the food, while Fabien told her about Olimpio, walking home one early morning and watching the maids and the mothers with sweeping brushes knocking the moths off the porch ceilings, off the lightshades and the lintels, the black moths bigger than the women's hands, black and furry moths as big as vampire bats, an indecipherable writing on their wings, the moths of Olimpio that were as much a part of Olimpio as the children and the rats and the hummingbirds and the cars. Once Mauricio spread a dead moth over his palms, saying it would make a perfect bikini. Fabien recalled another moth with spurs on its wings that he had chased out of their bathroom once, its golden mothdust on his face.

The next morning Fabien woke up in the trees. He was in Magdalene's room at the Santa Cruz campus of the University of California. From the balcony, all he could see was the redwoods, their crumbly bark oozing moisture, their everdark greenery covering the slopes. And the air was a pharmacy. He breathed its physic.

I'm starving, he said, and soon they were down in the refectory where a sign said 'the Devil drinks Nescafe', and Fabien ordered hash browns, bacon and scrambled eggs that Magdalene paid for, and then they came back to the room.

I heard a noise last night, he said.

The twigs, she smiled. They tap the glass.

He looked out again and there were other students awake now, girls high in the trees wearing pyjamas, girls in little shortie nightdresses up there in the branches, shaking out Golden Grahams or opening tubs of strawberry froyo while a pair of stellar jays dived through the foliage.

Wow, said Fabien.

My favourite birds said Magdalene. Aztec birds. And you know something?

What? Fabien was now stretching luxuriously on her bed, wearing the Audubon tee shirt moist with her redwood sweat.

All the students have been warned to keep the windows shut, she laughed. This is mountain lion country. But, you know what I really think?

What you really think?

I think a lion came in last night.

And she laughed again and stroked his tawny skin, and Fabien laughed and reached over for her orange juice.

Yes, I'll get you the union gig, she said, pulling the shirt over his head. But you have to promise one thing.

Only one thing? What?

No more Yesterday.

No. No more Yesterday.

And the jays came screaming past.

El Aziz

August 13, 3 a.m. Babylon, Iraq

Five hundred rooms? No, six. Six or seven hundred rooms. One day, I will count them all. They will come, I believe it, the fat Kuwaitis, the bankers with their pensions and their women dry as cork. They will come, because that is what we are told to believe. In that respect, nothing has changed here.

At Woodlands, there was an old man who gave me money. Steradent denture tablets, he'd say. More Steradent. Extra strength. And I would go to Tesco for him and bring the Steradent back and show him the packet and put it in his cupboard with all the other Steradent packets. And he would fumble in his purse for money, tell me to get more Steradent. More. At once.

And yes, I took his money. No one came to see him. No one looked in his cupboard. And then, after a while, he would give me his card to use at the Tesco cash machine. No relative had taken his card away. No neighbour. Thank you, Walter, I would say, as I held his cock and he dribbled into the bottle, teeth fizzing in the glass. In the dead of night. In the dead of winter. His cock in my hand. Thank you, Walter.

Yes, sometimes money is the easiest thing in the world. In my room with the pipes groaning I would look at the stacks of purple twenties from Walter's account. Pretty soon I knew the only transactions would be the ones I made. All timed and dated. When I started to take his money, Walter had seven thousand pounds. All he wanted was his teeth cleaned. All he wanted was his cock, the colour of a twenty, held between my finger and thumb. One drop. Two. His poison warm on my hand. Perhaps Walter is still there in room 23. There's some don't have the wit to die. There's some who grip too tight.

It's too hot to sleep. I rise from my divan and walk the corridors. Yes, I still wander at night. And sometimes I come to this other room to look out from the balcony. There is no number on the door yet, and the walls smell of plaster. I sit and smoke and think of the Andalucian palaces. Perhaps every man should own a palace. With egrets on the pools, their filthy nests. Every man should own a balcony and when he cannot sleep he should stand in the darkness and gaze out into the world.

Below me now the river people have lit their lanterns and the lights move quickly over the water, like someone writing there. Writing with fire. The cement mixers have stopped for the night. So even at the hotel there is quiet. When I listen I hear the river in the reeds. Twelve, fifteen years ago I would leave Aadam leaning under the Ishtar Gate, his cigarette my compass, and I would walk down to the Euphrates and take off my clothes and slip into the river's darkness and reach out with its velvet upon me, the shivering sheath the desert had warmed, that midnight had chilled to a black oil.

On the far bank I could hear the people's radios, sometimes a man singing, a man playing the uwd, overhear the heartbroken music of Baghdad, the great maqams of legend, of love denied and love forlorn, then a mother calling her children away from the Pepsi stall. A mother gathering her children from the dusk. And I would roll in those waters, swim and roll over and over, like something pale snared in the nets, a dolphin from the Discovery channel, a river bream leaving the shallows in the shadows, whilst the grains of the Euphrates mud would rise around me, Babylon's grains, the red Babylonian mud from the secret places now hidden by the river, the river that would take me if it could, as it had taken Nebuchadnezzar's bones, the edicts of the caliph, all the plastic bags from the suq.

And I touch the key I carry, the key on its chain around my neck. The key doesn't work now. I have tried it, but there is a different gate today. A different lock. When I ask about Aadam, people shrug. Aadam was the keeper, they say, the keeper of Babylon. But who keeps the keeper? And they smile as if they have said something wise. Something I should learn.

What they mean is that nothing stays a secret long. Even in this place, this place of all places, where the mouths of the innocents were stopped with salt and stones. Especially in this place.

Here at the palace, which is becoming one of the greatest hotels in the world, they are very good to me. I speak English. And English makes life easy, they say. Who say? The managers say, the mysterious men in their black Mercedes, they say it. These men park exactly where the earlier men parked their black Mercedes, the crocodile's men, who parked in a circle like a black sundial on the cliff above Babylon. Perhaps they are the same men. But Saddam has gone. At Woodlands I sat in the lounge one night eating chocolate money and saw a rope snap Saddam's neck. Heard the hangman's curse that sent him to hell, a hell deeper than Babylon's dungeons and latrines that now lie beneath the river bed.

Soon, they say, I will stand behind a desk in the marble foyer and greet the sheiks, the European politicians and the women who smell of frankincense, who are tanned the colour of the temple walls. There are such plans. They will dredge the river and build a jetty. Boats will come, cruise ships full of tourists eager to see our civilization.

But Aadam too is dead. He is dead with all the others. I remember a party of diplomats arrived once, unannounced. We sold them dates and maps. But they wanted to see Babel, they said. They wanted to see where the tower stood, where languages coiled like water snakes in the river below.

Certainly, said Aadam. So we locked the gate and took them outside the city walls, climbing high over the dunes, beyond the mosque of Ali, the women stumbling in their scarves and pashminas, the men in sunglasses, silk ties. And by and by we came to the crater, the quarry where Babel had been and still was.

Here, said Aadam. Here. Look.

And he pointed down to the last bricks, the Babel bricks, mudbricks they were of a shepherd's hovel, a few wretched walls where some beggar might spend the night and shit in the morning and wander on, blind with raki, soon to die.

Of course, the Babel babes didn't like it. The men in Ray Bans, they had come a long way, they said. And they didn't like it either. Yes, they hated this pisspoor and silent Babel we showed them. Hated it so much they refused to pay Aadam. And we all trekked back across the sand, sand in our shoes, sand in our hair, no one saying a word. Only Aadam, who was whispering to me as we led the way back. Never seek out trouble, he hissed. It is already on its way.

Tonight it is too hot to sleep. Even with its marble floor this room will be intolerable for the guests when they arrive. But when I stand at the desk in the foyer, the managers have explained to me that a great golden propeller will rotate above my head. That the air will smell of almonds. And maybe, I think, the air con will moan like the uwd as the elevators rise and fall through this labyrinth that the crocodile built and never visited. Yes, its breath will surround me, cool as the midnight Euphrates, tugging at the key that I carry upon my heart.

Lloyd

August 13, 9 p.m. The Travellers' Club, Pall Mall, London

They looked at me and I didn't flinch. No, not once. That's the first time I've ever used that word. Already I think I love it. *Flinch*. Almost a finch. Ha ha.

Last year, last week, I'd have, yes, flinched. Oh yes. But now things have to be different. So when those Nigerian hospital workers and the scrawny, squint-eyed, shifty Albanians stared at me, I didn't flinch. No sir. I just stared back. Just ignored them all. But gave this fit black girl a great look. And she glanced away. Yes, she flinched. But then she glanced back and smiled. And I smiled too. And then I gave her another of my new great looks. And she turned away again with this gorgeous grin on her face.

And then we were at Marble Arch and I was getting off. Getting off in my tuxedo on a summer evening, a man in a shiny black suit and red dickie bow, the crowds passing, the Greendown workers in their tabards trailing across Hyde Park, and me diverting to Speakers' Corner. Just to stand there. At the centre of the world. Just to whisper *actually Alice, I'm not boring at all.*

Got off there so I could stroll down Oxford Street. Strange to say, I'd never done that walk before. But it was a warm evening and the crowds seemed to part for my black suit and my red tie. Yes, that's what clothes do. Maketh the man. And on I went, all the way down and through Soho. At my own pace. With all the time in the world, saying *actually Alice* to myself, because I liked the sound of it. Actually Alice, the red buses, the black cabs, the swarms upon swarms of stressed-out faces coming out of the pit at Tottenham Court Road, they all seemed to pause and let me through. And on I went, across Piccadilly with the foreign students under Eros in each other's arms, and on into Regent Street, and I found it no problem at all. The Captain's Cabin.

A pub I'd never heard of. I had imagined John would say the Red Lion. Now that's the famous one. That's your traditional English boozer in its cosy alleyway. But John's canny. So The Captain's Cabin it was. And there sat John at a corner table. On time for once. John dolled up. A black suit, a black tie. So I was pleased with myself for choosing red.

Well smart, he said, hefting the bitters off the bar.

Not so bad yourself, I said. But, actually Alice, I knew I was 1-0 up.

I stood my round, of course. There were a few hoorays in, tanking up. But we sat there in silence. Looking at our watches. Then John said it was time, so we went back out into the summer evening and walked over to Pall Mall.

Just me and John, smelling the air, feeling the thrill. The thrill of London. Cheaper than dexies and better for you. And I couldn't believe it. There I was in my tux and there were these other types in their tuxedos and their smart caz and their inherited bling. Just taking it all for granted.

Money? I could feel it up my arse. In my nostrils. Money and history and empire seducing me, and me wanting to be seduced.

To be overwhelmed. Totally. These American kids passed us. All the correct brands. Their skin shining, their hair like hair that had been genetically improved. John looked at me. Outside the Royal Opera Arcade, pell-mell in Pall Mall, a race of warlike angels had come amongst us.

Clock them, he said, out of the corner of his mouth. Not a trace of doubt in their perfect teeth. The fears that infest us unknown in their blood.

We stepped aside as they strode ahead. In their white socks. In their imperious So Cals. Left us breathing the Tommy fucking Hilfiger of the master race.

Yes, you're right. I had a chaser with the second pint. Drop of Dutch. But that was two hours ago. And now I'm sitting by a roaring fire. Yes, a fire. In August. And my tie's awry and I'm full as an egg and there's a brandy in my hand and I'm thinking, this is it. The life.

But the occasion? Our birders' society annual dinner at the Travellers' Club, an arrangement that has lasted for one hundred and thirteen years. Mulligatawny, beef and roasters, spotted dick. Or lemon tart for the enfeebled. I had both. *Duw annwyl*, as my nan used to say.

John's off somewhere, pissed on the tawny port. Got into some argy bargy about this full Monty webcam thing. Seems the Royal has put a camera in a Montague's harrier's nest. Yeah, Britain's rarest raptor. On telly every night like *Big Brother*, but please, please, don't anyone tell me anything about Big Bro ever again. Actually Alice, I hate *BB*. So I backed John up on the Monty business. He's really outraged. There's a gang in front of another bloody fire in another bloody lounge, debating the rights and wrongs.

This Travellers' Club is a maze. All the African explorers were members, all the South Seas island hoppers, the Antarctic heroes. In this room there's a photo of some naked New Caledonians under their stone-age sky, drawings of painted Patagonians before they became extinct. Imagine it, running round bollock-naked on a glacier.

But it's Alice I'm thinking about. How she'd have loved this. The high life. Alice has a purple dress, just a sheath, all shimmery. I've seen her get into it, wriggling till it clings where it's supposed to cling. Very low cut at the back. Daring in fact, but Alice's back is her best feature. It tapers. Tapers like a candleflame. I've always told her that. Because she's a bit skinny up front, is old Alice. Two fried eggs.

Or she might have worn one of her short things, with black tights. Then, when Alice crosses her legs, she makes this rustling sound. Like something electric. Or a blackbird settling itself on the nest. It's just amazing, that rustle. You know, like the sound when a fire catches. When tinder takes.

I've been talking to Dave, the Kentish plover man, about Alice. You can see Kentish plovers all over the world but for Dave only Kent will do. So that's where you find Dave. On the pebbles at Dungeness. Training the binocs around St Mary's Bay. Even down the Old Kent Road. It's a quest, I suppose. Lots of the blokes here tonight have quests. There's Silvertown Clive and his overwintering whimbrels theory. Another chap says he's only interested in house sparrows. Most endangered London bird, he says. It's what London's all about, he says. Those little Cockney sparrers.

But as to Alice, well Dave listened and shrugged and said, yeah, women. That's what he said. And made a farting noise with his armpit. Forget her, he said. And remember this, he said. This club forbids women membership. Why do you think that is? So think on, my friend, he said. Think on.

And you know? Maybe that's what I'm going to do. Forget Alice. But I can see her crossing her legs and hear that electricity she makes, and when I remember everything we had, it's bloody hard.

John just passed through. Stuck a reciprocal brandy on the table for me, and is now showing off one of his ledgers. Seems there's an anomaly with a Sussex shrike. That's another word I like. *Shrike. A shriek. A strike*. Another word I never used till I met John, John who must be up at 4 a.m. tomorrow to tell the sorters where Minchinhampton is, or Zoffany Street. Back on the morning shift. His choice.

Zoffany, by the way, is where John and his mum live. It's also the last street in the London A to Z. As John keeps reminding me. Quite the traveller was old Zoffany. Shipwrecked on a desert island, he and the survivors cooked and ate a cabin boy. Straight up. Would have been right at home here.

There are birds at the Travellers' Club of course. Painting of a Great Auk, photo of a wandering albatross. And the mementoes of all these geezers who just had to get up and go. But me? I can't move from this leather chair. If there was an emergency, I couldn't budge. I'd sit here with all these books about aristocrats starving to death in the Thar desert, the plant hunters with seeds sewn into their clothes, or some toff sailing to Blighty with fifteen different tropical diseases in his blood and the feathers of a bird of paradise in his trunk.

But now Kentish Dave the plover lover is back again with a print-out of all his sightings. And here's a funny thing. Somehow my red dickie bow's come off. Somehow it's knotted itself around my fist. I hope it's not against club rules.

Zuzanna

August 13, 11 p.m. York Place, Bridgend, Wales

Dear o Dear o Dear Kazia

Because it's another Red Square moment. Sorry. But you know me. You know me better than anyone, don't you Kaz? You haven't written because of the wedding preparations. But I'll be there. Not sure yet if I'm coming on the coach or getting the Wrocklaw flight, then bussing it. But I'll be there. I'm so looking forward to it all.

But maid of honour? Rather spinsterish, don't you think, Kaz? Not that spinsterishness appals. No, spinsters intrigue. And do they spin or weave? Was Rumpelstiltskin a spinster? Was Shane Warne? Oh well.

Whatever, spinsters are sexier than just about anyone. I see myself with irongrey hair and a red headscarf, my bicycle bumping over the Kazimerz cobbles, haiku and a pot of basil in the wicker basket. I have a flat, with hollyhocks in a tiny garden. And I'm rather bad. Yes, bad. Which means good, of course. I'm on my way for an alcoholic supper at Alchemia after a great day's *Hard Expectations* at the Jag. I'm meeting a student with pale skin and long eyelashes. Sex indeterminate, but I think she's a he. Not that I'll be fussy by then. Hey, maybe I'm not now? Oops. Erase that.

Yes, maybe I'll have a reputation. Not safe in seminars. Keep the door open. O dear o dear Kazia, do you think I'm normal? I think I'm normal. But normal's not normal now. It's just I don't fancy the big bollocky men in their big bollocky Asda jeans. With their bollocky bull terriers. I like my meat lean, Kazia. As you do.

That's why I've noticed Virgilijs in the fair. Sometimes I watch him go round on the waltzer, round and round till my head is spinning, that's one spinster clocking another, Kaz, and it's like I've finished another vod! But then the ride slows down and Virgilijs is not a blur anymore. There he is, laughing at me, helping the children out of their seats. Like a kind schoolteacher.

He lives with Petr in a caravan in the Backs. Suicide Alley they call it, just off the Ghetto. It's so horrible there, it's rancid, Kaz. I thought the caravan would be utter squalor. But they've made it beautiful inside. There's no shower, so they have to cross the yard, holding their little flannels in the rain and the wind. To hide their manhood, is the expression you're searching for. How sweet is that?

Petr made some kind of soup for me last night, bellypork and beetroot leaves. That's Lits for you. Mostly we speak English, though Petr has Polish too. Petr's plump, and older. He's worked in Kaliningrad and tells mad stories about mad Russians, and has a tattoo of the Kaunas devil on his arm.

But Virjilijs is an angel! He reads the English newspapers from the bins, and says his favourite novelist is, yes, you've guessed, Charles Dickens. He did *Hard Times* in school! His tattoos make him look like the Roid Boys, but he's not half as pumped up. And Kazia, they're so trusting. They showed me all the money they've saved. Hundreds and hundreds of pounds, all in plastic bags under the caravan floor. Fifties, twenties, rolls of tens. They count it every night as a ritual.

You're insane, I whispered.

Now you know our secret, Virjilijs said, we'll have to kill you.

Then Kaz, after the meal and the cider and their Lithuanian moonshine, we went swimming. I kid you not. A midnight swim on the huge beach, and those two planets close together beside the moon. Are they Venus and Saturn? You can see them from over there, Kaz. Do you look up at the cosmos with your darling dentist and ponder the starry particles? Oh, I know you do, dear Kaz, I know. And we stripped off on the town beach under the lights strung down the promenade, people shouting and screaming in the Ghetto. As if they were drowning. And we ran and ran over the wet sand. The sea was way out. It was incredible, Kaz, I thought the sea had disappeared, even though there was a white line in the distance where the waves were breaking. And I was down to my grey bra again, Kaz, and I thought no, just do it, and I peeled right off. Knickers too. And so did the boys.

Now Petr, he's a little Lithuanian dumpling. But Virglijs? O Virgilijs is a Baltic shark. How he knifed through the neon surf under the lighthouse. Naked, Kat. All of us naked and wild. Wild as children naked in the night. And neither of them turned or said a word. Nice tits? No. Nice arse? Never. Just ran past me, feet slapping like fish, and plunged in and I plunged in and nearly died. Nearly died, Kat. On a hot August night at the fag end of Europe.

That shocked the homebrew out of me, the horrible cider we'd passed around in a plastic bottle big as a fire extinguisher. And yes, I thought. Spinster or married, boys or girls. What's it matter? I'll sit in Alchemia's candlelight and nurse my cup and remember the black beach under the neon. The promenade lights on their whistling ropes. Because that's the beach where I dived in head first, the beach where I thought, wouldn't it be great if the Roid Boys dived in, if the Mutant Crew dived in too, under Venus, under Saturn? Good conjunction or bad? Well, I don't know. But it must mean something, Venus and Saturn, twins in the sky.

And I felt as if I was washing it all away. Because if we can get out of our heads surely we can shed our skins. Washing all the *gowno* away. And soon the water was warm around me and I put my head under the waves. You know how I hate that, but I felt sleek and lithe. Felt free. The boys were whooping like swans. And then we all found one another and we walked back across the beach under the esplanade lights. But in the decent darkness.

And that's my pension, Kazia. When I'm down to my last few zlotys, or the red cents of the European Union, which God preserve, it's the beach I'll remember. The beach that will see me though my irongrey spinsterishnesses. Call it my intellectual pension. Yes, I'll remember running naked under the pink Welsh moon, my arse wobbling like floodlights on the water.

Don't worry, I'll write soon, Kaz, and tell you how I'm coming back, and when. But first let me work out all the other things I have to do. All this complicated astrology.

Love from the wild side, your Coney Beach Butty Baby, Zuzi the Banshee

Rhiannon

August 13, 7 p.m. The Broadway Dive, 2066, Broadway, Manhattan, New York

Yea, heavy. And still gigging. Still gagging. But it's going to stop. I'm in the Broadway Dive where Amir and I used to come. Once this bar had peanut shells all over the floor. Seemed a real pit, but it was the shells made it famous. Cleaned up now but at least it doesn't gleam. No, no gleaming. So it's bearable.

But the old woman's gone. She used to sit in the counter corner, skin like a beermat. Cracked blue heel hanging out of a slip-on. Peppermint schnapps right up to the bevel of the bar.

About two blocks away, the Plaza's shut. That's even harder to take, our favourite cinema becoming apartments. Think. I'm never going to feel that Plaza darkness creeping up my skirt again, the spongy red carpet with its dorito pieces. And all the posters went straight to collectors. Very knowing.

Yes, think. Because when you think you know New York, when you think at last you're used to something, they immediately tear it down and you're on the back foot again. Scuffling for dimes. The Afghan restaurant we used to love? That's gone too. Gone overnight. The Cedar Tavern? No more. All gone, all going, all up for grabs. And what's replacing it is not for me. Not for me because it's not my time. We all have a time. It comes, it peaks, it has an eternally sad falling away. All those little stones that make up a mountain? Falling away and slithering down? That's *scree*. Yes, scree. What a great album title. Scree. And I'm on the scree, honey. I'm going down. Screaming.

Does that sound old? Well at least I'm old enough to know what I don't like. Look, I'm not fucked and I'm not busted. But I'm facing up to things. Next week I hit the big five. The lion at bay. And next week I'll be home and if I ever come back here there'll be bigger changes than a cinema closing. Than some new landlord sweeping a floor.

Next week there's a party I don't want. My mum's idea, mum seventy and sexy, tanned by Marbella, not the tube, and mum's partner, a great big bewildered builder called Brian who lucked in big time, who's so generous to me I could cry, his champagne already in the booze fridge, yes, they've got one, they've got everything, Brian's hands so gentle on my waist that time we danced in the twilight, shirtsleeves down to hide his ruined tattoos, a gold hooped earring that might have made him rakish, but doesn't, because there's no gypsy cool in Brian.

Dad too. I'm taking Dad to the shindig. Dad who might nurse a shandy in his wheelchair and sneer at the canapes. Sourpuss Dad, last explorer of the vinyl frontier. Yes, fifty. Dad's girl is fifty. Fifty, her empty womb. Fifty her hairy nipples and fifty her loose front tooth for which no tooth fairy has a remedy. Not that Brian wouldn't write a cheque. Not that Brian wouldn't be absolutely desperate to pay.

And, you know what? I'm going to take Brian's money. Oh yes. Because teeth are different. Teeth count. Especially here, teeth count. They count in the united states of teeth, they count here in the Manhattan of teeth, and on the Broadway of teeth

teeth still and will count. Even above 100 Street teeth count and will count more with every passing year. Teeth will count as they tear down the cinemas and build the highrise. Teeth will count as they sweep the floor and put the Guinness up to seven bucks. Teeth will count all right. The currency of gleaming teeth. I think of my father and his codeine-killed brown stubs. Nicotine brown, my old man's mouth. Goat breath.

But, as I said, it doesn't gleam here yet. Not quite yet. So I push at my tooth with the tip of my tongue and make a big smile at the room. Then take another black mouthful. Pouring the blackness into myself. Which might be a lyric. Oh yes, oh boy, another lyric. The waters, these black waters, these black waters of oblivion. Only some bastard has got there first.

I've tried, but I'm having problems keeping up payments on the Inwood place. The landlord wants to know about the next six months. Yes, I hear you. Ask Brian. Tap good old Brian, because it's easy for Brian, Brian with the hot tub he doesn't use, the golf clubs and golf cart he doesn't use, the computers he never switches on. Because Brian is a simple soul. What Brian wants is the midnight-blue Alpha Romeo Spider with that creamy leather interior.

The same colour as meadowsweet, Bri, I said to him.

Is it, Rhi? he beamed. That's nice.

Brian parks his motor at the golf club where he doesn't play. Or Brian stays home because Brian has the full Sky package with 24-hour sport on the telecinema. Let's see. Aussie Rules. Snowboarding. Girls in little gold pants playing beach volleyball. And panels. Panels of pundits talking stats and transfers, lists of the greatest-ever Kenyan middle distancers, the best Brazilian World Cup freekicks. Ultimate's the word the pundits use. So Brian uses it. A lot. Everything is always ultimate for Bri. The big man's word in the big man's world.

Oh, and my mum. I think Brian still wants my mum. But Mum is older than Brian, and on dodgy ground because of it. Her face is lovely, heart-shaped and strong. But as to the rest? Someone left the cake out in the rain. Now if Bri had anything close to an imagination, she wouldn't get near. But there's no accounting for lack of taste. So, yes. I could ask Brian about the apartment.

Course, love, course, he'd say, delighted. Have to come out there one day, won't I? Glad to see you doing so well.

You know, sometimes I feel Brian looking at me out of his life of Brian and I can guess what he's thinking. Bet she's never had a shag. That's what Brian's thinking. Well think all you can, Bri. But if I'm going to tap him twice, maybe it's not for the room. Because Amir says he's given up on the US. Amman's the place now. The place for film, for digital, the place for Amir. Where his parents happen to live. His melancholic mother. Cheap, he says.

Amir wants to make a film about shepherds in the desert. Their life in a landscape like another planet. No water, black rock. But a purple sky all shot with stars. Then, a film about the Tower of Babel. Amir says he knows where it is. Or before that, a short piece called 'Suq of Souls', about the market he took me to in Amman. You see, Amir's bored with the tours. Film's the future.

Move on, he laughs. Or else.

Or else what? I say.

Or else I send you back to McDaddy's in Big Stone City.

Not Big Stone City, I say. No, daddy, no.

Now I cross to the bar and pick up a Jacky Dee, double, because this is my last before the gig. It's a special gig tonight. In a museum. Usually they have classical duos there, or po-faced poets from the shorn lawns of academe. But I've been visiting the Roerich for months now, a hidden-away brownstone over on the rather discreet One Hundred and Seventh Street. Hey, that's a verse. Don't worry, I'll remember it. And I love it at the Roerich. So quiet. Some days it's only me and the paintings, the smiling Buddhas of copper and bronze. Yes, the hush of the Nicholas Roerich Museum is the biggest kick I'm getting these days. Where I can look into myself and out the other side into the universe.

Seriously, I've become contemplative. Contemplation rules. I wander the museum and look at the paintings of Tibet, the monks in the mountains, the monks contemplating away like fury. Yeah, those monks. Sly or what? And the weirdness they believe in. So tonight I'm going to do all the contemplative songs I know, including my little ode to Topaz Street, which is the title track of the next album, and my song about Dad, spark out on his couch, my songs of vigil and songs of loss, all the soft songs off the CD, the CD here with me now, my precious amulets these CDs, my album that is selling slowly but still selling.

Because that's all I want. That's all I ever wanted. My music for the people to hear, locked up in these silver circles, holy to me as Tibetan prayer bowls, the sound I make, the sound I'm making, paying the bartender and crossing Broadway, out amongst the poor people now in the heat, this heat stinking of the Texas T Rotisserie and the Mexican dry cleaning, and who knows where these poor people will sleep tonight under all this glass, all this concrete, the subway trains running under my feet, the 1 train, the 3 train, the rivers of shit, the rivers of rats, and yes I'm ready as I'll ever be because I'm getting where I need to be and that's exactly where you'll find me. On the brink.

Rachel

August 13, 5 p.m. Zichron Ya'akov, Israel

Go to Fatoosh, everyone said. If you're in Haifa, you must try Fatoosh.

The woman next door drove me to the hospital the first few times. Then she pointed out there was a bus. Some people wouldn't dream of taking the bus. For obvious reasons. But after a few journeys, everything seems fine. In Haifa, I go by taxi to the hospital, and am with David for two hours, two afternoons per week.

But David's friends at Sachs say we should come back to New York. So that's what I'm thinking. Back where I started. Or didn't start. Not back to West End Avenue, because the apartment is sold. But what about those new places down by the water in Battery Park City? they ask. The ones the Slovakians are building. So modern. And the river walks are fabulous.

Maybe. I look at David in his blue gown and think he should be home. David's a Manhattanite. His sister is there on 107 Street. Yes, Rebecca should see him again. I know she will never come here.

At our place in Zichron I sit where David sat, on the ridge in our garden, looking at the Mediterranean. There's a triangular view of the sea, like a page turned up.

Yes, time is slow. That's what I like. Olives drop and I pick up the rubbish the mongooses have pulled out of the bin. There is a family of mongooses in the undergrowth between this and the next house. I see them in the early morning. They are clever, yes. It's as if they're learning. And they're big. I would never chase them, as David used to, back into the undergrowth. David in his shorts and sandals, waving a collector's magazine. His glasses glinting.

The doctors say he might soon be discharged to somewhere nearer me. But his friends want him home in an apartment by the river. Beside the Hudson that flows both ways. With a live-in carer, they say. Leave it to Sachs. Yes, David was good to the bank. And the bank remembers its own.

One afternoon the nurses were changing him and they said it would take some time. See the town, one suggested. I know you're back here on Thursday.

So I went to Fatoosh. The taxi dropped me under a palm. All I had to do was step out from the car and sit down under a parasol. A boy came up and took my order. Then when he brought my coffee he placed it too near the table edge. But I wasn't paying attention. I was looking around. Office girls eating salads. A few men on their own, smoking at smaller tables. They had already noticed me, every one.

So this was Fatoosh. I went to the Ladies and passed through the dark little bar with its awnings and rugs, the pipes with their glass bulbs on the table. And I thought of Robin in the saloon, the propellers of the fan overhead, her shoulders bare. Robin would have liked Fatoosh. She smoked all the time and would have investigated it here, although I don't think women are allowed. To smoke, that is. Mind you, it's nothing strong. They say the tobacco's mild, and that each smoker can mix in ingredients of their choice. Lemon or mint to cool the throat.

I said to David once, when we were outside, sea gazing, what about a pipe? I had had two glasses of the Baron's white. I don't think David heard. But if Robin were here, we'd do it together. Two Scherezades, Robin and I, with no one to hear our stories.

When I arrived back at my table there was a disturbance. Someone had knocked my cup over, and the coffee had spilled everywhere. A waitress was cleaning up. And the men were still looking at me. Lizards, I thought. With lizard throats. A little like my own. I wear a silk scarf now. David has bought me quite a collection.

Oh, it's you, I heard a voice. A young woman stepped from behind the palm tree. It was a girl I had spoken to once on the bus. A tall girl, Arab blood I had supposed, who had sat opposite me all the way from Zichron. Her English was quite good.

I'm sorry, she laughed, and I noted the laugh. My friend is so clumsy.

Her friend was a dark-skinned man. Thirtyish, stylish tee shirt that said 'System Ali', jacket hooked over his shoulder, a Gold Label in his other hand.

My apologies, he beamed. Of course, I've ordered another.

In the end, they took me back to Zichron. I was amazed. The man drove what he insisted was a Ford Mustang. Five litres, he said. I had it imported. Hold on.

When we started, I could feel the whole car sway.

Fishtailing, he laughed, as I looked in surprise across at him. As you say in America.

The girl was in the back seat. She was wearing a leather miniskirt and her knees were pushed up into the air. How her foal's legs gleamed. She showed a tiny blue triangle. Like the sea. On the bus she had been dressed in uniform.

During the journey they both asked me questions. I think they were intrigued. I told them about 9/11. I explained as best I could how Sachs had survived the banking crisis, and about the imaginary apartment in Battery Park City. Its big windows, its river walks. I told them about it in impossible detail. Until it became real in my mind.

In the end, I was wracking my brains. What more could I say? What else from my life that was somebody else's life? Of course I said nothing about Kazimerz and Krakow. There was nothing to say. Then I remembered the automobile.

David owned an Impala, I said. We would drive those straight Florida highways. When it rained the car was like a barge in a river of rain. A barge on the Hudson.

And I could see David, both hands clutching the steering wheel, staring ahead, eyes wide, through the streaming glass.

Impala? the man said. And whistled.

Super Sport, I added.

Mm, he said. V8.

It was a Chevrolet, I said helpfully.

Oh Yes. Drove my chevvy to the levee, he laughed. And looked across.

When we pulled up at my gate, the girl climbed out after me and stretched. Skinny as a Haifa street cat. But the honey of her.

We'll see you again, she laughed.

And so they do. A week later they walk into the garden where I'm waiting under the olive tree. David and I always used to sit here as night fell. Blue evening sun. Yes, darkness comes quickly in Zichron. The cedar seeds hang like black stars, there are lights in the wineries and the polytunnels on the plain below.

Sometimes the pneumatic drills sound after dark. There is so much building here, the older people in the supermarket throw up their hands.

The girl is Ranie, the man Feroz. To put me at ease, they tell me they are both Christian. And I smile and say nothing because I have never told anyone my religion. It is not part of my dream. But others dreamed it about me. As to David, he had no time for those orthodox Williamsburg couples, the men in ringlets, the women's hair tied tight under their wigs.

Yes, they are intrigued. When I told them about David walking north in Manhattan on 9/11, the dust on his shoulders, they seemed to think he was a hero. They were sure they had seen him on TV. And I was thinking the same thing. There was a famous image of a man covered in dust on that morning. A survivor, staggering through the choking clouds. That's the man I was describing. Because David didn't go to work that day. He watched it on TV in his study.

And those figures, falling from the twin towers? I thought one might be me. Falling and taking so long to fall. Yes, that must sound strange. But it's what I felt.

I'm not sure why I let Ranie and Feroz think David was a hero. A survivor. But other people make up their lives. Other people have dreamed my life. Why shouldn't I do the same?

Ranie is so stylish. She makes me feel stiff as olive wood. She tucks herself into the back seat and soon Feroz says we are on the Yitzhak Rabin highway. Traffic is slow.

I like speed, he says. This isn't speed.

For a while we are stuck behind a van carrying sheep. The sheep's faces are pushed against the wire netting of their pen. Feroz drives close to the van and the sheep stare at us as we stare back into their yellow eyes.

They told me to bring a swimming costume, so I had to buy one specially in the high street. I suppose we're going to the beach. I haven't swum since Florida but I'm not scared. Not bothered either about showing my body on the beach, my olive tree body with its grey leaves.

Feroz plays CDs and looks at me to check my reaction. Arab trance, he says. Electro. Good stuff.

And yes, I like it, like it because it repeats itself over and over. Round and round the music goes. Just a few notes, and Ranie is laughing and singing in the back while Feroz is impatient with the traffic. When they talk to one another it's in Arabic, although I don't pretend to be able to tell Arabic from Hebrew.

It's comforting that I can't understand. That I'm cut loose from language. As our speed picks up I'm free to look out at the landscape, the soldiers at bus stops, the helicopters like black wasps.

Now I can tell we're not going to the beach. We seem to be heading inland. The earth is dry and thin with ribs of rock and dark boulders choking the streambeds. Stone is winning its war with water.

After two hours we are in the desert. Rock like rust. Grey and gold grit. But Feroz slows and we drive off the road. Below us are a few huts made of planks and plastic sheeting. There is a camel too, and a lorry supported by flat stones.

And here they come. The children have seen us and they are running uphill from the hovels, running barefoot over the famished earth, the soil like cement dust. We stand outside the car and the heat seems to suck all the air from my lungs and Ranie gives me sweets and a few shekels and then the children are swarming around saying *mun-nee, mun-nee* and their enormous eyes are pleading, their faces filthy, their clothes in rags, impossible rags, and we give them all we have and show our empty hands and then we are back in the Mustang and it fishtails as it starts, oh yes, I have learned that word just as Feroz learned it, and one of the children touches the car and recoils in shock and the tyres send a cloud of dust and gravel down the hillside, and the bigger children are running after us and laughing, laughing in this parched and barren place, and we are back on the desert highway and the three of us are laughing although I don't know what we are laughing at, no I have no idea at all.

The camel never lifted an eye.

There, says Ranie.

And I look.

There.

A gleam. There are saltbushes now. Even trees in the sulphur-coloured rock.

Again a gleam.

We're there, she says.

Ah, I say.

We thought you'd like it. Because we love it. The Sea of Salt.

The Dead Sea, I say.

Very dead, says Feroz. But fun.

Ranie takes me to the women's changing room, which is a shock. So much olive wood. So many grey olive leaves. But it's all part of the dream, I say to myself, and soon we are walking down the path to the water where Mr Mustang is waiting for us in his striped Speedo's. Feroz is thicker round the waist than I had expected. At the tide's edge there are people daubing themselves with black mud. Some of them are completely covered, their teeth flashing in their faces.

Don't get the water in your eyes or nose, laughs Ranie, and she winces in over the stones, and I follow as best I can and do what another woman is doing, lowering herself into the water, dark here where the lake bed has been churned up.

And then I am floating. My head facing Israel, my feet towards Jordan's bare hills. Floating in the steaming air, the sulphur in my nose, the salts already slippery, a kind of soap on my skin, slippery because the dead cells are peeling, that's what Ranie says, the dead skin being burned away.

Ranie and Feroz are swimming east to where the water is clear. But I think I will stay here in the shallows. Floating. Floating in a dead world. Floating under the red cliffs, under the scrolls of red rock. As Robin floated in her pool, blowing smoke rings at the sky. Just as David is floating, I think, in his shadowy room, and the Bedouin children are floating in their sea of bitter dust.

They say my name is Rachel. They tell me I am seventy years of age. I know my name is Rachel. I know I am seventy years of age. But no matter how much I know I know I know nothing.

Postscript: a note from the neolithic

I stop at once. Then crouch down. Nothing is moving. Nothing but a blade of grass five yards away. The only blade that shivers. Something has brushed it. Or someone has passed by. As I look, the grass stops trembling, that one grass stem, one arrow in a lynxskin quiver, and soon it is invisible amongst the other grasses that grow out of the sand. And there is no sound at all. Not a breath in this crater under the ridge. All the world, my home world, silent.

I guess a cricket has leaped from that stem into the marram. Making it shake. It's hard to tell because the sun is strong. But I love those crickets. I love to see them perch on my wrist. Such grave faces they have, under their paint, their faces squeezed into helmets. And I love to feel the crickets thinking. How they think. They might explode with their thoughts, surely, because such crickets have many thoughts. They would be like broom pods crackling in the heat. Shellfish in the fire.

But the wolf has paid no heed and the wolf would know and she is not concerned. Now she looks around and wonders why I have stopped. The sun catches her right eye and her pelt is the colour of an oystershell. A bee-eater, all red and blue, flashes past. Yes the wolf would know. That's why I never feel afraid when the wolf is with me. Because the wolf hears the unhearable. Brush of the buzzard's wing. Cricket flight. And the wolf sees the unseeable. I know my eyes are keen but I am blind compared to the wolf. What she sees I will never know yet I know she sees it. Yes I wish I was a wolf. A poor wolf, unhearing, unseeing, but still a true sort of wolf.

I have tasted her breath and it is a scorching wind, hot as this sand dribbling under my skin, the sand path that comes up from the beach and across the plain and over the ridge and into the crater and runs on behind me into the hollows and hillocks and becomes a green way and vanishes into the trees, the first line of trees of the forest, the forest that masses behind the dunes and seems to grow no matter how many trees we cut or burn. Tall birch. Willows with moss. The forest I visit only with the wolf, so dangerous it is, my father tells me, my brother warns. Yet I go there. On my wanderings I have come to the trees, paused, and stepped in to that darker world of perfumes, sighs. How I long to say what I have seen. To make my stories and tell them at the fire.

Now up we go to the crest. It is all sand here. But roses grow out of the sand. Only the rose faces are visible, the stems buried, the thorns hidden. So that the crater side is white with rose petals. Children's faces, I always think, as if someone is pulling them into the ground. How good it is to come here in the afternoon, yes this afternoon, and lie on the incline amongst the roses. Somewhere there is water for them. But they need so little. They hoard the dew, my mother says, the droplets from the sea frets that roll up the slopes and vanish. And their lives so short.

Sometimes there are lizards here but not today. Just one snail, with horns like father's divining rods. Don't worry, snail. I'll leave you be. And the wolf climbs ahead with her paws in the sand and even she finds this difficult. How she sends the roses to their ruin. But she is never mindful of the trail she leaves. Perhaps that is her one mistake. Not like me. I take care where I step. Everyone says I float upon this ground. That I never leave a sign. Now, I don't disturb a petal as the sand flows beneath me in its streams, but even my breasts under the vest must drag against its warmth.

Small breasts, my brother claims. Well, like pine cones even I would say. But cockleshells to him. Black teats of a fox.

Yeah, yeah, I say. Look who's talking. Not even half a man, you puny piss-stain. Cuttlebones where your muscles should be. Slow as a dewcat with your cock.

And he sniggers and cuffs me and I rumple his hair and he goes off to his chores and I to mine. Pulling out gorseroots for the fire. How the thorns stay in my hands and heels, hot and golden, nagging all day. But it's the needles burn the best. Fine fuel. And how dreamy the flowers smell when I crouch under the bush. Before I cut I listen to the yellowhammer singing above me. Little goldsmith of the gorse, my mother names him. My mother names all things. She has given me my first tattoos, her nib a splinter from a spindle tree.

There, she laughed. Wolf girl. Brave girl. And kissed me with her fishy breath. And went back to tending the garden in a clearing of the gorse. She grows her radishes there and tall alexanders. But also her herbs, muttering songs over them. Songs with strange words, but she'll teach me soon she says. Herbs for headaches. For women's bleeding. Herbs to make you horny and herbs to make you smell nice. Herbs for delirium. Herbs for snakebite swelling and joint swelling. Herbs to anoint the sacred skin of the dead.

And then I'm off to dragging branches from the beach, salty boughs that burn green as copper. And checking the nets. And pulling the seaweed out of the nets. And opening oysters. And smoking the dogfish we trap in the rockpools. Or filleting bass. Biting out their bones. And gathering seaweed. And making the fish stew for the night, putting in a mullet head, its eyes dulled as if with bubbles of sand. Pieces of eel, gutted with a razorshell. How the brew bubbles. Then cleaning the pots. And picking the ticks out of the skins. And cutting my sister's hair and hiding my make-up from her. And mending our clothes. And checking the nets. And checking the nets. And pulling the nets through The Dafan. And diving with my knife. And duelling with crabs in the crevices. No wonder we all smell of fish. And woodsmoke. No wonder my hair is stiff as rope, washing the smoke out of it in salt water because the fresh is drying up. Yes, the spring is low, lower than last summer. It's getting warmer, my father says, crabmeat in his beard, the firelight on his tattoos. Warmer every year. You should bathe in the sand.

But I love making the stew. Picking the roots and the rocket and the fennel bulbs to go with the bass the men catch. Sometimes I hide in the rocks and wait for turnstones. I follow their wet footprints which look like tiny arrowheads. I go creeping in the boulders, all the gutters red with anemones, on through the carpets of kelp. The turnstones are gossipers and never expect the net. My brother casts it well. I'm clumsy. And not much meat on those birds: just roasted salt and crunchy bones. When they fly away it makes me dizzy. How they jiggle, all of a zigzag.

Yes everyone cooks. Everyone except the simples. Who only eat. Because if you don't cook you're a fool. A simple. You're a danger to yourself. To the families that live with us you might as well be dead. So I must look out for something. Never go home empty-handed, is one of the main laws. You never ever do that.

So I'm looking as I climb. Maybe strawberries for my pocket. There are so many here.

Strawberries, my brother will mock. Those finches' hearts. Yet still he'll cram his face.

Forage, father will say. You have to forage. And I'm one of the best. Once I brought home honey twisted round a stick. Now everybody does that. And once an egg. But not the normal eggs, seagulls, curlews. This egg was huge and green. Its shell was rough as hemp, covered with craters. And maybe it had just been laid, but by what bird I never saw. Still warm, it was on a ledge of sand, and took both my hands to hold it. Like a drinking cup.

How carefully I carried that egg home and even my mother was surprised. Such an egg, she laughed. Clever girl. And though I've searched everywhere since, I've never found another. No one has. Perhaps we should have waited for the egg to hatch so we might tell what type of bird it was. But father was hungry. He said it was a swan. We made an omelette for him with marjoram, and he shared it with me. The egg bringer he calls me. Honey twister. And yes, that night he told us tales.

But now the wolf is at the top, up to her belly in sand, sending an avalanche down upon me and on I go and yes, here is the crest, the highest part of all. For even she is panting. Froth on her ragged gum. She shakes the sand out of her coat like seawater. But this is where we watch. This is our pinnacle. And the sea is calm and the tide coming in and blue as a mussel shell it looks, day after day, not a storm for weeks, not a rain cloud, the mussel beds already half hidden, the waves white against them and white around the reef that lies a mile off shore, and look, and look. Because. Because a boat. Between the rocks of the inlet. A big boat. Bigger than I've ever seen before. And now our drumming starts.

*

I am wary coming off the ridge but when I arrive on the beach my father is already there, and my brother and some of the other men. They are laughing and not afraid because there are only two people aboard, allowing the tide to bring them in, waving, calling out, standing up unsteadily. Sitting down again. And it's not a boat but a raft, a long raft that is soon beached. Some of its timbers are painted blue. It is stuck on a rock shelf that rises out of the sand, so that the two sailors have to wade ashore, staggering out of the shallows.

You're drunk, spits my father. Filthy drunk. You might have drowned.

And we help them on to the dry sand and they collapse before us. One man, long hair and beard, his tunic dyed red. And a woman, skinny as a boy, her hair cut short, her arms covered in tattoos and insect bites. The man is laughing. He sits up and shakes his head.

Dogtooth already has, he says. Well, he must have. At least he wasn't with us when we woke up. Probably slipped overboard in his sleep, the silly bugger.

The woman looks round. Bastard beer was stronger than usual, she grins. Hell of a brew. But we'd welcome another. Dry as ashes, aren't we? And burned.

Our men are looking at the raft, wedged on the rock.

What you carrying? asks one.

What's it look like?

Like a bloody big stone.

Got it in one, says the woman. Bloody big stone.

The stone is three men in length and one broad. This load is lashed to the raft and I can hear the hissing of seawater evaporating down its sides.

Now where's that drink? asks the bearded sailor.

Soon it is dark. We sit around the fire and the drunk man, who doesn't seem so drunk now, regards the wolf with a narrow eye.

Maybe it's appropriate, he says. It was wolves who first owned fire. Of course you know that. But the pack leader wandered off, looking for wolf food. Deer or lizards or worms. Worms or a child of woman. A wolf eats anything. So the pack left fire behind and fire cried out as it burned low. Fire was lonely. Fire was frail. Fire was almost out, only sparks left in the dark. Weak as glow worms. But a woman heard fire crying and she came and took it. Thought it an abandoned bairn. She blew on it and the brand burned. She fed it straw. Nursed it. Soon it was burning twigs. Then she took it home and now it's people who own fire. Not wolves. That's why you never see wolves at a fire.

Raised it from a cub, my father says. That's why it's not afraid of the flames. Where you coming from?

West just now, says the man. Been sailing about a week, but there's no wind, only current.

How far west?

Where the land ends. Mountains, a maze of coves. They're a rough lot down there. The wild bunch we call them. They wave sticks at you or axes made of slate. I ask you. And bad hair. And terrible tattoos.

Rank smell too, said the woman, sucking out an oyster. It's poor country and ignorant people. They speak like bears. *Umph, umph*. Like that. *Hurrumph*.

I think they drink blood, says the man. And I'm sure they drink piss. A disgrace to mankind.

They used to say west is best, laughs my father.

Not now, the man scowls.

His companion, I see, must be hungry, because now she has a plover's egg. Only yesterday I picked it from the scrape. Speckled, triangular. Easy to find if you know where to look. But isn't everything? The plover pretended to have a broken wing. It limped away, hoping I'd follow. But I knew where the eggs would be. Stupid bird, what could it expect, making a nest on open ground.

My brother is drinking beer with the others but I'm not allowed yet. At least, not in public. But there are plenty of times the girls have taken a jar up to the crest and swigged it round and giggled and gone moony-eyed and the wolf has lain with us in the sand with her muzzle between her paws. Eyes closed. Ears up. Girls' day off, we call it. Forget the nets. And we paint our symbols on each other's skin, or make the stories we want to tell. That's when I think of our twilight fires, with owls calling and cockchafers dive-bombing the camp.

Like my story of the forest. One month ago. I was foraging, of course, without much luck. Going over the tops away from the sea, and soon, I hardly noticed, but soon I could see I might reach the line of trees. Yes, it was hot. There were flies on me. The orchids had erupted, violet and hairy. A viper, very dark, mottled like a wildcat, dreamed in the sand. Such are the summer days. And there were the trees and the wolf was with me and when we reached the trees the wolf paused but I steered past her and she followed and soon I was further into the forest than I had ever been before.

Brazen is how my father describes me. Brazen hussy, he laughs. My little belter. I like that. It makes me feel I'm brave. So this hussy walked on with her wolf and it was cooler, and the green shade divided my body into thousands of squares and spangles. Like plovers' feathers.There was grass on the forest floor and white flowers. We stopped to listen, the wolf and I. Not a breath. Or maybe gnat whine. Sap rising. And soon I could smell water. Really smell it. The wolf could smell it too and so we crept low, completely silent, as there was light coming through the birch.

Such a pool I had discovered. Green water with green rushes round it. The sun shattering on the surface. No one had told me about this place. It wasn't part of the stories. But there would be fish there. And grebes perhaps with freckled chicks.

I held the wolf's rope tight and we slid under the last branches. Grass ran down to the rim. The pool was full of lilypads and some were in flower, white and golden. Now here's the story. Amongst the lilies was a boy. A boy swimming. He might have been diving because he surfaced as we settled down to look at the pool. A real boy. But what a boy. He stood up in the water and his skin was white. The whitest skin I had ever seen. Blue-white as whey. A spurt of milk. And his hair was white. Like a crown. And I could see his eyes were red as if he had been crying a long time. Strange red wounds his eyes were. Buried deep in his face. He was staring straight towards us but I knew he couldn't see. We are the invisibles, after all. The invisible people who can hide in sand. In seawater. We are mother of pearl. We are betony. The bleached bones of hyenas dug out of the dune.

And then he turned around and waded to the other shore and pushed through the rushes and was gone. Skinny boy. Arse a white conch. Sharp elbows and knees. Then only the dragonflies were left but he had been no less curious than that tribe of cannibals.

To tell the truth, the wolf was not much bothered. As if she knew him or understood his mystery. One of the simples perhaps.

After the boy left she went down to drink. I stood up to my knees in the pool and it was icy. No wonder he had no dick. Come back you little fairy, I wanted to say. I'll do you no harm. I'll crown you with a lilypad. But then I looked round. I was a long way from home. Who else was there, I wondered. Who was looking at me?

Because I know the stories. Of the people who were here first. The old people who have different words. No, they're not all dead, my mother says. They can hide better than us. And they've learned how to disappear. Into thin air. My brother's been far into the trees. He has to go further than me to prove himself. But he said he was scared by the silence. He also told me of the wind in the forest and how the trees shook, branches falling, branches rubbing against branches in the storm's language. I heard a sobbing, he said. It was the grief of trees. But the silence was worse.

Those strangers are still talking. As if they know more of the world than us. Travel broadens the mind, they say. The strangers you meet will teach you things. But the man especially won't learn much from us because he doesn't ask questions. I hate people who don't ask questions. It's a kind of insult. And anyway, I don't think bears speak like they said. *Umph, umph*, they said. *Hurrumph*. No, it's not like that.

Because I remember a bear. A brown bear sitting on a dune. Oh sad lord, I thought, as I watched him sucking a root. Resting he was. Perhaps grieving for something. Then he picked up one of the stones in the sand and looked for beetles. Like mother taking the lid off the cookpot. And just like mother he put the stone back exactly in its place. The one right place so that the stone fitted the stone's shape. A young bear, legs apart, scratching his armpit and muttering to himself. Too hot in his fur I suppose. Then he swarmed off through the sand.

No, west ain't best, the sailor is saying. Anything but.

It's our bread the strangers don't like. The loaves are old with a blue crust. They feel hot. But our beer is strong and there's yellow meat on the crabs. We're cooking shellfish in a pit under the fire. This isn't one of our usual camps, and we haven't taken the strangers home to the ravine. That's where our houses are, which can't be seen from the tops of the dunes or from the sea. That's also where our spring is. It's the perfect hidden place. Though it's true, we can't hide smoke. Instead, we've stayed close to the raft which is moored in the rocks. Now the tide is full with starlight in it and firelight in the pools. As my brother says, these midnight barbecues are our favourite meals. Really special occasions.

You know? says the man. I've been up and down this coast a score of times and thought there was no one here.

Looks like a desert from out there, says the woman. The back of beyond. You must like it like that.

Then she glances at me and smiles.

How can you live in all this sand? It's bad for the skin. And aren't there snakes? Long snakes?

Lots of snakemeat, smiles my father. And there's some of us wear snakeskin shoes.

Very trendy, says the man. Look, don't get me wrong. I've been worse places. Marshes with blue lights. Pools black with mosquitoes. We like it here. Might stay for a bit if that's all right.

What about your stone? asks that oaf, my father's brother.

That heavy bastard? Total nightmare. I've had it with all those stones.

We turn to where the raft is tied. The stone is a black

treetrunk in the firelight. A fallen pillar. The only shelter on the raft comprises stakes bound together and an evergreen roof.

You know how many of us it took to bring that monster from the mountain? How many days? You know how many of us were needed to get it on the boat? And then you have to know how to sail the boat. How to steer. How to navigate the coast when sometimes there's no land at all and you're reading the stars and thinking about this useless cargo of a useless rock. How it might just slip you under a black wave. Like it did to Dogtooth, poor sod. Like it did to two of those labourers down west. Toppled straight off the wagon, didn't it? Broke their backs. Writhing about like squabs, what could we do? Had to stove their heads in. Couldn't leave them in pain. Good men apparently. And all the time it's just another stone for the bloody temple.

Temple? asks my mother.

For the gods. The bloody gods.

Everyone is silent. Then my brother sniggers. Someone snorts. Soon we're all laughing.

Hey, a toast, cries my father. To the gods! The bloody gods.

The bloody gods! we shout. And we all drink, even some of the girls, waving our cups.

The stranger brandishes a crab claw and continues.

Don't worry, folks. You can trust me. I've been everywhere. These gods are not so terrible. I mean, the so-called gods. Once down the coast I met these people that worship a whale's penis. That's right. This old cock the size of a totem pole. All the old men bowing down to a fish's pizzle. I ask you. Hilarious.

He takes a long draft.

And what temple? asks my mother.

Four days sailing east. Then two weeks on the wagons.

Big job, says the woman. Huge job. But it pays.

Dogtooth might not agree, says the man. But, yes, big earner. Got these engineers in, haven't they. Greaseballs and little dark types explaining to everyone how to build it. Can't understand a word. But talk about meticulous. What goes where. Drawing their lines. Measuring their plans to the titchiest blade of grass.

And the priests, says the woman.

Oh, don't get me back on the priests, groans the man, pulling his beard. Self important? Sanctimonious? Like who cares where the sun rises? I ask you. It's got to be somewhere, hasn't it? The sun has to rise. Is that really like… important? Droning on about the new maths. What's wrong with the old maths, my father would ask. Count up to ten and you're made. You're in business. Then there's all the others coming over. Smiths. Brickies. Astronomers. Those astronomers are a weird lot. And surveyors. Like what's to survey? Anyway, pass that flagon.

He belches out of the darkness. Then continues.

This other journey, last year, I was kipping in a cave down east. Nice and dry, big fire, and aye aye, I notice someone's been scratching shapes on the walls. Red deer they looked like. Maybe rhinoceros. So, I thought, right. I'm going to have a go. But no animal claptrap. I'm going to do a man. I'm going to draw myself.

He looks round.

Yeah. Myself. A self-portrait. Well, why not? The way I see it, I can do anything. Jack of all trades, that's me. So why not be an artist? And pretty good it was too, my drawing. I scratched it in and used some of the yellow ochre they'd been digging. There was an ochre pit just down the hill.

What happened? my father asked.

Didn't like it did they? Not one bit. Had to wash it off. One of the priests in a ponyskin got miffed. So I calmed him down. But then this silly old bugger with antlers on his head started a real strop. Offensive he said it was. Insulting. The bloody gods wouldn't like it...

The bloody gods! shouts my father. And, shrieking, we drink again.

So all night, says the visitor, as a kind of apology I had to sit around reciting that poem. You know. Endless long verses we all had to learn? Warriors and maidens and holding out for a hero? Maybe you don't have it in this desert, no disrespect. That poem about the deerhunt that goes on for two years?

The poem or the hunt? I ask, and everybody cheers.

And all the warriors die one by one? asks my father.

That's it.

And they meet a magician?

You got it.

And a sea monster?

Well, I'd say it was a basking shark, most likely, says the man.

And everyone gets pissed?

For a whole year, says my father's brother.

Predictable, isn't it, says the man.

Too pissed to fight? laughs my father.

Completely wasted.

Yeah, we got that poem too.

Goes on a bit, doesn't it?

I'll say.

But some good lines.

Oh yes, some good lines.

When I look up again the fire's still burning but everyone's asleep. A moth with eyes on its wings is floating around. Both the visitors are spark out. That's what usually happens to boozers. Oblivion. They're very trusting, I must say. The shorthaired woman was carrying a rawhide bag and it's here at my feet. Carefully I look inside. Her dyes, her powders, her contraceptives. Some shreds that might be hashish. Nice knickers. A different top. Knife with a turtleshell handle. Cuttlebone necklace she's dyed pink. Probably used madder. And a drawing, a map it looks like, scored in bark. Where the temple of stones is, I suppose.

Yes, I might wish to be like the shorthaired woman. I think she must have a great heart. Free to roam, and a sailor too. Tough and skinny and a scar on her belly. Maybe they pulled a child out of her. Tomorrow I must ask her name. She is quiet but she listens to all. And yes, I am learning from her. She told me she speaks three dialects. That she once saw a woman whipped with nettles for taking her food first. A soupbone. But perhaps that woman was starving. Perhaps the bone was for her children. It's still so primitive, she says. Not only bears hurrumphing round the world. Men too. Men eating their own fleas. Men scratching their scabby balls. Makes me cringe. Like mother says, men's minds are made of mud.

Silently I slip away and go to the raft, placing my hand on the hemp bands, the stone itself. The sea is not far off now, glittering like birch. But these summer nights are never really dark. The worst they get is that colour at the far edge of a rainbow. It can still be light enough to forage, if you're brave enough.

Already the stone is dry and warm. I like the man too, boaster that he is. Taking up all the air, all the room, the firelight on his face. But I like storytellers and if the woman goes with him, and a woman such as that, he must be, what? Honest? Brave? No, something else. But I don't have that word either. That dark edge to the rainbow.

Perhaps they will stay and the stone will rest on the shore. And perhaps they'll decide to build their temple with the rest of the new people and we will wait for a higher tide to free the boat. Perhaps I will go with them. And perhaps not. The sea frightens me. From the ridge I've seen the storms. Once I watched as a black wind, spinning like a spindle, travelled from the other coast. It smashed ashore here, swept through the inlet and raced along the ridge. It was full of bird voices, birds imprisoned in its black branches, birds falling exhausted from its prison. And there was lightning, white as coral, growing out of the sea. And thunder all around, its sulphur in my throat sickly as medicine. That's why we hang holly at our door. Mother has planted it above the ravine and it is our guardian tree.

I'd miss everything I know. The curlews at dusk, their cries the saddest cries, the happiest too, because they are calls to home. Come to the fire, they say. Come home from the dark. And the lichen that grows on the grey stones. Yellow as eggyolk, its tiny leaves. I'd miss that.

This sand is home, the sand that hides so much. What did he say? A portrait of himself? Trust an ugly man to decide that. Haven't we always drawn in the sand here with our sticks and watched the seawater bubble up in our footprints, washing our tracks away? The girls draw the boys. The boys draw themselves carrying spears. My mother sharpens a holly stick and draws the moon for planting, the moon for harvesting. My father draws the whale that once came to the bay, its waterspout tall as a tree.

Drawing started in the sand, not in caves. But we have an understanding with these visitors. We could cut their throats. Or they could cut ours. Father said we were watching their boat a long time before it came ashore. Because we only drum if a boat lands. This time we decided to show ourselves. There was no danger.

So I'm borrowing the woman's handbag. I'm going to use her lipstick. Such a colour she paints herself. A mauve, a purple. She must be a gaudy orchid when she has the need. There are rocks all around where I might draw. But here, the surface of their temple stone is smooth enough. I might picture the wolf, of course. Here she is, snapping at the sand fleas that jump out of the weed, her pelt pale as driftwood. Sand people know that any fool might draw, might make their mark. But what can my painted finger make? A bird, a boat? Myself? And what's a rhinoceros anyway?

About the Author

Robert Minhinnick works for the environmental charity, Sustainable Wales, and is co-founder of Friends of the Earth Cymru.

A new edition of his *Selected Poems* (Carcanet) is due in 2012, together with a critical book and appraisal from Seren.

He has twice been awarded the Forward Prize for Best Individual Poem and twice the Wales Book of the Year for his collections of essays.

His other books include *Fairground Music: the World of Porthcawl Funfair* (with Eamon Bourke) from Gomer; *Sea Holly* (Seren) shortlisted for the Royal Society of Literature Ondaatje Prize; *The Adulterer's Tongue: Six Contemporary Welsh Poets* (Carcanet).

Robert Minhinnick is glad to acknowledge a Creative Wales award that has enabled him to undertake the writing of *The Keys of Babylon.*